DEFEN̶S̶E̶L̶E̶S̶S̶
hearts

USA TODAY BESTSELLING AUTHOR
MEAGAN BRANDY

DEDICATION

To the one who holds the weight of others in silence,
your strength amazes me.

SYNOPSIS

After months of silence, here she stands on my front porch, waiting to be let in again. But it's the same play every time, and I know how this ends - I give her all I have and she carries it with her on the way back to him.

I should turn her away, but I won't. Couldn't do it if I tried.

Because no matter how many times she pops back up, pulls me in and drags me under, it will never be enough. I'll always want more.
More of her.
More for us.

And she'll always choose him.

"I'M PREGNANT."

My mouth opens, but words fail me as I stare at the girl in front of me. I have to have heard her wrong. No way in *hell* did she say—

"Parker!" she snaps, and I blink back into focus. "You heard what I said. Stop talking to yourself."

"I wasn't—"

"Save it. I know you, remember?"

"I'm sorry, but I, uh … need a minute to process. I wasn't expecting … *that*. Or you."

Lips pursed; she shoulders past me into the house. Her nose turns up with judgment tightening her features as she takes in the simple style of living my best friend, Lolli, and I have settled into. Sure, it's beachfront, but it doesn't scream money. Guessing that's what she expected.

"Wow. I would have left my hometown for all this, too." Sarcasm streams from her mouth as she leans against the back of the couch, her arms folded over her chest.

I wanna argue with her, defend my home, but she has a right to be upset with me.

I left her behind when I moved here, all without considering how it would affect her.

But I had to. I had to get out—for me.

When Lolli asked me to move to California, to live here with her and go to college, work for her company with the promise of taking it over once I graduated, it was almost a no-brainer.

Only a fool would walk away from that. So, I packed my shit and took off the day I graduated.

Doleful eyes search mine before cutting right to look out the window, and immediately, I feel like shit.

She must be scared, anxious, and unsure of everything in this moment.

Fucking pregnant.

With a sigh, I approach her, gently latching on to her biceps.

She tries hard to avoid it, but her faux strength fails, her emotions winning over. Tears fill her eyes as her bottom lip starts to quiver.

When I pull her close, she fights our nearness but only for a few seconds before she breaks down and gives in, turning to sob into my chest.

"Hey," I whisper. "It'll be all right," I tell her, knowing it might be a lie.

"I'm s-scared."

"I know you are." I kiss her hair, and she cries harder. "But we'll figure it out."

"Mom's gonna kill me, Parker," she wails. "I don't know what to do. I can't let her find out."

I swallow my words.

Payton still doesn't get what our mom is. She still trusts in her. Still loves her. Just because Ava Baylor is dead to me, that doesn't mean her daughter isn't still wrapped around her little finger. There are so many things Payton doesn't know.

But, right now, this is bigger than any of that.

My sixteen-year-old sister is pregnant. This is a problem.

I rub her back as she pulls from my embrace.

Wiping her nose with her sleeve, she sniffles. "What do I do, Parker?"

"I don't know, Peep, but we'll … it'll be fine. Come on." I take her hand, pulling her into the kitchen to make some hot chocolate. Sure, it's July, but this is Southern California. The beach is my backyard, and the air is chilled.

Once it's ready, she hops up to sit on the countertop and I hand it to her, earning a small, one-sided smile.

While she blows into her cup, watching the marshmallows melt, I look her over. Her blonde hair is pulled up high, a long, straight ponytail hanging behind her. Her clothes are designer. I know because it's the same shit my mom wears.

The tan heeled sandals with way too tight, too damn short dark jean shorts and a three-hundred-dollar sweater, which now has snot on the sleeves, screams, *look, but don't dare come close enough to touch.* Superior. I hate it.

"Talk to me, Peep."

She sighs and peeks up at me, finally looking like a little girl who's talking to her older brother. "What do you wanna know?"

"Everything. First, how the hell did you get here?"

"I …" She cuts her eyes right and then back. "Bus."

I scrub my hands down my face. "And if I hadn't been here? I haven't been home consistently for weeks."

"Well, your little roommate would have been here, right?" she sasses. "What? Would she not have let your little sister in? Only accepts you if a dick hangs between your legs?"

"Payton."

She rolls her eyes. "Please. I'm not your kid, Parker. You don't get to scold me."

"Look, I get it. You're pissed at me. Fine. We'll deal. But rag on Lolli when you know jack shit about her, and I'll drive your ass right back to Alrick. And not because I'm choosing sides, so reel your little neck roll in. Don't go making your mind up about her without giving her a fair chance. Don't be like Mom."

"Whatever," she whispers, only half giving in.

"Back on track. Pregnant?"

"Yep."

"And Mom doesn't know?"

"Nope."

I nod, shifting to look out the window a moment. "Who's the father?"

She gives me a side-glance, and her lips pull to the left.

"Payton."

"He doesn't know either."

"Payton."

"It's not important right now!"

"*Payton.*"

"Fine!" She hops off the counter and takes a step toward me. "Wanna know?" Her eyes widen as her eyebrows lift. "Deaton Vermont."

My mouth opens, and for the second time in a fifteen-minute span, I'm speechless.

Deaton Vermont. Brother of Kellan Vermont.

Kellan Vermont, fiancé to—

"She knows."

My eyes jump to hers, and she reads the question right.

"I … needed help. I didn't know who else to—"

"Yeah. Got it." I clear my throat and nod, excusing myself to my room where I lock myself inside and pull out my phone. Dialing a number I never thought I'd have a need to call, I bring the phone to my ear.

It takes three and a half rings, and then she answers.

The few deep breaths on her end have me holding mine.

I'm just about to hang up when she speaks, soft and low, "Hey."

One word. One insignificant, tiny, meaningless word from her lips, and my head swims. Hundreds of thoughts I've pushed away and just recently have been able to keep gone come crashing back into the forefront of my mind.

One gentle, airy whisper, and I'm drowning again. Suffocating.

"You two talked."

I lay my forehead against the wall, letting out a strangled, "Yeah."

"Good."

I swallow, forcing myself to speak, "What if I had been gone? She'd have been stuck here, having never met Lolli before, not knowing what to do."

"I only wanted to help."

I spin slowly, leaning against the door, my chin dropping to my chest. "Don't."

"Parker ..." she breathes. I picture she's backed herself against a wall, her head tipped against it, those eyes squeezed shut. "I'm ... sorry."

"I know you are." I inhale deeply. "You always are."

"Don't be like that."

A saddened chuckle leaves me before I can stop it. "How would you like me to be?"

She's quiet for a moment before clearing her throat. "Should I head home?"

My body shoots up straight. "What?"

"I can. I—"

I drop my phone from my ear and storm from my room, my eyes narrowing in on Payton as I make my way around the corner.

Her face scrunches as she chews her nail, both an apology and confirmation.

Damn it.

I shake my hands, hang up on the call, and stuff my phone in my pocket before stepping up to the door, and in what feels like slow motion, I look out the peephole.

All the air leaves my lungs.

There she is.

All perfect hair and ironed clothes, leaning just the way I pictured. But against my porch? Never would have expected that.

She looks to the screen of her phone before tucking it into her chest. Her head dips, and a sheet of caramel hair falls over her shoulder, hiding her. Blocking her from the world. It only lasts a minute before she steels herself, stands tall with fake bravado, and smooths out her blazer.

With a quick glance at Payton, I turn the handle, taking a deep breath in an attempt to settle myself.

But it does nothing to calm me, and the second I open the door, the moment her eyes hit mine, it's as if they never left. Like always.

She tries not to show it, to pretend like she doesn't feel the same. And she's gotten better at hiding it throughout the years, but I don't need to see it in her stance or measure it in the way she breathes—even though I can. It doesn't matter how her eyes widen only slightly, just for her lids to drop even lower in the end. Or the way the pulse at the base of her neck speeds up, just from being near me. She could try to hide all these things, and it wouldn't matter.

All those little telltales are there, but I need none of them because, somehow, her feelings radiate off her body and seep into mine. It's always been that way for me and my secret friend. My secret everything.

"Parker." My name barely passes her lips, but the attempt at nonchalance almost kills me as much as her need to use it. She gives a small smile. "You planning on inviting me in?"

I wanna turn her away, tell her it's best she go home. Back to her life.

Back to him.

But I can't, and that's the problem.

I couldn't turn her away if I tried. And, as much as I wanna hate her, be cold toward her, I can't. Won't. Because, at the end of the day, no matter where life takes us, something pushes us right back here, with her standing right in front of me.

My smile starts slow, but once it cracks, it only grows.

Instantly, her shoulders relax, and she sears my soul with a smile of her own.

"You've never needed an invite before. Why you waiting for one now?"

She smiles wider but tips her head to the side, again hiding behind shiny, straight hair.

I place my hand out for her to take, and her eyes slowly shift from it to me before she finally places her tiny one in mine.

"Welcome to California, Kens."

CHAPTER 2
PARKER

My head pops up when Kenra steps around the corner. She freezes for a second before taking the last few steps toward the couch, choosing to sit on the ottoman in front of it.

"Payton's asleep," she tells me quietly, and I nod. "Where's Lolli?"

I glance at the clock behind her. "Should be on her way home."

She watches me for a moment, her head tilting slightly, before a small smile finds the corner of her mouth.

"What?"

She shrugs, glancing off only to bring her eyes right back. "It's just … it's good to see you; that's all. I haven't seen you since—"

"Since I came back from Mexico, and you stopped by to find out if I slept with my best friend?"

She opens her mouth to speak but rethinks her original thought and tries again. "My brother was real messed up after that, Parker. I just needed to know if we should still hold out hope for those two."

I scrub my hands down my face and glance away.

Over spring break this year, a bunch of us went to Mexico. Nate, Kenra's brother, had been dating my best friend, Lolli, for the better part of five months, and shit hit the fan while we were there.

His jealous ex-hookup, who also happens to be Kenra's ex-best friend, went crazy and set it up to make Lolli think he had slept with her and made Nate think Lolli played him. They split because of it.

Lolli, having no idea how to process such emotions—she had been closed off from the start—didn't react all that well, and when the night closed in and I helped her drunken self to her room, she asked me to stay. I wasn't sure I should at that point. She was vulnerable, beautiful, and broken, and I was lost in my own mind, unsure of how to deal with my own issue—her role in my life at that point being one of them.

But I loved her and knew I needed to be there for her, like she would do for me, so I stayed.

She asked me to kiss her that night, and I thought about it. Almost did, but in the end, I couldn't. She didn't belong to me, and I knew that as much as she did. She didn't want me. She wanted the pain to go away and didn't know how to make it happen.

That next morning, Nate found me in her bed and flipped his shit. And, apparently, word got back to Kenra because, not two days later, there she was, on my doorstep.

It wasn't fair for her to show up, and she had no right to the truth. Hell, she was engaged to another man and we hadn't talked in months. But that didn't stop me from wanting to give it to her. She has a power over me no one ever has. One I'm betting no one ever will.

Every time I think she's gone for good, that maybe I can start to push forward, she shows up and pulls me right back in, right back under.

With a sigh, I look to her.

"How long will you stay?" I change the subject.

"I don't know," she whispers, her gaze flitting back and forth between mine.

I watch moisture start to build, clouding her auburn eyes. In my peripheral, I see her hand lifting, but I don't break eye contact. I've missed those eyes too much to look away, and who the hell knows how quick they'll be gone this time around.

I force myself to sit still as the tips of her fingers skim along my jaw when all I wanna do is pull her in.

"You have stubble," she whispers, eyes still locked on mine.

With a deep inhale, I stare at her.

"I miss you, Parker."

"Do you?"

"Yes," she admits quietly.

"Just not enough?"

She blinks, her eyes dropping to the floor, and a tear breaks free, sliding down her cheek.

"Kens," I whisper, my ribs constricting as I reach to wipe it away, "don't cry."

She shakes her head, laughing lightly. "Sorry, I just … nothing is how I thought it would be."

When my brows pull in, she waves me off and shifts to stand, as if that were enough of an explanation.

"Is there somewhere I can rest for a while? I'm exhausted. Long ride."

When I don't move, my eyes still trained on hers, she sighs and gives me something.

"I … miss my mom and dad." She waves a hand around the room. "I miss Nate. I didn't know, or I didn't realize I wouldn't see much of them when I … when Kellan …"

"Right." I clear my throat and stand before she can say anything else. I don't want to hear about all that quite yet. I need a minute to wrap my head around all this—her here. My sister here, pregnant. "You can lie down in Lolli's room for a bit —she won't mind—and I'll get the other guest rooms ready for you guys."

Her eyes swing between mine, and she nods.

"We, uh … Lolli and I are barbecuing tonight, so dinner's covered," I let her know as I usher her into the room.

She looks to the bed, slowly closing the door.

"Kenra."

Dispirited eyes find mine.

"Don't worry …"

She can't help it, and like I knew she would, she laughs as she responds, "Be happy."

I chuckle and grab the handle, pulling the door closed myself before she looks at me again.

Once their rooms are ready to go, I make sure everything is out for dinner. Then, I sneak out the back, making my way to Lolli's oasis—a pergola in the sand that overlooks the ocean. She added a hammock under it for me, to the right of the swing Nate hung for her, so she and I could come out here together or on our own and just … be.

I lie back and look across the ocean at the California sky.

My sister, sixteen and pregnant. With a Vermont, no less.

And he doesn't know. My mom doesn't know. Payton doesn't speak to our dad, so he and his partner, Clint, for sure don't know.

Yet she told Kenra.

Last I knew, Payton didn't even *like* Kenra. Sure, it's because she was—*is*—a bratty teenage girl with a stick up her ass—not her fault necessarily. My mother raised her to be Ms. Alrick Falls—to stand taller against anyone who thinks they can see eye to eye.

Clearly, things have changed, and maybe they did a while ago. I guess I wouldn't know. I haven't seen or talked to Payton in a year, thanks to my mother. Haven't slept under the same roof as my baby sister in over three years since I left my mom's to live with my dad.

But how much could have happened that would make my sister trust Kenra? Or was she just desperate? And if so, why?

And why did Kenra have to come here, *stay* here?

11

Kenra Monroe is in California. In my house.

But not as mine, not that she'd ever be.

That has been clear since day one.

"There's a Monroe in my bed, and it's not the one I'm fuckin'."

My body shakes with laughter, and I turn my head to peer at Lolli as she makes her way over.

She grins and hops on top of my feet, making the hammock wobble.

"Hi, Lolli Bear."

"Hero." She slowly drags out her nickname for me, a single dark brow arched high.

"How was your trip to UCLA?"

She tips her head, narrowing her eyes on me. "Okay, I'll play along, but know it's not working. You *will* spill the beans. Buuut my trip was fantastic. Nate's killin' it out there. It's only camp, and those coaches are practically jizzin' in their jeans at the thought of what he can do." She wiggles her eyebrows. "Pretty sure one *really* wants to know what he's got goin' on."

I laugh and look to the ocean.

Lolli doesn't say anything else but watches the waves crash against the shoreline with me.

And this is why we work. She gets down; I pull her back. I lose my grip; she steadies me. She could tell I needed a minute, so she made me laugh and then gave it to me.

When I sigh, she adjusts herself, so she's lying opposite me, our eyes locked.

"She's in your bed because my sister's in mine."

When Lolli's eyes go round, I nod. I told her all about how my mom refused to let me see or talk to Payton over the last year. She knew it wasn't something I liked to talk about, so she never pushed.

"Payton's pregnant."

"Shut the hell up!"

"With a Vermont."

Lolli's jaw drops.

"Yep. And Kenra brought her here *without* telling my mom and then decided to stay along with her." I eye Lolli, and she eyes me right back.

"Okay." She nods, holding a hand up. "We are so talking about this Kenra thing, like, in five seconds, but holy mother of shit, Payton is pregnant *with a Vermont,* and your mom has no idea?"

"That's what Payton says."

"Think your mom will call here, looking for her?"

"Nah. She doesn't think Payton would ever step outta line and disobey."

"Ha! She's a horny teenager. Course she will."

"Not helping."

"Wasn't supposed to." She laughs and nudges me with her knee, making me laugh with her.

I look to my hands, pulling off my class ring and putting it back on, my thoughts on Kenra. "I can't have her here, Lolli Bear."

"So, I'll tell her to leave."

I grin at that. Instant and complete support, no questions asked—that's how Lolli loves. And I love her for it.

Kenra is Nate's sister, Lolli's future sister-in-law, but that doesn't compare or get in the way of what she wants for me— pure and uninterrupted happiness. Now, if it came down to me and Nate, my ass would be grass, and I'm okay with that.

When I look to her, her forehead pinches, understanding dawning.

"You can't have her here ... but you don't want her to go."

I tilt my head, nodding.

"Shit."

Damn straight.

"Ugh. I hate when it gets hot like this," my best friend, Liv, complains, dabbing her arms with a towel.

"Maybe you should get in the pool then," I tease.

Her mouth drops open as she looks at me in horror. "Seriously?" Her perfectly drawn eyebrows lift. "Half the varsity football team is here. I wouldn't be caught *dead* with pool hair in front of them."

"Then, why did you insist on a pool party? Why not let my mom have the barbecue at our house, like she wanted?"

"I swear, Kenra, it's like you're the youngest of our little duo." She shakes her head and lies back against her lounger. "Sometimes, you can be so dense. Having it *here* meant my dad would invite Mr. Prescott and inviting Mr. Prescott meant he'd extend the invitation to the rest of the football team."

Ah, right.

My brother, Nate, made the varsity team as an incoming freshman, which is a huge deal in this football town. So, of course, Liv thought a party was needed for that, so here we are, in Liv's backyard, surrounded by their friends and classmates along with some upperclassmen I've yet to meet, but I recognize them all the same.

Liv's parents, who live *way* outside their means, have no idea what overkill is and went all out with this luau-themed party.

I shrug and look back to the others messing around in the water. Some are swimming, others are chicken fighting in the shallow end, and some are sitting on the edge, dipping their toes in.

I jump when cold water hits my stomach, and my eyes fly to my brother, who's cracking up from the edge of the pool, a pool noodle in his hands.

"Don't even think—"

Before I can finish my sentence, he bends and blows through one end, the water squirting me right in the face.

"Ahh!" I jump up, laughing.

When Liv shrieks beside me, I turn to her, laughing even harder.

She looks up, her eyes hard, but forces a smile when she sees it was Nate who got her wet.

"If you wanted me to get wet, Nate, all you had to do was ask." She gives him a flirty smile, and he spins around, completely ignoring her.

For the past two years, she's been all about Nate and trying to get him to pay any bit of attention to her. I'm glad he has no interest; it would be so awkward for our friendship if he went there.

I could never tell her that though. She thinks I'm in her corner. If they were right for each other, I totally would be, but she's ridiculously needy, and Nate's not known for kissing anyone's ass.

"Kenra, hand me a water. I'm dying," Nate whines.

"Get out, and get it yourself," I quip.

He gives me those big brown puppy-dog eyes he's perfected over the years.

I should let Liv get it since I know she's dying to and is seconds away from offering, but he'd hate it.

I groan and go to grab him one from the ice chest. He is my baby brother after all.

I get about two feet from the water, ready to toss it to him, when he tries to dart out and grab ahold of my legs, just like I knew he would.

Expecting his trickery, I toss the bottle in the water and hop back, laughing, but gasp when I slam into someone behind me.

A firm grip latches on to my bicep and waist, and my body freezes, goose bumps spreading across my exposed stomach despite the heat.

Scared to look but intrigued even more, I peek over my shoulder, coming nearly face-to-face with tan, smooth skin and deep blue eyes.

He stares at me for a second before the corner of his mouth turns up, showing off a small dimple on the left side of his cheek. "Hi."

My eyes fly to his, and his grin grows.

Embarrassed, I pull away.

"Hi." I clear my throat when my voice comes out scratchy and try again. "Hey."

He opens his mouth to speak, closing it when my brother yells from the water, "Baylor! Where've you been? You were supposed to be here an hour ago!"

Baylor, as my brother called him, scratches the side of his head as he glances off. "I, uh … just stuff at home."

"Mom bein' a bitch again?"

"Austin!" I glare at my brother's annoyingly obnoxious best friend, but the guy beside me simply chuckles. I'd say it sounds a bit forced, but what do I know?

"What?" Austin shrugs innocently.

Nate dunks him and then turns back to us. "Get your ass over here, man. We're about to play volleyball. Show these seniors what's up."

"All right." The guy nods.

Nate glances from him to me when neither of us makes a move to step away.

"Oh, right." Nate rests his forearms on the edge of the pool. "Parker, this is Kenra, my little—"

"Big."

"Sister. She's a prude."

"Nate!" I shriek, horrified, a flush growing up my neck because *oh my God*!

Parker laughs the comment off, looks my way, and then moves past me to set his stuff down on one of the loungers.

I escape quickly, walk over to the cooler once more to grab myself a cold drink, and then make my way back to Liv.

Right as I go to sit, my eyes lift just in time to see Parker reach back and pull his T-shirt over his head.

His back is facing me, and I can't look away, my greedy gaze locked on the smooth curve of his shoulders. When his hands come down to adjust the waist of his swim trunks, my eyes follow, slowly trailing the length of his arm and neck. His hair is shaved at the sides and grown out slightly at the top with soft blond strands lying all over the place. It's a dirty-blond, brightened by the summer sun.

As if sensing my appraisal, he turns around, catching me staring at him. When I don't look away—because my brain forgets to tell me to—he does, his chin dropping to his chest, looking like he's fighting a smile as he makes his way to the pool.

He—

"Seriously?"

I whip my head to the right, finding a sickened Liv.

"What?" I say too quickly, too rushed, and any hope in pretending I wasn't ogling my brother's friend goes out the window. I clear my throat and lower into the lounger beside her.

"Ugh," she grumbles in disgust. "Don't even go there, Kenra. He's a *freshman*."

"So are you."

"Yeah, and you're not. Besides, if you're gonna help me climb the social ladder this year *and* hook up with your brother, you need to set your sights higher. *Way* higher."

"I wasn't even checking him out, so chill," I lie, forcing my eyes to the opposite end of the pool where the varsity team has gathered, ready to play against Nate and his friends.

Kellan Vermont instantly catches my eye, like he's been waiting for me to look his way, and winks.

I smile at him and look around to the rest of the group, but feeling his eyes still on me, I glance back. Sure enough, he's still staring.

He's cute with dark hair and light-brown eyes. Richer than dirt and kind of flaunty about it, he drives a shiny little convertible and takes up two spaces in the front of the school when he parks. He's *that* guy—the one everyone looks at when he walks into a room.

"Now, *that's* more like it," Liv mumbles quietly, covering her mouth with her hand. "That's exactly the type of guy you need to make the next four years worthwhile."

As a sophomore, I only have three years left, so I can only assume she's talking about her own high school experience. But maybe she's right.

Maybe being seen is what I need. I laid relatively low last year, but now that my best friend will be with me in school every day, maybe we're supposed to be the girls everyone else is dying to be.

I look back to Kellan.

If anyone could make that happen, it's him.

"Maybe you're right." I stand when he waves me over. "It could be fun." I look to Liv, who is beaming at me, giving me the courage I need to walk across the cement to the senior boy beckoning me, but on my way, my nervous eyes avoid his and shift left, colliding with Parker Baylor.

He looks at me and then cuts his gaze in the direction my feet are headed and back.

With a lick of his lips and a small pinch in his brows, he focuses back on the game.

Once at the edge of the pool, I lower myself in and take the bench seat in the deep end. Kellan floats right in front of me.

He smirks, reaching up to slide a hand through his wet, dark hair. "Hi."

I blush instantly, and he chuckles. "Hi."

"Why don't you sit here and cheer me on? Be my good-luck charm?" He stares at me with those dark eyes, and I force myself to swallow.

Unable to speak with his attention focused on me, I nod, making his smirk grow before he turns his attention back to the game.

A few minutes of boys yelling and shouting pass before my eyes wander again, finding Parker leaning against the edge, talking to a pretty redheaded girl.

The girl stares at him, completely captivated, but he doesn't seem to notice and continues chatting with her and her friends. But, after a moment, he squints, and shifts slightly, glancing toward the deep end. His eyes skim the water, stopping when they find me through the net. There's inquisition in those blue eyes; it's strong and overpowering, sparking an instant curiosity I've never known. Never felt the need to explore. I bend one knee to push off the seat, getting ready to stand, when an arm snakes around me, and I'm pulled further into the water.

Kellan grabs ahold of the diving board, pulling us beneath it.

His dark eyes roam my face before locking on mine. "Go out with me tonight."

He's not asking, but I guess he probably doesn't have to.

He's Kellan Vermont.

High schooler by day and college student by night. Future state senator, according to the rumors.

And he wants to date *me*?

"Okay." I smile, and he awards me with his.

He leans in to place a soft kiss to my jaw, the dip of his shoulder allowing me to look past him and right into a pair of blue eyes staring at me in the distance.

Those blue eyes drop to the water, and for the remainder of the party, they never find their way back to mine.

Σμυρνιός

"So, who's gonna call Nate?" Lolli asks as she swings one leg over the picnic-style seat on our patio, ripping open a bag of chips.

"You know you want to." I grin, laughing, when she sticks her food-covered tongue out at me. I close the lid on the barbecue and turn toward her. "I'll call him, but don't you think she should be the one?"

"Course I do. That doesn't mean she will."

"It's not a big deal, Lolli Bear."

"Ha!" She swings her other leg over and leans on her elbows, turning to look at me. "Come on, Hero. Who are you talking to here?"

I glance off, nodding slightly. I want to explain everything, but what happens when I do? Will she understand on the level I need her to?

"Hero."

I look back to her, and she smiles softly.

"Stop. It's me. We can either chat … or I can whoop your ass in some sports trivia?"

When I laugh, she smiles brighter.

She's right. I could tell her anything, and she'd still be right here with me. My Lolli Bear.

"Remember that day back in Alrick when you asked me if I messed around with Kenra? I told you she showed up at my house, drunk and crying, because of her douche boyfriend, and I let her sleep in my bed before waking up next to her."

"I'm not sure the douche boyfriend was mentioned, but yeah, I remember that. I noticed how nervous she got when she saw you at her engagement party at their parents' house."

"Yeah. You're not the most perceptive person, but you did pick up on that," I tease.

She throws a chip at me, making me laugh.

"What?" I grin harder. "It's true. Everyone could see Nate had it bad for you for weeks before you two made it happen. Everyone but you."

She throws a lime this time, but I dodge it, and she laughs.

"Yeah, well, we're talking about you right now, shithead, so don't forget the part about your morning man's salute to her ass." She grins, winking to let me know she's trying to make this easy for me. "I believe the words you used were, 'Woke up, appreciating her ass.'" She raises a brow, and I raise one back with a smirk.

"You've gotta admit it, Lolli; it's a nice ass."

She starts laughing again, and I find myself chuckling with her.

I turn to check on the meat. "Anyway, she showed up at my house that night, but that wasn't the first time we'd hung out." I glance back to find Lolli giving me all her attention. "That was my junior year, her senior year."

"Okay …"

"The first time was my freshman year. She walked by my dad's house, alone, in the dark."

I remember everything about that night.

It was the first time I ever felt someone was listening. *Really* listening. Not just to hear, but to understand. And not by force, but out of want, maybe even a deeper need than even we realized at the time. Whatever it was, she shone some light on me that night.

But it was also the second time Kenra Monroe walked away from me for Kellan Vermont.

Kenra

Jealousy. That's what's burning through me as I hide just inside the sliding glass door, watching Parker and Lolli relax under the sun, chatting and cooking together, completely at peace—what I assume is a typical evening for them.

I couldn't sleep, knowing he was under the same roof as me, so eventually, I gave up and came to find him … but he has Lolli to keep him company, to laugh with.

I want to know what weekend dinners on a California deck feels like. I want to be simple, small town again. Not that this place is small town; it's not. But I want to *feel* that—the purpose of everything around me.

And the only time I can is when he's within reach.

But he's never *truly* in reach. He's so far beyond my range. I stand five foot seven, three feet away, and couldn't pull him in with a ten-foot pole.

I watch from where I stand, as she laughs at something he said, noting the crinkles that frame his eyes as he peeks at her over his shoulder, not missing the subtle smile she gives in return.

It's as beautiful as it is devastating.

On one hand, my heart is full for him, for him having someone he sincerely connects with. A best friend to lean on who gets him and knows what to give with a simple look. A look that speaks volumes to him.

And on the other hand, I don't want her to have any of it—his pain or his happiness. It's disgusting and selfish—I know this—but it's true.

I step closer until I can hear his voice and allow it to run through me. I don't even listen to the words, just close my eyes and lean my head against the wall, his mere presence calming me like nothing else can. His voice, digging deep, pulling at the buried pieces of myself I've missed … that is, until he starts talking about the night I made my first mistake.

Sophomore Year

"Come on, baby. Just hang a little longer." Kellan rubs his nose in my hair, and I force myself to stay still for a few seconds before slowly pulling back.

I've been trying to leave for an hour now, and every time I mention it, he distracts me, and I end up staying longer. But people are getting to the point of regrets, so I know I need to leave before I witness drunken mistakes.

"I can't. My parents will flip if they find out I'm still here."

"Nate's here, and he doesn't look any kind of ready to leave."

We both turn to see Nate pulling some half-naked girl down onto his lap.

"In fact"—his voice deepens, and he brings his lips to my ear—"he looks like he's just about to get the party started."

Ew.

Kellan's brown eyes, slightly clouded by alcohol, come back to mine, and he slowly moves closer, caging me against the wall. "Stay. One of the rooms upstairs is for me. Will makes sure it stays clear, so I always have a place to crash at the end of the night." He licks his full lips. "We can have our own party."

My brows draw in, and I swallow, slight panic kicking in. Kellan sees it and starts rubbing circles on my stomach just beneath my shirt. He leans in to kiss my neck the way he's found—and taught me—I like, a move that causes me to relax into him. His hand skates higher, caressing my ribs, as his mouth drops lower, warming my skin with kisses to my collarbone, and my breathing speeds up.

When a small, involuntary, sound makes its way up my throat, I feel his lips stretch into a smile against my skin before he immediately pulls back, grabs my hand, and all but drags me up the stairs.

The lights are off in the room he leads us to, and he doesn't bother to turn them on when we enter. He locks the door and quickly moves us, pulling me onto the mattress with him so that we're facing each other.

His focused stare makes me feel irresistible, like I'm just as desirable, if not more so, than the older, more experienced senior girls downstairs.

Struck with the want to please him, I lean in, making the first move, and press my lips to his. I softly kiss him, but he's quick to take control, and he immediately shifts, pulling me closer as he grabs on to the sides of my face, directing me.

At first, my kiss is hesitant, but when he slides his hand up my stomach and lightly squeezes my breast over my shirt, I open my mouth wider, allowing him in more.

He continues to kiss me, and I try to lose myself in the moment, but I can't. I'm timid, and he senses it.

With a huff, he pulls back and looks down at me. "You don't want this?" His voice holds a hardened edge.

"I'm just ... I don't know ... nervous maybe?"

At my response, his features soften, and he shifts closer again, whispering, "I can be gentle. Promise." He kisses my cleavage, and I hold my breath. "It'll be hard to control myself with you—you're so damn sweet—but I will, if gentle and slow is what you really want."

I squeeze my eyes shut as his fingers inch the V-neck of my shirt further down.

"I think I should go," I whisper.

All his muscles lock up. He turns to stone above me and hovers there for a second before all but jumping off.

"Yeah. All right," he agrees, already making his way out the door while I'm barely pulling myself up.

I walk down the stairs, alone, Kellan having disappeared from sight, and search for Liv. I don't have to look far, spotting her in the living room right away with a red Solo cup in her hand.

She smiles instantly when she sees me and pulls me close, turning from the conversation she was having with a couple of varsity cheerleaders.

"Isn't this awesome? I'm having so much fun!" She hiccups and then giggles before sipping her beer.

"You're drinking?"

"Jesus Christ." She rolls her eyes and then narrows them on me. "Yes, *I'm drinking*, duh. It's a party, Kenra. That's what you do at parties."

"Not everyone drinks at parties, Liv, and I figured you wouldn't be since you wanted to drive tonight." I wave to a few of the girls who say hi to me and then look back at Liv. "I'm ready to go."

"What? No!" Her gaze slides past me, and I turn to see Kellan making his way toward us.

Liv pinches her lips to the side as her eyes come back to mine. She pulls her keys from her jeans pocket and hands them to me. Really, she shouldn't even be driving since she only has her permit, but her parents don't seem to care.

"Here. Take my car."

"Go back to your house without you?"

"My parents are gone, so what's it matter?"

"I'm not sure that's a good idea."

Kellan steps up and throws his muscular arm around my shoulders. "Don't worry about Liv, babe." He pauses for a second, staring her way. "I'll make sure she's taken care of."

"You sure?"

He pulls his brown eyes from her to look down at me, an easy smile on his lips. He nods, looking her way. "Oh, I'm sure."

I turn to give him a hug, and he squeezes me with the one arm wrapped around me. I figure he'll walk me out, but when I step away and he offers to grab Liv a refill, it's clear I'm on my own. I look for Nate to see if he wants a ride but don't find him. When he doesn't answer his phone, I decide to let him figure it out himself, and I make my way toward Liv's car.

With a push of a button, the engine fires up, but before I can reach for the handle, a voice calls out, "Leaving already, huh?"

I yelp, jumping slightly, and search the darkness for the culprit who scared the crap out of me.

I squint when I see him sitting in a lawn chair. "Parker?"

He chuckles quietly. "Guilty as charged. Didn't mean to scare you."

"Why are you sitting there by yourself?"

"Why you leaving a Will Roberts party by *yourself*?" he challenges, straining for playful, but strangely enough, I hear a slight testiness in his voice.

Pushing the little button, I turn off the car and walk around it to see him better.

"Well, Liv should be leaving with me, but she decided to stay a bit longer. I was just about to head to her house." I lean against the passenger door. "Why are you not at the party?"

He shrugs, leaning back in his seat. "I'm not much of a party guy."

This surprises me. He's pretty popular at school. He hangs with the older crowd; most of the athletes do. I guarantee there are a bunch of girls who wait around in the halls, hoping to get a glimpse or a word from him.

Parker's cute.

He's got that sweet face, soft but firm. With dirty-blond hair and crystal-blue eyes, he definitely catches your attention.

And, now that I think about it, I haven't seen him at any of the parties Kellan has brought me to since we started dating a few months ago.

I glance behind him at the simple home.

I might have never been to Parker's house before—never had a reason to—but I know it's closer to Kellan's side of town. Big and fancy.

I mean, my house is big and beautiful on a mesmerizing piece of land, but it's modest and heartfelt, having been created from scratch at the hands of my dad.

The side of town Parker and Kellan live on? They have dog walkers and use golf carts to pick up their mail … at the end of their driveways.

"My dad's place." He tips his head toward the house.

I nod, crossing my arms over my chest to show him I'm settling in, that he can continue to talk and I'll still be standing here when he's done. He nods, understanding my move.

"My parents are getting a divorce. Been a long time coming."

"Are you … do you live here now?" I ask him, dropping my gaze to the grass.

When he doesn't answer, I peek at him, finding him staring at the house.

Finally, he looks back to me. "Is it weird that I want to?"

"Um …" I'm confused by his question because how would I know?

He chuckles lightly and stands, moving to the dark porch, out of my line of sight. I assume he's leaving me standing here, that maybe I asked the wrong question, but when I push off Liv's car, ready to leave, he emerges with a second chair. Setting it beside the other, he drops back down and looks up at me.

He doesn't say anything, but the shadow of the moon is hitting his face just right, showing me the hope that someone will stop and listen, that I'll listen, and the fear that he read me wrong moments ago.

For some reason, I want to hear what's on his mind. It's like I'm being pulled to him, and the sudden weight on my chest will only lift with his spirits, so I move to sit in the seat he's placed right beside him.

"Tell me, Mr. Safety," I mention his position on the football team in attempt to ease him and I'm rewarded with the slight tip of his lips. "Why would it be weird for you to want to live here?" I ask him, turning my head to once again take in the simple home.

It's a basic tract home, looks exactly the way the house two doors down does, but it's got a nice paint job, and the yard is well kept. There are even some plants in big pots lining the walkway.

With a broken grin, he takes in all the things I did, his head nodding as he looks back to me. He stares for a moment, and I let him, allowing him to look for whatever it is he feels he needs to find in order to share his worries with me.

"My dad's never around. He'll be gone for days, sometimes weeks, at a time, only to come home for a night or two before he's"—he sighs—"gone again."

There's a crease in his blond brows and small wrinkles beside his eyes that tell me this is not only a disappointing fact, but it's also painful. This hurts him.

"It hasn't always been this way?" I guess.

He shakes his head, turning to look the other way. "It about three years ago." He licks his lips and then looks back to me. "He used to go to every game of mine in peewee football, every practice even, until one day, he just … stopped. Just like that."

I shift in my chair, tucking my legs half beneath me as I place my elbow on the armrest and lean closer. "You never asked him why?"

He gives a botched grin. "Is there an answer that would make it okay?"

My gaze travels over his gentle features before returning to those soft blue eyes. "No, Parker, there isn't."

He gives a barely there nod.

"Yet you still want his home to be yours." I glance to the house again in thought. "That means ... there's an even bigger reason you'd rather live here with a man who's made you feel as if you were less worthy than in the home you were raised in with your mom."

Eyes open and intense, his stare digs deeper than the surface, searching for something I can't name, but feeling the depth of his reach. When a deep exhale leaves him, my attention is drawn to his mouth.

I take a sharp breath, watching, staring, as he licks his full lips in what seems like slow motion.

"Kens," he whispers.

My eyes reluctantly return to his. "Sorry," I whisper, feeling a blush that—thank God—he can't see in the dark. "Tell me why you don't want to stay with your mom."

He goes to open that distracting mouth of his again but stops when his eyes travel over my shoulder. My gaze follows his, and I tense when I see Kellan walking this way, a giggling, drunk Liv under his arm. He laughs, as equally drunk as she is, and moves the arm from her shoulders to her waist right as his eyes lift, finding mine in the dark.

He freezes for half a second, and then his gaze cuts from me to the boy beside me and back, narrowing. Making quick work of it, he deposits a confused Liv against a random car parked in front of hers on the curb. She follows his line of sight, and her eyes shoot wide before she laughs, shaking her head.

"Ken ... baby." Kellan walks closer, so I stand from my seat. "What are you doing over here? I thought you left for Liv's house a while ago."

"I ran into Parker on my way out and stopped to chat a bit." I glance around him, seeing Liv now on her phone.

His jaw twitches slightly as he turns to Parker. "Well, since you're still here and Liv's parents are gone for the night"— Kellan steps in front of me, his arm wrapping possessively around my waist—"I'm gonna come spend all night with you," he whispers, his voice purposefully loud enough for Parker to hear.

His insinuation is obvious, and my ears burn instantly.

Too embarrassed to speak and make it clear that he only means we'll likely sleep in the same bed, I give him a tight grin, allowing him to pull me toward Liv's car.

With a quick glance back, I find Parker watching me.

I want to apologize for leaving so suddenly. I want him to understand that I heard his pain. I need to let him know I want to hear the story I think he needs to tell. I want to learn everything there is to know.

I want to stay.

But I do none of those things.

Instead, I walk around to the driver's side and slide behind the wheel, wondering at what point I became "Kens" to the near stranger I just left behind.

And, even more, why I liked the sound of it.

———

I blink away the memory, quickly wiping the tears that have slipped down my cheeks.

God, I remember every second.

I fell for the blond-haired, blue-eyed boy next door that night, but I was too stupid to know it.

CHAPTER 5
PARKER

When the sliding glass door opens, Lolli and I look that way to find Kenra hesitantly making her way toward us.

"Hey, you feelin' any better?"

She tucks her hair behind her ear with a tight smile, moving to sit on the opposite side of the table. "A little."

"Shouldn't we wake up Payton?" Lolli asks, pushing the plates of food toward Kenra. "I mean, she has a person in her. It probably needs to eat, right?"

While my head snaps back, my face scrunching in horror, Kenra fights a grin.

"What?" Lolli shrugs.

"Not sure I'm ready to hear all that."

She waves me off and then flips me off. "Get over it. She got dicked, dick delivered its dick spit, and now, little dicky deserves dinner."

When I gape at her, she glances at Kenra with a grin, and we all start laughing.

I wipe my hands on the towel and then take a seat beside Lolli.

"I wonder ..." She picks up a hot link and flops it in front of me, making me choke on my water.

My hand shoots out to slap over her mouth, and she bounces with laughter against it.

"No more talking about my little sister getting … just no."

Lolli winks, so I drop my hand and bump her with my shoulder.

"But, really though, should we wake her? I haven't even met her, which is bullshit."

"She's not very friendly, Lolli Bear. And you know why you haven't met her."

My mom kept her locked away with every excuse as to why she couldn't be near me. Who the hell knows what she told Payton to get her to stop trying to reach out?

Lolli nods. "So, leave her be?"

"Yep. The drama queen will stir some shit soon enough. Let's prolong it."

Lolli laughs and dips her hot link in the mustard on my plate.

When I glance at Kenra, I find a slight crease on her forehead as she considers Lolli. Instantly, she senses my attention, and her gaze flicks to mine.

I see the questions there. She wants to understand my relationship with Lolli, but she can't figure it out.

And she doesn't need to.

It's our friendship, and we've made sure everyone around us understands that.

We settle into eating, and I can't help but notice how Kenra keeps glancing from the water to the trees on the other side of us.

She likes what she sees.

Her deep, cleansing breaths and long, slow blinks tell me so.

"'Kay, well, since it hasn't been mentioned yet, I'll ask," Lolli announces and then leans her forearms against the wooden tabletop. "Are you gonna call your brother and let him know you're here?"

Kenra sits taller. "My being here doesn't concern him. He has no reason to know."

Ah, shit.

Lolli's lips pinch to the side, and she nods slowly. "Right. I guess I can understand why you'd take my asking as me getting into your business or trying to stir some shit 'cause *that's what girls do*, right? My bad."

She stands to leave, but I keep my eyes on Kenra.

She's not getting where Lolli's going with this, and that's a damn shame.

Lolli doesn't say anything else. She's learned when to rein it in for the most part—that, and she's not sure where the line is when it comes to hurting me by tearing into Kenra. I'm not sure where that line is either, to be honest.

When I stand and start cleaning up, Kenra's fork hits her plate with a loud clink.

"So, she storms off, and all of a sudden, you're done, too? You sure you—"

"Stop," I tell her, not in a shout, but stern enough for her to know I'm serious.

"Stop what?"

I gape at her, trying to hold myself back but fail. I lean over the table, invading her space a bit. "Don't come into *my* home and start unnecessary problems because you're jealous."

She gasps. To an outsider, it would come across as a *how dare you* gasp when really, it's a *you can't say it out loud, but you did* gasp.

"Don't deny it. I can see it, Kenra, and it's misplaced. I'm gonna go inside but let me tell you the way Lolli's mind works, and you can decide if you should feel like crap or not." I push off the table and stand tall again. "Nate hasn't seen you since your engagement party in *November*. You didn't even show for graduation. If he finds out you were here, a couple of hours away, and you didn't care to try to see him, he'd beat himself up, wondering why that was. He doesn't know what you're going through since you don't share anything real with your family. Hell, I don't even know what you're going through."

"That's not fair," she whispers.

"But it's true." I shrug a shoulder. "Look, you have a brother close by who misses you, and his girl is inside this house right now, driving herself crazy because she knows the hurt it'll cause him when he finds out. Hurt that she'll then feel because she loves him."

She stares at me, lost for words.

I sigh, speaking softer this time around, "She's good, Kenra. You know that. You met her and instantly loved her for him. Don't let mine and your problems get in the way of that."

Teary eyes search mine. "We don't have problems," she whispers.

My chest constricts. "You're not mine, Kens," I gently tell her, pain I didn't mean to show clear as day. "And that's a problem for me."

———

Two hours pass before I've finished up my studying for the night. Closing the book, I toss my notes on top of it and make my way down the hall, pushing Lolli's already cracked door the rest of the way open.

"Sorry," she whispers from under her pillow, making me smile.

"Not your fault." I shuffle in and drop next to her on her bed.

"Payton ever come out?"

"Nah. I think she's still knocked out."

"Kenra go to bed, too?"

"She walked that way, so I'm thinking, yeah."

"She's different than I remember. Off somehow."

I squint at the ceiling. "Yeah, she is."

"You got any thoughts on that?"

I nod into the pillow even though she can't see me. "She's not happy, Lolli Bear. Kellan's a dick. I think she's … breaking slowly. And I think it's killing her inside."

"Why do you say that?"

"Her eyes tell me so."

We grow quiet for a few minutes, both lost in thought.

"I'm calling Nate in the morning."

At that, Lolli throws the pillow off her head, a mess of dark hair and blue eyes meeting mine. "Yeah?"

"Yeah." I stare at her. "She needs it, needs her family. She hasn't been home in eight months. Maybe, if she spends a couple of days here, around you and Nate … me, she'll feel more like herself again. At least for a while."

"And then … what? She leaves again, goes MIA for who knows how long, and turns icy?"

"Icy?"

"All the cool kids are saying it."

A chuckle leaves me, and I push up to sit on the edge of the bed, dragging my hands down my face. "I'm hoping she'll remember how it felt to be a part of a real family. Maybe, if anything, she'll at least call you guys more."

"Pretty sure she has no desire to *anything* me."

I shift to face her. "This isn't her, Lolli. She's lost. She needs someone like you."

She slightly shakes her head. "And if it's you she needs?"

"I'm there as much as she allows."

"And you're okay with that?"

"It's complicated."

"You deserve better."

"So does she."

"Parker Baylor"—Lolli gives a small, proud smile, pulling her blanket to her chin as I stand—"always the hero."

I grin and turn off her light. "Night, Lolli Bear."

After peeking in on Payton, finding her snoring softly, curled up in a fluffy ball of cotton, I check in on Kenra.

I didn't think she'd be asleep yet—she was always a night owl, my nightingale—but she is. Lying across the blankets with her hands tucked under her cheek, she looks every bit a pristine fairy-tale princess. Exactly like Kellan wants her. Prim and proper, perfectly groomed.

Is this who she's become?

The girl who gets stared at but stares through everyone.

That world was never for her.

She comes from two amazing parents whose love runs deeper than coal. A family who loves her with everything they have and raised her to be strong and independent and free.

That's the only reason they didn't fight her on moving away to a bigger city and playing trophy to Kellan and his political followers. They think it's what she wants, and maybe, at one point, she did. I honestly don't know for sure. But I can see the wear it's taken on her.

She's pale and her eyes are empty. She's unfulfilled and unsure of what to do about it.

And to make matters worse … Kellan is an asshole. So, it's not like she's there, unhappy with her surroundings but treated like a queen at home.

She is treated like a queen but by the fake people around her. And that's only because they're afraid of their king, so again, none of it's real or right.

She belongs under the sun with flip-flops and a smile.

She belongs here. With me.

Grabbing the blanket off the chair in the corner, I lightly drape it over her, watching her eyes flutter behind closed lids.

Right before I exit the room, she stirs, and I'd swear, I heard her whisper my name, but I don't look back to see if she's awake because the thought of her dreaming of me hurts too much to bear.

CHAPTER 6
PARKER

Σωτηρίας

W HEN I COME AROUND THE CORNER, I CAN'T HELP BUT LAUGH. "Really, Peep, ice cream at six a.m.?"

She shrugs and brings another bite to her mouth. "I'm drowning in my sorrows. This is what they do in the movies, so figured it should work."

I pull a water bottle from the fridge and then look back to her. "I don't think your kind of dilemma can be fixed with mint chip."

"Worth a shot." She pops a shoulder.

"What are you doing up so early anyway?"

She rolls her eyes and glances out the window at the beach. "This is nothing. Mom makes me wake up at four thirty every morning to work out before getting ready."

I study her when she says this, and her face scrunches slightly, her lips pinching together.

"How long has she been doin' that?"

Payton swings her eyes back to mine. "Since the day you moved in with Dad."

"You were thirteen."

"And eleven pounds overweight, according to her."

"What's going on, Payton? Last I knew, you and Mom were

thick as thieves, and I couldn't get past it to get to you. What happened?"

Payton laughs humorously and hops off the kitchen island. She smacks the lid on the ice cream and roughly places it in the freezer. "You want me to sit here and recap three years of my life that you weren't a part of? Hard pass, Parker."

She storms out the back door, and I follow, quietly closing it behind me. "Come on, Peep. We have a lot to work through on our own, but we have to put that aside and focus on what's happening right now. You're having a baby."

"I know!" she shouts, spinning to face me. "I. Know. I'm having a baby. I'm a freaking reality TV show, Parker!" She starts pacing, throwing her hands out as she talks. "I'll be a laughing stock at school. I'll probably get kicked out. I can kiss art school good-bye!" She drops, so her knees are bent, her ass practically scraping the ground. "Oh God. My showing will be canceled. No way will they want a sixteen, —seventeen by then —big, fat, pregnant girl representing their program." She takes a shuddering breath.

"Hey, hey … calm down. Hang on." I drop to her level and bring her up by her shoulders, walking us over to the patio sofa. "Come on, sit."

"I ruined everything. I'm such an idiot."

"Payton, stop. I know your mind is racing right now, but first, we have to figure out what we have to do. Like doctors and what to do about Mom. And I need to know if that guy will be calling to look for you. And, eventually, I wanna hear about this art-school stuff 'cause last I heard, you wanted to be Miss America when you grew up."

Despite how she's feeling, that earns me a light laugh, and she peeks at me before looking away. "A lot has changed, Parker."

"Yeah." I sit back, and she allows me to pull her with me. "I guess it has."

"That her?"

I look were she's pointing to find Lolli running along the beach, headed home. "Yep."

"She runs ... for fun?"

I laugh. "Among other things, yeah. It's peaceful for her; she enjoys the physical part of it, but it's also a necessity."

"What do you mean?" Payton asks, watching Lolli as she grows closer.

"Lolli isn't what first impressions will tell you. But she'll only show you if she feels it."

"So, she runs to escape?"

"To escape. To understand. To believe." I look at Payton and find a small smile on her lips.

"I can get that."

I'm about to ask her how, but Lolli hits the bottom step and slowly jogs up. "Hey. It's fuckin' hot already."

"It is no kind of hot. It's six thirty in the morning on the beach in Oceanside."

She pops her hip out as she screws off the lid to her water. "You run your ass six miles, and then your opinion will count."

I grin at her, and she smiles back, her eyes cutting to Payton.

After taking a drink, Lolli steps closer to her. "Hey. I'm Lolli. I'd shake your hand, but I feel like you won't appreciate the sweat and sand."

"Not so much, no." Payton crosses her arms over her chest.

"You hate me?"

Payton's eyes dart to mine before going back to Lolli. "Nooo. I don't even know you."

"But your brother came here because I asked him—among other personal reasons. I imagine that felt like the knife in the gut and created instant hate for me. I just want you to know that, if you feel that now, it's okay; I get it. But you won't forever. Promise."

Payton looks at Lolli like she's an alien.

"Lolli likes to keep things out in the open, clear the air with honesty. It's a problem sometimes." I laugh, and Lolli shrugs.

"So, you just blurt out what you think or feel and expect others to be okay with it?" Payton sasses, head shaking and all.

Lolli laughs lightly and looks past us. "No. I just want to make sure people know where I stand, is all." When she looks back to Payton, Lolli's blue eyes are warm, and she smiles softly. "I *am* happy you're here, Payton."

Payton nods, uneasy.

"All right. I'm gonna take a shower and then make some breakfast for us." She heads to the door but stops and turns back, once again smiling at Payton. "Congratulations, by the way."

Payton freezes, and Lolli disappears through the door.

"I ... didn't think she knew."

"I might have told her yesterday."

Payton shakes her head. "It's fine. I just ... it didn't feel like she was judging me."

"She doesn't see or feel things like we would in certain situations."

"Why?"

"She lost her family the night before her seventeenth birthday. She was at the hospital with her grandpa, and the nurse came in to say her parents had an accident. Right after, her grandpa passed and Lolli shut herself down. Until Nate. He's managed to get to her."

"But you couldn't?"

I lick my lips and look off. "I did. Just in a different way."

"But you hoped for more?"

"Everything is how it's supposed to be, as far as Lolli is concerned."

Payton grabs my arm and drags me to the door. "That's not what I asked, but I get it."

I smile at her. "I love you, Payton."

"I'm mad at you, Parker, but I love you, too."

41

She says she's mad, but I have an inkling she understands why I left our mom and moved in with our dad. It'll be a long road for us to get back to the tight relationship we had as little kids, but I have no doubt we can.

I toss my arm over her shoulders. "Come on, little sis. Lolli makes some mean French toast."

CHAPTER 7

KENRA

Σμιζνιὸς

With a deep breath, I smooth my shirt out, making sure there are no wrinkles, and force myself to take a look into the mirror. Silky, straight brown hair and my plain face with nude shadows and lipstick, both tones that Kellan picked out for me. He says it's classy and understated in a professional way.

I came home with a rose-colored lipstick one day, a free gift I didn't want or ask for, but the lady at Sephora gave it to me anyway for my birthday, and he accused me of trying to gain attention. He said I'd look like a cheap gold digger, and that wasn't the impression he wanted me to put off. So, he rolled it all the way up and broke the stick. I wondered if he thought I'd dig it out of the trash had he simply thrown it away, but I didn't ask. It would have done nothing but cause an argument.

Avoiding my own eyes, I look myself over again, and once I confirm not a hair is out of place, I exit the room and head for the loud chatter in the kitchen.

I expect them all to grow quiet as I come around the corner. For Lolli to scowl at me and Parker to look away, but that doesn't happen.

In fact, Lolli continues laughing as she turns and gives me a quick, "Hey," before returning to her food. Parker winks at me, pushing the chair at the end of the table out with his foot for me to join them. Even Payton is smiling as she takes a bite.

"I wasn't sure if you liked sweet shit for breakfast, so I started to make some omelets, but then Parker said you and most vegetables weren't friends, so I scratched that. Anyway, there's a bunch of random crap, but it kinda works." Lolli nods, dipping her eggs in a pile of syrup.

"Thank you, Lolli. I'm sure it's great." I manage to speak without my voice cracking as conflicting emotions begin to take over. I've done nothing to deserve their kindness.

Lolli licks the syrup and starts on another bite when the door flies open, and voices flow through the house.

My forehead creases along with theirs because I wasn't expecting multiple people.

"What the fuck—" Lolli starts but squeals when Nate comes around the corner.

Pressure builds on my chest while I watch him ignore everyone around us as he makes his way to her, and her eyes track him just the same. She shifts to stand right as he bends to scoop her up, squeezing her tight against him. She laughs into his neck as he laughs into her hair before she pulls back and looks to him. It's only for a second, hardly a glance, but I feel the *I love you* that neither has spoken but both communicate in that moment.

I glance away when he kisses her, my eyes landing on Parker, finding lines framing his eyes as he pulls his eyes from the couple as well.

I try to study his facial features, but when he looks at me and gives a small smile, I can't decipher where the sadness came from.

Is it because Nate is here?

Because Nate's kissing Lolli, and Parker wants to be the one?

Or could he possibly, maybe, be wondering what it would be like to have that feeling for himself?

I stare at him, and he stares back, his head slowly tilting as he attempts to study me, as I did him. Right then, I'm pulled from my chair and spun around.

When Nate drops me to my feet, I smile up at him with watery eyes.

"Aw, Ken." He chuckles, slightly rocking me. "Don't cry. I know you missed me, but damn." He grins when I smack his back.

But he's right. I did miss him. So damn much.

"So, you're not mad, Kenra?" Lolli asks and turns to her.

"Mad?"

"Well, yeah. I mean, yesterday—"

"Uh," Parker cuts her off, and my eyes fly to him in suspicion, "you didn't tell us you called Nate."

My brows knit at the center and then it clicks. He was going to call Nate on his own even though, last night, I never said I wanted to see him.

I should be upset, but I'm not. Especially when those blue eyes tell me they're proud.

A sliver of light finds its way inside me.

I glance at Lolli, and she too gives a small, almost unnoticeable nod, having picked up on Parker's diversion.

I thought long and hard about what he said to me, about how Lolli knew how Nate would feel, and I was disgusted in myself even more. I should know and understand my own brother, who has been a part of me all his life better than the girl in his, right?

Truth is, I was afraid to call, afraid to see him. He's my baby brother and the last person I'd ever want to let down. I worried he'd see a different person when he looked at me, like he'd see through the mask I've painted on. But seeing him now, I'm glad I did. I've missed him.

"Wait." I turn back to Nate. "I heard more than one voice …"

Nate grins, and the other intruders pop around the corner.

"Surprise!"

I look between them all, and my emotions threaten to overflow.

My cousin, Arianna, runs up to me first, squeezing me tight around the neck. "I missed you!"

I latch on to her, fighting as hard as I can to hold it together. Some tears slip, but I manage to keep them at a happy-tear level when, really, I want to crumble right here and now.

Next, Mason, Ari's twin, shoves her out of the way and gives me a quick spin and kiss to the cheek. I'm passed down the line from there.

Brady and Chase, Mason's best friends, and lastly, Cameron, Ari's best friend, all greet me in hugs and kind words.

I pull back and dab at my eyes, smoothing my shirt down once more. "What the heck are you guys doing here?"

Ari gapes at me, and Cam makes an *mmm* sound like I'm in trouble.

"Seriously?" Ari asks as she hops onto the countertop.

"I just mean, how'd you get here so fast? Were you already on your way?"

Ari's eyes search mine. "You didn't even read any of the messages I've sent you? Or listen to the voice mails? What the heck, Ken?"

I open my mouth to defend myself, to say something, but what could I possible say? She's right, I never checked any of her messages.

She sees the struggle I'm having and gives a small nod, quickly hopping off the counter and making her way to the table. "Make me some French toast again, Lolli?"

My eyes cut to Lolli, and I glance between her and Ari and the others. And I see it.

They're all comfortable here.

Brady and Chase are digging in the fridge while Mason is now sitting on the counter Ari just jumped off of, and Cam is filling a cup of something.

They've been here, enjoyed summer days together like we used to do as kids.

"Guys," Parker speaks, pulling his worried gaze from mine when I glance his way, "this is my sister, Payton. She might be here, hanging out with us, for a while."

The group looks to Payton like they just noticed she was here, and they all take turns greeting her.

Eventually, everyone finds a place to sit, and we eat and chat a little bit. Mainly, they talk about summer, and I listen to all the things I've missed, feeling like the outsider at a table full of my own family and close friends.

I glance at Nate, finding him and Lolli in their own world. He's maneuvered himself, so he's behind her, and she sits between his legs. One of his arms is on the outside of hers, caging her into him, as he eats around her with the other. Every few seconds, he runs his hand down her arm, brushes her fingers, whispers in her ear, something. Every single time, she smiles even though he can't see it. But he knows because, after she does, he smirks to himself. They are completely and utterly entwined.

It's one of the most beautiful things I've ever witnessed. It reminds me of my parents and the love they share. But, watching my brother and his fiancé, you can't simply see it. You're forced to feel it. What it's like to be consumed and to consume.

For someone like me, it's a sharp pain in the form of reality. Forcing me to remember the weight of a war no one knows I'm a part of. It's a heavy exhaustion that's never rejuvenated. A hunger never satisfied. I'm not consumed by the man I'm with but controlled. Owned in a devastating way with no out.

I look to my plate and push my strawberries around.

I know Parker's eyes are on me, but I don't want him to see what I'm feeling right now, and he will. He always has.

CHAPTER 8
PARKER

Σμιγμάς

"Where are we goin'?" Kenra laughs as I pull her through the trees and down the thin dirt path.

"Did I hound you the entire drive on Wednesday when it was your pick?"

"No." I hear her grin and smile to myself.

"That's right. No. I was a good boy and sat through two hours of Selena Gomez music—she was lip-syncing the entire time, by the way"—Kenra snickers behind me— "all without complaining. I think you can make it through a five-minute mini hike without asking questions."

"Okay, fine, I'll stop asking."

I stop walking and turn to her with one brow arched high, knowing damn well she's got a clause coming.

She smiles wide, and I inhale deeply, smiling back.

She's infectious. Everything about her screams to everything in me.

I lick my lips, the corner of my mouth lifting. "Let's hear it."

"Piggyback ride to the destination." She nods once, lifting her chin at me, and I grin. She bobs her shoulders in triumph.

Crazy girl.

"All right, piggyback ride it is." I nod, and she claps her

hands, but I catch her off guard and step closer to her. "But you, Kenra Monroe, are off your rocker if you think you're the one who is winning here."

Her eyes crease at the edges but only for a moment before her cheeks turn as red as her swimsuit.

I smirk as I spin around and glance over my shoulder at her. "Hop on, Kens. Wrap those long-ass legs around me."

I'm betting her jaw has dropped a bit, what with the few moments of hesitation. Finally, her little hands land on my shoulders, and she hops up.

I catch her when she jumps, hooking my hands around her thighs, and start back down the path.

After a few steps, she giggles near my ear, her hot breath and silky sounds traveling past my waistband. "Whatcha thinkin' 'bout, Nightingale?"

"About you, Mr. Safety. Just you." She sighs, and her hold around my neck tightens a bit.

"Just me, huh?" I tease, clapping my hand against her thigh. "This I gotta hear."

She smiles against my cheek. "I like when we do this ... take off for the day, just us. It's been a fun summer."

I swallow, wishing I could see her face right now. "Summer's not over yet; we've still got a couple of days."

"You're right," she speaks low. "A couple more days."

Uneasiness has my face scrunching, but I don't ask because, finally, we're within view of our stopping point.

Kenra gasps, and her legs and arms tighten in a death grip. "Oh, hell no! No way, Parker Baylor!"

I laugh and keep forward, toward the water.

Now, she starts flailing, attempting to kick her legs so that she can get down, but all it does is make her flip-flops fly off her feet.

"You put me down right now."

"Nuh-uh. No way." I grin and tighten my hold, so she doesn't fall.

"Wait. Uh, my keys!"

"Left them in the glove box with your phone *and* mine."

"Shit," she whines in a panic. "My clothes! I need to take off my clothes."

"Eh," I tease, "I'm not opposed to that, but they'll dry."

"If you jump in that water with me on your back, I'll—"

She cuts off when I quickly shift, pulling her around my front, her legs now wrapped around my back. Her chest rises on a deep inhale, and it takes her a minute to remember what she was about to say.

"You'll what, hmm?"

Her eyes flick between mine. "I'll make you pay for it, Baylor."

My grin is slow. "I'd love to, Monroe." I squeeze her thighs, and those golden eyes grow darker, a burnt-honey color now.

"You gonna throw me in that water?" she asks, her hands slowly shifting to rest on my biceps.

"Nope."

"No?"

"I'mma let you take these clothes off, just like you said you wanted."

She laughs lightly. "Oh, really? All because I wanted, huh?"

"I mean, I see that little scrap of red around your neck. Gotta admit, I'm curious as to what the rest of that thing looks like."

Her chest grows pink, but she likes hearing what I'm telling her. Her little tongue curls up behind her teeth, and she smiles a bit. "You gonna put me down then?"

"Nope."

She laughs. "No?"

"Not till you promise you'll do it."

Her eyes narrow playfully. "Do what?"

"Whatever I request."

I grin, and her chin dips just a tad, those pretty brown eyes of hers staying on me. I can see it in her stare, her want to do whatever I ask. Finally, she rubs her lips together, giving me a small nod, and damn if I don't want to lean forward and pull her bottom lip between mine. But I don't.

I slowly let her legs slide down my waist until her feet hit the ground. "Strip."

She smacks me, and we both laugh.

While she gets undressed, I move over to the tree and lay our towels across one of the branches. I kick my shoes off, stuffing my socks inside, and then toss my shirt on top of them.

When I spin around, Kenra's facing the water, her ass in a tiny red bikini, facing me.

I suck my lips between my teeth and will my dick not to get hard.

My eyes follow her frame, sliding across the curve of her back, as she ties her hair up in a knot.

"Want me to shake it for you?" she teases, glancing back with a smile.

I grin and take a step closer. "Hey, you can't blame me. You're the one dressed in red. You're the muleta, and I'm the bull."

Kenra laughs loudly and spins to face me. "Okay. I'm undressed. You're undressed. Now, what exactly did I promise to do?"

I wince, and she tilts her head, her eyes narrowing.

"Parker ..."

I hook my thumb over my shoulder, and her eyes shift to look.

"Ha! Yeah, freaking right!" Her wide eyes come back to me, fear clear as day, which she tries to hide with slight anger. "A rope swing? I told you what happened last time I tried one. I swung back around and hit the tree."

"I hung this one myself and tested the shit out of it. Found the furthest out branch I could. The trajectory could never allow you to swing back and hit against the tree like that. I promise."

"Parker ..." She shakes her head, rubbing at her palms as the facade falls. "I can't. I'm scared."

"Exactly," I say, and her eyes swing back to mine. "I know you're afraid, and that's okay. You had a bad experience last time, and it left a little scar. You said you could never do it again. Well, I wanna show you that, yes, you can. We're gonna take the bad and replace it. I wanna erase the bad with a good."

Her steady gaze holds mine for a long moment.

Finally, she licks her lips and gives a slight nod.

I reach a hand out for her to grasp, and together, we walk over to the rope swing.

"I'm gonna go first."

"'Kay," she rushes out in tight panic as she surveys the water.

"Hey." I turn to her, running my knuckles over her cheek, and she brings her wide eyes to mine. "I've got you. Trust me."

She smashes her lips together, giving me a jerky nod as she steps out of the way.

My movements are slow, so she can study my approach, and she does.

I grip the rope and walk backward, over the tree's roots. Placing my hands above the top knot, I pull and then run the few steps until I'm jumping over the edge of the bank and slinging across the water, letting go right when it hits the widest point.

Her shrieks have me smiling as I splash into the water.

I pop back up a second later, and she's peeking at me through her fingers.

"You're crazy!" she shouts through a huge smile. "I can't do it!"

"You can!" I shout back, moving off to the side to tread the water as I wait for her. "Come on, girl. Get your ass in here!"

She grabs the rope and starts bouncing on her feet, switching hands as she wrings out the other. With a squeal, she pulls hard as she stares up at the branch the rope's suspended from. "Parker Baylor, I swear to God ..." She looks back at me. "Are you sure?"

"Come to me, Kens!" I shout through a grin.

She laughs through her nerves before stepping back, as I had, and running forward. She screams the entire way and lets go at the perfect moment, her little body dropping into the river.

"Woo!" I shout, proud as hell of her, and swim closer.

She pops up and turns to face me, a huge smile on her face.

A loud laugh leaves her as she looks from the swing to me before she lowers her head into the water and starts swimming on her back. She doesn't say anything, just smiles at the sky with her eyes closed, and I'm struck with a realization I only guessed at before.

She is, without a doubt, everything I could ever want.

Kind and gentle but spunky with a splash of sass. She smiles with her heart and hurts with all she is. She's more than I ever knew a person could be. She's the light I've never known but now crave.

At the beginning of summer break, I was worried because she was still seeing Kellan even though he hardly ever came home from college to visit her, and the brightness in her eyes wasn't so easily found. But two weeks out of school, they split, and I've had her all to myself since. It only took those first few days for her spirits to lift.

She flips over and starts toward the shore, so I follow.

We pull ourselves out of the water, and she moves to sit on one of the large rocks lining the opposite side of the tree, watching me as I move to take a seat beside her.

She reaches up to push my wet hair off my forehead, her eyes locking with mine. "You wanna take away the bad?"

"Yeah, Kens," I admit, my voice quieter than intended. "All of it. Any of it. Always."

She fights a grin, cutting her eyes to the side before sliding them back to me. "I might let you."

"You will."

A laugh bubbles out of her at that. "Oh, yeah?"

I nod, my eyes leisurely shifting between hers. "Yeah. Maybe not today or tomorrow but eventually. Meanwhile, I'll be around."

"Why?" she asks, studying me with bright eyes.

I shrug. "Can't really explain it. All I've got is, because I want to. Maybe because you never judge me, and you know everything about my fucked up life. Maybe because, when I get rocked on the field, you show up to make sure I'm all right. Or how you think of me on days you should be spending time with your own family, all because you know I don't really have one of my own anymore. Because you share all of yourself with me. Your happy, sad, mad. You give me these things, do these things for me, because you want to. Because, even though you haven't said it out loud, you like me on a deeper level than friendship calls for." I run my thumb over her cheek as it turns my favorite shade pink. "You do all these things because you want to. Well, I wanna wait for you to need me like I do you. Because *I* want to. Because you're worth it."

"And if I'm not?" Her forehead creases slightly, and I give a half smile. "If I mess up or disappoint you?"

"I'll want you regardless," I answer honestly, instantly, and she stares with parted lips. "Always, Kenra. No matter what."

"That's quite a promise there, Safety," she whispers, her hand on the rock, shifting to touch mine.

"It's a solid fact, Nightingale."

She smiles into her lap and then stands, making her way over to the rope swing again. She grins over her shoulder. "See you in there." She winks, and then she jumps.

All brave and beautiful like.

CHAPTER 9
PARKER

As a group, we walk down to the beach and set up shop. The guys start passing around beers as the girls ready themselves to sit and chat on a blanket. But, when Payton continues past, making her way to the beach, Lolli starts to follow.

Our eyes lock, and she winks, letting me know she's got this.

With a sigh, I turn back to the guys, finding Nate frowning at Lolli before sliding his eyes to mine.

"My sister's got some stuff going on right now," I tell him.

He nods before looking off.

The guys start talking football—all of them are set to play in college: Mason and his buddies for Avix University, Nate at UCLA—but I can't focus on the conversation.

My gaze keeps sliding to Kenra, watching as she talks with Ari and Cam. After a moment, her eyes find mine, and a small smile plays at her lips before that sheet of hair blocks her face from my view.

I didn't think she heard me yesterday when I tried to get her to see the choice she made was the wrong one, but when Nate showed up today, I knew I'd dug deep, reached a part of her she seemed to have lost. Her calling him took courage she herself mustn't have known she still had. And him showing up with the rest of their gang, their cousins and friends they've known since they were little—that's the best part.

Maybe seeing everyone, spending some downtime with them, will help her find another piece of herself. Little by little, we could all help her find her way.

Payton and Lolli start back for the group, laughing as Lolli's hands fly all around in conversation.

"So"—Lolli digs into the ice chest, handing Payton a water and grabbing herself a soda— "Al called."

Al is Lolli's CEO and advisor, my new mentor.

She smiles, making me laugh. "Is he really coming?"

When I nod, she squeals, gripping Nate's arm in excitement, gaining the attention of the girls a couple of feet away.

"Is who coming?" Mason questions as Nate hikes his brow at Lolli.

"Number one receiver in all college football before he transitioned into becoming the number one quarterback, eligible for the draft next season." Lolli smiles wide.

"Wait … Noah?"

All our eyes snap toward Brady.

"How the hell do *you*, of all people, know *that*?" Cameron grins.

"Dude," Brady starts, hitting his chest, "I know shit. I almost beat Lolli at sports trivia, remember?"

I smile wide as the entire group, aside from Payton and Kenra, starts cracking up.

"Bro, no." Mason shoves him, and Brady shoves right back. "Kalani whooped that ass."

"*Lolli*," Nate corrects on a growl.

Mason winks at him.

Kalani is Lolli's real name, but only Nate and her aunt call her that; it's their thing.

"Fuck all of you. Watch." He points at everyone individually. "I'mma show you. And you're talkin' bout Noah Riley, aren't you, Lolli, baby?"

"Brady." Ari shakes her head.

Nate growls again.

"Course I am Brady." She pops a brow at Chase and Mason.

"Wait, Noah Riley from Avix?" Mason questions.

"Yep."

Chase nods. "We met him at camp this summer. He's good."

"He's not just good. He's *damn* good." Lolli brings her eyes back to mine. "I want him. Bad."

"Dude!" Mason cries right as Nate snaps, "Baby!"

All the girls laugh.

"You can't say that shit!" Mason frowns.

Nate turns to shove him, spinning back to Lolli. "You'd better watch it, gorgeous," he warns with a sharp brow raised.

She only smiles wider.

Both Nate's and Mason's frowns deepen.

Lolli calms him with a hand on his chest as she turns to me. "Seriously though, he's coming to Oceanside?"

"Yep. Guess he's got some buddies vacationing around here this summer, and he's coming to spend his last free week here."

"Hell to the yes." She gives me a high five.

Nate and Mason continue to pout.

"What's wrong with those two?" Payton whispers to Ari, not any kind of quiet.

The group laughs.

"Oh, don't mind these boys." Cameron smiles as she hops up and makes her way to a scowling Mason. "They're a little insecure—"

She's laughing and running off, Mason hot on her heels before she even finished her sentence. The group follows, headed for the water, but Kenra instead veers left, and I smile to myself.

She's spotted it—the pergola, the swing Nate gave Lolli that once belonged to their parents.

I give her a minute, just observing as she hesitantly steps

under the open wood. Her fingers trail the links that hold the swing in place, but she doesn't attempt to sit.

"I can't believe my mom let this thing go," she says quietly through a smile.

I lean against the beam. "She knew what it meant for the two of them. She was happy to make Nate and Lolli happy."

Kenra nods.

"She'd have done it for you."

A chuckle mixed with sadness escapes her, and she shifts to face me. "I know." She steps past, running her fingers over my hammock as she looks to me.

"The swing is Lolli's spot. This is mine." I grab on to the rope it's suspended from. "I come out here when I need to process or just need a minute to breathe." My eyes search hers. "We all have hard days, Kens. We all have weak moments, but you have to find your strength and reach for it."

Her golden eyes crease at the edges, and she glances off.

"I haven't been a very good daughter, Parker." She looks to her brother in the distance. "Sometimes, I think I should just walk away from everything back home and embrace the life I'm in. Let Lolli fill the hole I dug into my parents' hearts. But it's the only piece of me I have left." A sad laugh leaves her. "Isn't that selfish of me? All so I don't lose myself while they sit around, wondering what they did wrong, why their daughter won't come home for the holidays or simple visits anymore, why I have an excuse or reason they can't come see me when they ask. And they ask all the time."

Pressure builds against my ribs as I listen to her speak. "Talk to me, Kens."

She watches the others play in the water, her lip twitching when Mason lifts Payton by the legs and runs into the water with her. "She's happy with Deaton."

My gaze hardens, and I look to my sister. "Don't lie to me, Kenra."

"I'm not," she whispers. "Deaton ..." She hesitates a

moment. "He isn't his brother. He's good." Her eyes come back to mine, and she offers a small smile, knowing damn well she just admitted Kellan's not but letting me know that's all she's gonna say on that. "Payton loves him and with good reason. He loves her just as much, if not more."

"Then, why is she freaking out? Why did she run here, away from him, like that?"

"I think she knows, once he finds out, it'll all be real. He'll want every piece of her, and I'm not so sure she's made a decision yet, as far as the baby goes."

"You mean, she might …"

Kenra shrugs and looks to the water again. "I don't know. Maybe. Maybe adoption. She's young, Parker; she has her whole life ahead of her, plans. I don't think she's ready to think about it yet."

I nod, running my hand across my jaw.

"He'll look for her, Parker. He knows her inside and out. It won't take long for him to figure out where she is."

"And, when he finds her … will Kellan find you?"

She's quiet for a moment before vacant eyes meet mine. "He won't have to. I'll go back on my own. We both know that." And then she walks away.

CHAPTER 10
PARKER

Σμυρνός

I knew the minute Kenra called, something was wrong. Her silky voice was cracking, and she kept pausing as she talked. *Um* was every other word and followed by a deep inhale.

It's been the same thing every few weeks since she took Kellan back right before school started. She fights with him and ends up here, crying.

I hate everything about it. I hate that she's upset, that he's the one who upsets her. I hate that she lets him, and no matter what he does, she forgives him.

I hate how, every time it happens, hope sparks inside me, and I think, just maybe, she'll see. Maybe she'll admit to feeling what I feel when I'm around her. She never does.

But tonight is different. She's hysterical, upset like never before.

I walk back into the living room with a bottle of water and drop beside her on the couch.

"Talk to me, Kens." I rub her back, and her body sways closer to me. "What happened?"

"L-Liv," she cries.

"You want me to call Liv?"

"No!" She hiccups through her tears. "No. She …" She starts crying harder, her head dropping to her lap.

"Kenra, listen, I know you're upset, but if you don't tell me what's going on, I'm gonna figure out a way to find out for my own damn self."

She sniffs a few times, nodding slowly. I hand her the tissue, and she turns away to wipe her nose and runs her fingers under her eyes.

"I … so Kellan said he would call me when he was headed over to get me, but a few minutes later, Nate popped in my room and said he was on his way to the party if I wanted to ride with him. So … I did."

She starts crying again, and my muscles tense, intuition making me rigid.

"Kellan's car was there, which was no big deal because I knew he was helping set everything up for tomorrow. Tonight was only supposed to be a few of us. Well, Nate went straight for the garage, which was open with some guys moving stuff around." She keeps her head straight but shifts her eyes to mine. "No one even saw me get out of the car."

"Keep talking, Kens."

She gives me a half-smile that doesn't meet her eyes. "I found Kellan."

I nod.

"With Liv." Her voice cracks, and she crumbles again.

Bending at her waist, she cries into her knees, her hands coming up to fold over her hair.

Damn it. I knew it was worse.

Kellan, I'd bet, had done it before, cheated while away at college. But I never would have expected this from Liv. From what I've learned, they've been best friends since they were little.

That's a hard blow.

"Kens." I drop in front of her, running my hands along her

thighs, trying to comfort her. I'd do anything to make her feel better, take away her pain. "Tell me what to do."

Her head lifts slightly, those caramel eyes muddled as they move slowly between mine. "Let me stay."

I swallow. "You wanna stay here? For the night?"

She nods, her eyes dropping to her tearstained jeans.

"What will you tell your parents?"

More tears come, and she quickly wipes them with her sleeve. "They think I'm at Liv's."

"Right."

She looks back to me. "Please, Parker."

I should say no, offer to take her home, but I won't. I want her here as much as I want to be the one to make her feel better.

"Course you can stay. Want me to make us something, put a movie on?"

"Can we just … go lie down?"

I nod, my forehead pinched.

When I stand and reach for her hand, she stares at it for a moment. Then, she places her palm in mine and moves to stand in front of me.

I'm supposed to step back; I know that. But I don't. Can't.

She looks up at me, her free hand lifting to rub the center of my chest, before turning and leading me to my room.

She's been in here before but never to stay. She shows up, unannounced and at random, and we hang. Usually, it's when she's sad, but sometimes, it's when she's happy. Like, when her cousin, Arianna, came to visit over the summer, Kenra showed up at my house just hours after they dropped her and her twin brother, Mason, at the airport, gushing and glowing about all the fun they had had over those few weeks. It was the happiest I'd seen her in months.

I hand her a pair of basketball shorts and a T-shirt, and she smiles gratefully, slipping into the hall to change in the bathroom.

Right as I'm pulling an extra blanket from the closet, she

walks back in, her face fresh and clear of all the makeup marks her tears left behind.

I give her a soft smile and pull the comforter back for her. "Sheets and pillowcases are clean. It's yours for the night."

When she frowns, her gaze quickly dropping to the floor, I walk up, bringing her eyes back to mine. "Don't do that, Kens, not with me. Don't shut down. Tell me what you want."

A smile pulls at her mouth, a real one. It's small and clouded by sadness, but it's mine, which makes me smile in return.

"I want you to stay with me."

My hand caressing her chin slows. "In the room?"

"In the bed," she whispers, her eyes filling with tears once more, so I nod. I could never deny her.

She walks around me and climbs under the covers, choosing the space next to the wall.

I close and lock my bedroom door, crack my window for a breeze, and then climb in beside her.

She's quiet for a few minutes before she speaks, "How could I have been so blind?"

"This is in no way your fault, so don't even for a second think it was."

"It's just … God. My best friend, Parker? How could she? And, not that the time frame matters, but the night before formal? I must look like such a fool," she whispers. "He only came home to go with me to the dance, and now, this?"

"This isn't something you should have had to see coming, Kenra."

"I think I need … I don't know what I need."

"You don't need this," I whisper. "That's for sure. You don't need to be lying here, having been betrayed by two people you should have been able to trust."

"I know," she agrees faintly.

I know she's falling asleep, her emotions proving too much for my nightingale.

"You need someone who will be there for you, Kens," I

quietly tell her, staring at the ceiling. "You need someone to take care of you, not hurt you like this all the time."

"And what do you need, Parker?" she whispers as she slips into slumber.

You.

The score's twelve to six with fifteen seconds on the clock. Cape Carl has no choice but to go long if they hope for any chance of scoring. If they get it and make the extra point, they'll officially knock the Knights out of the playoffs.

I drop back, staying deep, and watch as the receivers go out for a pass. When the quarterback steps back, ready to fire, my feet start moving, and right before the ball is set to drop, I shoot past, picking off the ball and cutting wide. I hear the crowd go wild, and I smile against my mouthpiece. I won't make a touchdown; most of my guys didn't see me coming, so there's little to no blocking. But my team moves forward regardless.

I tuck my shoulder and take the hit as I'm shoved out of bounds. But it's no matter. The clock runs out, and the celebration has begun. I hop up, watching the varsity team cheer us on from the sidelines as they prepare to take the field for their game, and the announcer pumps the crowd, telling them the junior Knights will advance to the JV championship game.

I spot Kenra against the fence, jumping up and down, as she screams her congratulations.

What I wouldn't give to go over there, lift her by her waist, and spin her around. Instead, I grin her way, and she winks.

My entire team creates a straight line, ready to be announced one by one and escorted across the field—the typical closing for when the Knights advance.

Most everyone here has a parent or girlfriend waiting to walk with them, but Dad's out of town, as usual, and my mom couldn't be bothered with the idea—not that I wanted her here, but still. So, I prepare to walk on my own.

The announcer calls on me, and I begin taking my first few steps.

I'm not embarrassed, and walking alone in no way bothers me, but it must have bothered her because I don't make it four feet before her soft hand slides in mine.

My gaze snaps to her, my heart rate rising with the flush of her skin. Her eyes are a little puffy from her crying last night, but she's still stunning, just gorgeous in her tight little jeans and Alrick high hoodie.

She looks forward again, so I do, too.

"That was some interception back there, Mr. Safety," she speaks low, pausing as we make it to half-field for the school photographer to get her shot.

I chuckle, grabbing her hand and shifting so that she's holding on to my arm instead. "Thank you, Kens. And thank you for this." I glance at her, and she smiles, quickly glancing off with a nod. "I didn't expect to see you here tonight."

We step past the people on the sideline and turn to each other as I drop my helmet in the grass.

She shrugs. "I wanted to be here to watch you win," she teases, but her eyes crease at the edges, showing her true sadness.

"Well, I'm glad because I was thinking …" I trail off, and she eyes me playfully. "What if you came over again tonight? After everything with Liv and Kellan, you were planning to skip the dance anyway, so come over. We'll hang, distract each other."

She nods, subconsciously looking in the direction of the varsity team where Kellan is chatting with his old coach. "Yeah, maybe you're right." Her eyes come back to mine. "I think I'd like that." She tries to say it strong, but she's bummed out. She wanted to go to formal and probably still would if it were just another fight between her and Kellan, but this time is different.

"You staying to watch Nate play?"

"Well, I don't want him to disown me, so yeah." She laughs.

"All right, so about nine?"

She grins, shocking me when she grips my bicep for leverage, bringing her soft lips down on my sweaty cheek. "Thank you for being you," she whispers before making her way back to her friends, all of them looking from me to her with a frown.

I ignore the questioning glances I get for having Kellan Vermont's girlfriend escorting me across the field. Little do they know what he's done or that they're over. And, of course, none of them have a clue that she slept in my bed last night or that she's spent more time with me than him in the past two years since he's been gone. It's no secret he only pops up on random weekends. People will chalk her walking with me up to her being the sweet little people-pleaser she is. And that's all right. No need for them to know our business.

I hurry from the field to change and head out, planning to shower at home.

As expected, it takes a good fifteen minutes to make it out of the parking lot, but once I hit the road, it only takes a couple minutes to reach my house. As soon as I kill my engine, I head inside, rushing to get things ready.

It might have seemed on impulse, my inviting Kenra over tonight, but I planned on calling her right after the game. From the moment she left this morning, I've been thinking about her having to miss the dance because of the assholes who wronged her. Losing them both in the same night was tough.

And I can't accept that, her unhappy and feeling like she is missing out on something, so I'm bringing formal to her.

I move the couches, pressing them against the wall, and the coffee table to the spare room. I hang white lights I found in the garage, framing the living room and entryway.

Once I step off the stool, I check the frozen lasagna I threw in the oven the minute I got home, seeing I've got just enough time to shower and change before the timer goes off.

It takes longer than planned to have everything ready, but when she's still not here twenty minutes later, I start to worry.

Kenra is never late. In fact, she's always early, so something must be off.

I dig my phone out of my gym bag, finding no messages from her. I try her phone, but it goes straight to voice mail.

The only thing I can do is wait, so I do.

Two hours go by before I hear a car pulling up outside. I hop off the couch and hustle to the door. When I pull it open, my gaze narrows.

Car after car pulls forward, and it hits me, irritation heating my skin as, one by one, Alrick's finest exit the vehicles, all in their formalwear.

She went with him.

Right when I get set to slam the door, a group of laughing senior girls stumble up my yard, pausing when they see me standing in the doorway.

They glance from the house to me. "This *is* where the after-party's at, right?"

I'm two seconds from turning them away, just about to direct them next door, when more people walk up behind them.

"Parker!" Austin, one of my teammates, walks up with a couple of other guys, smacking my shoulder as he steps past me. "Where do you want the keg?"

And I just stand there as they begin to shuffle inside, the giggling girls following behind.

I should tell them this isn't the place, that the setup inside the house, the lights and food and music, is all for a girl who never showed.

But I don't. Instead of turning them away and having a pity party of one, I pull a fake smile for the people who continue to walk up, thanking Austin as he pops back up with a red Solo cup in hand for me.

These people, they need something I can give them, unlike Kenra.

I've never been the partier—I prefer to keep to myself really —but from tonight forward, I'll give them what they need.

I pull out my phone and take a quick picture of the entryway full of dangling lights, lost hope, and eager teenagers. I post the picture to Facebook, letting everyone know where the party is.

Tonight, I'm getting plastered, anything to erase the mental image I've cooked up of Kenra dancing in Kellan's arms.

Σμνρνιδς

"So, what's up, Ken?" Ari asks, smiling at the waitress as she sets down our drinks. "Tell me all about the hustle and bustle of this lush life you're living. Has Kellan's campaign started yet?"

I lose myself even more in another little lie. "It's busy but in the best way. Kellan is really dedicated and hopes to make some positive changes in the community. He—"

"Seriously?" Cam interjects, her straw between her teeth.

My eyes fly to her.

"Cameron—" Ari starts.

Cameron rolls her eyes. "Uh, no." She sits forward, crossing her arms. "I've known you forever, Kenra, been going on your guys' family vacays since before I could fucking walk. Don't feed me this politician's wife's bullshit answers."

I freeze a moment, looking between the two.

My shoulders sag, and instantly, my eyes start to water.

She's right.

God. I can't be real with anyone anymore.

"Busy. Life-consuming and … fake." I sniffle, smiling at Ari when she reaches across the table to grab my arm. "But at least I have Kellan there at the end of the day," I lie, trying to smooth out my confession some without giving too much.

"Yeah." Ari nods, the pinch of her eyes telling me she doesn't buy my little cover up in any way. "I didn't think it was all that glamorous. I mean, you ordered salad and water, hold the dressing. That sucks," Ari teases, knowing I won't go in to detail on the topic.

I find myself relaxing some.

"Since you haven't been checking messages," Ari tactfully shifts the subject and I'm grateful for it. "Did you hear Brady's parents' put their beach house in all our names as a graduation gift?"

My eyes widen. "I didn't. That's some gift."

"I know!" Ari squeals, excited. "It's insane! Our parents said they wanted to make sure we stayed close, and sometimes, college can drive wedges between people, so they banned together and bought into it to ensure we all have a common place to land. I guess Mr. Lancaster, Brady's dad, suggested their place since it's the largest and the rest agreed so they divided it equally between us."

"So, will you live here and commute to Avix?"

"Nah." Cameron waves her hand. "We're three hours away, and our dorms are already paid for. The boys are on scholarships for football, so we're gonna play full-on college kids and get fucked up and do stupid shit."

"Ha! Fat chance! Mason's gonna have you on lockdown." Ari laughs.

"Girl, I wish he would. In fact, I *dream* he would. Tie me up, tie me down, bend me over. I want it all from that man." Cameron smirks.

Both Ari and I grimace at the thought, and Cameron laughs. "What? Like you don't want all Chase would give." She points to Ari.

It's common knowledge that Cameron has feelings for Mason and has since they were little, but he pretends he sees her as a little sister when we all know that's crap. He cares for her just the same.

And Ari and Chase have tiptoed around each other for years, but no one in their little group dares say that out loud, not with how protective Mason can be.

"That's the problem. Chase won't *give* me anything because he's too loyal to Mason. Mason is his best friend. I'm just his best friend's sister."

"That's bullshit, and you know it," Cam quips. "He'll give in eventually. You've just gotta give him a little push." She turns to me, playfully narrowing her eyes. "And I've got my suspicions about you, Miss Prim and Proper and I Wear Cardigans in the Summer. There's a freak under all those layers; I can sense it."

Instantly, I grow self-conscious and tuck my hands under the table to pull at my sleeves.

There's a freak under here all right but not the kind anyone would want to find.

The kind you hide.

"Oh, Ari!" Cam starts, and the conversation is quickly taken over by gossip.

An hour later, we pull up to the beach house. The girls walk around the side, but I head in through the front, so I can put my things away.

When I walk into the kitchen, Lolli glances up from cutting some watermelon, offering a small smile. "Everyone's out back. I think they're gettin' set to head back to the water for a bit before it starts getting cold."

I nod, glancing at the group through the floor-to-ceiling glass that makes up the back wall of the house.

"Do you want to borrow something to wear?" she asks, not looking at me. "I have some suits that have tags still, so it wouldn't be weird, if that kind of thing grosses you out."

"I … no but thank you." I pull at my sleeves.

Lolli starts to nod but sighs instead and drops her knife in the sink with a bit more force than necessary. I eye her for a minute as she hastily cleans her mess, tossing the fresh fruit in a bowl. She picks it up and is set to walk around the counter

71

but instead drops it and spins to me with a pinched expression.

"This is one of those times where I should really shut my mouth, but I've never been real good at that. I'll probably get in mad trouble for this—from both boys—but I just ..." She trails off, her gaze narrowing. "Why did you come here, Kenra?"

"I brought his sister here," I answer quickly. "She needed my help, and I wasn't about to leave her to figure it out on her own."

Lolli stares at me with a blank expression. "I know we haven't gotten to hang much, and I'm sure, under normal circumstances, things would be different, but I don't like stupid shit. You and I both know you could have dropped Payton at the door or gotten her a plane ticket, sent him a text, something. But you didn't. You came here, and you stayed. I know you two have unfinished business."

I freeze, panic running through me as I dig my nails into my palms. "Excuse me?"

"I don't know everything," Lolli admits. "But I know enough to be concerned. You trip him up. Bad. Your relationship isn't mine to understand; only the two of you know what this thing between you really feels like, but you have to know you'll knock him on his ass this time around. And if you do, be prepared for someone else to step in and catch him as he falls."

My chest grows tight as I watch moisture build in her eyes.

"I need you to figure out what you honestly hope to gain from all this before you leave. Then, either stay away or only come back if he asks."

I start to shake my head, ready to argue without a leg to stand on, but she lifts her bowl and walks closer to me, so I stay quiet.

"I don't want to hate you, Kenra," she whispers when she reaches me, and tears cloud both our eyes. "And Nate would be real disappointed if I did. Make up your mind on how things end. If not for your own sake, then for Parker's."

With that, she wipes her eyes, squeezes my bicep for a second, and then heads out the door.

And I'm left staring in the kitchen of the man I can never have but can't figure out how to let go of.

But she's right. I know she is.

It's not fair to keep coming back like this.

He didn't have to open the door for me at any point over the last four years, but he did. Every damn time. And, every time, I left him, knowing he needed more from me.

And this time will be no different.

When the sting hits, I look to my palms. Fresh blood sneaks from the crescent shapes of my perfectly manicured fingernails that broke through the skin, and a saddened chuckle escapes me.

Even my scars are perfect.

Slowly, I turn to look out the back door. The second my eyes find him, his lift, locking on to mine.

Deep creases form instantly at the edges of his beautiful blues. A soft blue I wish I could get lost in.

He sees it. The inevitable.

I should leave now and get back before Kellan starts asking questions.

I should leave.

Parker shifts to stand and pulls open the sliding door.

He stares into me, his chest inflating with his deep, sorrowful breath as he places his hand out, silently asking me not to go yet.

My nose starts to tingle as I fight back tears.

I know the right thing to do, but I do the opposite and place my palm in his.

My heart constricts in my chest as his hand squeezes mine, and he pulls me through the door, gently ushering me toward the patio chairs to join Payton and Lolli.

When I break eye contact with him, I spot Nate staring with

a frown. He looks pointedly from Parker to me and tips his chin in question.

I give a small shake of my head, and he lifts a hand to rub at his chin before looking away.

I used to be a girl I could be proud of. I used to be honest and kind, and I used to love.

Now, I'm a liar. Selfish and weak.

It's okay if Lolli grows to hate me. It's okay if they all do.

Because no one could possibly hate me as much as I hate myself.

The moment I drop onto the cushion, Mason turns his attention to me. "So, where's your fiancé, Ken? Busy saving the world one charity at a time?"

I feel all eyes slide to me, and I force my practiced neutral expression. "He is campaigning, yes. He's in Colorado right now, strategizing."

When Payton scoffs into her cup, my eyes fly to her, and she looks up, mouthing, *Sorry*, before cutting her eyes around the group.

"That's cool, I guess." He nods but narrows his eyes on me. "That leaves you alone a lot, doesn't it?"

"Yeah, sometimes, but I also go with him every few trips."

Kellan says he needs people to see how important having his loved ones near is to him.

"So, how come you don't come stay with us at the beach house the rest of the summer? Or with your parents?" He frowns. "I don't like you being by yourself."

"Mase, leave her alone. She has a new life there that she can't just leave whenever she wants," Ari defends.

"And she's in the middle of planning a wedding," Cameron adds.

The muscles around my heart tighten along with the invisible leash around my neck.

"How's that going, by the way?" Cam turns back to me.

I force my eyes not to look his way, but I do look at Payton, who frowns at the girls, shakes her head, and keeps eating.

I turn back to Ari and Cameron's gleeful faces. "I ... well, you girls got the invitation. It's at the fanciest resort in Hawaii."

Cameron laughs. "Yeah, but tell me about the dress and the hair, flowers ..."

"I, uh, don't really have all the details. The resort is handling everything."

Both girls frown instantly, and I notice Parker walking off in my peripheral. My heart sinks a little more.

I get it, the looks they're giving me. As a child, I was the girl who dressed up in every gown and heel her mother owned and picked from the planter I wasn't supposed to touch to make the perfect bouquet. I'd beg for bridal magazines and scrapbook everything for future reference.

I wanted the veil and the roses petals and the most amazing of grooms.

I'll have a veil, but it might as well be black.

I'll have rose petals, but all I'll see is blood stains I can't erase.

And the groom, he'll be waiting at the altar with the heaviest of chains and a keyless lock.

My wedding day will be the day I say good-bye to myself completely.

"While this is fascinating in the most unfascinating of ways —no offense, Kenra, baby," Brady teases, "I say it's time for a quick round. Who's in?"

Everyone but Payton and me follows him inside.

"I don't get you, Kenra." Payton shakes her head. "I really don't."

I don't respond but move to go look for Parker, finding him a few dozen feet off the shoreline.

For a few minutes, we both say nothing, staring out at the midnight ocean.

As dark and daunting as it appears, it's also welcoming, offering the promises of a home inside its unforgiving waves. A place free of shame and disappointment.

All you have to do is hand yourself over, and it'll welcome you with open arms.

"Why do you stay?" Parker whispers into the darkness, and I lower myself to sit on the log beside him. "I've racked my brain a thousand times, trying to understand it, trying to see through your eyes, and I can't. If anything, I imagine things are even darker from where you stand. I know you walk around, pretending everything is fine, acting like you're happy, and for a long time, I believed it, believed you wanted him instead of me. I thought marrying him is what you wanted, but I ... I see the defeat in your eyes, Kenra. I feel it every time I look at you." He shifts toward me, but I can't bring myself to meet his gaze. "So, what's it really about? What does he do for you that keeps you there? Is it because you love him?"

At that, my eyes fly to his.

"It's ok, Kenra, you can tell me. *Please* tell me. I just want ... I need to know. I need you to tell me you're happy and in love with the man you've chosen to marry because I'm not seeing it."

Tears fill my eyes for what seems like the hundredth time since I arrived. All I've done since I've been here is cry and ache and wish for things that can never be.

Why do I stay? What a loaded question with so many answers, none of which I can share with him.

I wish I could. I want to tell him every last thing there is to tell. Hear him say that none of it matters, that we're worth more than the aftermath that would follow should he and I get together. But the risk is too high and the reasons too many.

So, I do what I do best, something that won't shock him in the slightest, as sad as it might be.

I stand and walk away.

Truth is, once upon a time, I thought I loved Kellan.

And it was the saddest, most demeaning few minutes of my life.

Σμυρναϊός

ONE YEAR AGO

Parker laughs loudly as I squeal and dive for my inner tube.

"It is so not funny, Baylor!" I shout through my fit of laughter; all while being equally freaked out.

"Oh, it's funny." He grins, running his hand through his dirty-blond hair.

"There was a fish sucking on my toe! That's scary! And disgusting!" I whine, and he laughs harder. "You know what? Screw it."

I hop off quickly and flip Parker's inner tube over, so he splashes into the water. We've been floating for two hours now and are coming up to the first bend of the river that lines my house.

He pops up, and I see the mischief in his blue eyes.

I ditch my inner tube and start for the edge of the water, but before I can climb out, he wraps his arms around my middle and pulls me back into the water, bending at the knee to submerge us to our shoulders.

I start squealing, and he laughs into my neck. It only takes a second for my voice to die down and the feeling of his arms around me to set in. I glance over my shoulder, locking eyes with him.

The left corner of his mouth tips up slowly, and he shifts me so I'm cradled in his arms.

"Not afraid of the fish anymore, Kens?" he whispers, and his gaze drops to my mouth.

Heat makes its way across my skin as his eyes continue to shift between mine and my lips.

"You're so damn beautiful, Kenra."

I blush and look down with a smile. "I'm a soaking mess."

He lifts my gaze with a finger under my chin. "You're perfect. Inside and out."

I stare at him, my body somehow shifting closer to his without permission. "Thank you, Parker."

When his fingers twitch against my skin and his head lowers the smallest of fractions, I breathe, "We should go. I … have plans with Kellan for dinner."

He stares back a moment before he licks his lips and looks away, depositing me back on the ground. "Right, yeah. This is about where we parked the other ATV, right?"

I clear my throat, nodding. "Yeah, I'll grab the rafts and—"

"I'll grab the rafts. You climb out and fire that baby up."

I nod and make my way out of the water. "Hey, Parker?" I turn back, finding he's already staring after me. "I'm sorry I bailed on you the night of the dance. Things with Kellan are—"

"Don't sweat it, Kens." He gives a half smile, one that doesn't quite meet his eyes, but his words are genuine. "I'm glad you called me today."

I smile back and head up the hill.

After we get everything put away, I run inside to change, dropping my wet swimsuit over the porch railing on my way back to my car, then I drop Parker off at home.

I knew my parents and brother would be gone for the weekend at some football camp a few towns over, so I wanted to have some fun with my friend. I haven't been brave enough to show up at his door since that night a few months ago, but I'm getting ready to leave for the summer, heading to California to jack around with my cousins before I have to come back here and decide what to do with my life now that I've graduated.

And since my dad and Nate don't exactly know about my friendship with Parker—of course, my mom knows some—I thought today would be the perfect day to float.

As I make my way up my driveway, my forehead pinches.

Kellan is standing there, leaning against the beam of my front porch, so I park and make my way to him, finding his stare locked on my wet swimsuit.

"Hey, baby," he rasps, his eyes slowly lifting to meet mine.

I swallow, suddenly feeling a little unsure. "Hey, I didn't know you were coming."

With a slight tilt of his head, he eyes me. "No? You told me your parents would be gone, remember?"

"Right. No, yeah." I shake my head. "I just … thought I was meeting you somewhere."

He nods, but then an easy smile finds his face, and I breathe a sigh of relief. "Come here, baby."

He holds his arms out, so with a smile, I move to hug him.

When I pull back, he laces his hands through mine and kisses my knuckles, making me grin.

"Come on, let's go inside. I need to take a quick shower, but then I'm all yours."

He smiles and pulls me closer. "I have a surprise for you."

"What?" I playfully narrow my eyes, and he smiles wide.

"Nope. Not telling. You take your gorgeous self into the shower, and I'll see you when you get back downstairs."

With that, I release his hand and make my way to my room. Perks of having a carpenter for a father, my brother and I each have our own bathroom.

It takes me about twenty minutes to get showered and changed, and then I'm making my way down the stairs, the smell of fresh marinara making my stomach growl.

He's cooking for me?

I hurry into the kitchen. "Something smells good."

He spins quickly, a bright smile on his face. "Baby! No peeking. Go relax on the couch. I prepped at home, so I only need a few more minutes."

"You sure you don't need help?" I lift onto my tippy-toes to try to see past him, and he laughs, rushing toward me.

He grins as he kisses my lips, forcing my steps backward. "Go, beautiful. Let me spoil you tonight."

Placing my hands on his strong shoulders, I lift myself and softly kiss him.

"It's spaghetti, isn't it?" I whisper.

He laughs loudly before gently nudging me the rest of the way out of the kitchen.

With a smile, I turn on the TV to some random rerun of *CSI*.

Only a few minutes pass, as he promised, before he comes in to get me.

"Aw …" I gush when I see the table has been set for the two of us, two large plates of homemade meatballs and fresh bread waiting to be eaten. "Kellan, this looks amazing. Thank you."

He pulls me in, brushing my wet hair over my shoulder. "I wanted to do something nice for you, show you how much I appreciate you. You've stuck by me through some really crappy things, Kenra, and I need you to know that I'm so grateful. So lucky to have you."

I smile and lean in to kiss him before taking a seat at the table.

We talk a bit about what to expect over the summer and his schedule for next year.

Kellan took AP classes all through high school and early college courses since sophomore year, so he technically entered his first year of college with a junior's credits. He's insanely smart and business savvy.

Once we've settled into the living room, we cuddle beside each other on the couch, and I can't help but enjoy the easiness of the night.

We've had many ups and downs, but over the last few

months, Kellan has been great. He's come home almost every weekend to see me, and always makes sure I feel included when we go places with his friends. He hasn't pushed or pressured me in any way, like he used to. I was so young when we first started dating, so naturally, I was timid. But lately, I find myself being the one trying to get closer to him, and he always lets me lead.

So, when his fingers start to skim across the exposed flesh of my side and my core grows warm, I'm the one who shifts to face him, the one who moves to straddle him.

His eyes grow darker, lids heavier, as his hands slide higher.

I look from his eyes to his mouth. Then, I drop my lap against his and kiss him.

It only takes a moment for heat to build, and my hips start to rock against his.

His hands lift to cup my ass, and he breaks our kiss for a moment. "Tell me this is okay, baby."

I grind against him as my answer, and he squeezes harder, lifting his hips to meet mine.

After a few minutes of heavy kissing, I need more, so with shaky hands, I lift my shirt over my head, and his mouth instantly comes down on my heated skin, making me whimper.

At the sound, he shifts us both, so he's hovering over me, and I wrap my legs around him, bringing his hard-on back to rub against my clit.

We've messed around like this several times, and it's always fun, but tonight, this friction isn't enough, so I nudge him slightly and move to kick off my pajama pants and underwear.

He groans and looks from my naked body to his clothed one and back. In response, I bring my hands to his pants and undo his belt, slowly dragging his clothes from his body as nerves start to kick in.

He feels the tremble in my touch and brings his hand to my swollen clit to help distract me, and it works. I pant against him, bringing his face to mine to kiss him as he works me over.

"I have a condom," he whispers. "If you think you're ready."

I freeze for a moment, but when I do, his finger slides inside me, and my back bows.

Kellan tosses the throw from the back of the couch to the floor and moves us onto it. He pulls a condom from his discarded jeans and quickly places it on.

I open my legs for him to settle between, and he kisses me slow, his tip now positioned at my entrance.

"It's gonna hurt a little."

I nod and open my legs wider.

He works his way in with gentle care, kissing and rubbing on my body to soothe me as he does. It burns more than anything at first, but slowly, it goes away, and the stretch of me opening for him starts to feel more like a teasing pressure.

I lift to kiss him, running my palms across his warm skin, and he fiercely kisses me back. His movements speed up as my hands roam all over his heated skin. I can't say for sure, but I think I finish as he gets ready to.

He brings his eyes to mine, softly running his fingers across my cheek as he rocks into me. Gently pushing my hair from my face, he skims his swollen lips against mine as he groans with his release.

I stare at him as he stares at me for a long moment afterward and smile softly when his hand sinks into my hair.

"Kenra ..." he whispers, his eyes searching mine, and I run my hands up his chest. "You have to know ... he'll never have you like this."

My hands freeze against him.

"You will never be his," he says, his tone measured and low, and the hand in my hair starts to tighten.

My eyes widen as realization sets in.

"You will stay away from Parker Baylor." His grip deepens to the point of pain, and I whimper beneath him. "Or I will *ruin* everyone you care about."

With that, he quickly pulls out, not caring how bad it hurts as he does it and hops up. He tosses the dirty condom near my head and pulls on his clothes while I lie there, tears building in my eyes, my exposed body and still-open legs visibly shaking.

"Just a heads-up, you'll be canceling your little trip to California tomorrow. Go to bed, Kenra. We'll go over the rules and consequences in the morning." He snatches my phone from the coffee table and heads for the kitchen. "Don't think about sneaking off. You'll regret it if you do. You're eighteen now, and I'm done playing games."

Afraid and unsure of what just happened or what to do, I run upstairs and climb into my bed without bothering to clean myself off.

I cry myself to sleep.

"I don't know why Danny puts up a front. He's obviously in love with Sandy. Why not just tell her?" Lolli squishes her lips to the side as she clicks off the TV, tossing the remote with a pout.

I laugh, jerking my knees that she's sitting across, and she frowns my way. "Not everybody can swallow the honesty pill like you can, Lolli Bear."

"But wouldn't it make life so much easier if the world wasn't full of such pussies?"

I laugh louder right as the front door swings open, and Nate's and Kenra's voices fill the room behind us.

They step around the couch, and Lolli smiles up at Nate, who bends to meet her with a frown.

"Baby," he speaks against her lips, "love you, like Parker enough. I'd hate to have to kick his ass … so get yours off him."

Giggling, she reaches up, and he sweeps his hands under her tiny frame, lifting her. She winks at me over his shoulder as he drags her off.

With a shake of my head, I look to Kenra, finding her down-cast eyes on me.

"You have fun?" I ask, patting the spot on the floor beside me.

Smoothing her clothes down, she walks closer but chooses the space on the couch instead of at my side, so I shift to see her better.

"I did. We went and checked out my cousin's cabin, visited with Ari for a bit, and then we walked along the beach a while." She glances away, her eyes pinched at the edges. "He talked to me about everything that happened between him and Lolli last year, told me about graduation and his summer so far."

She smiles softly, a true smile that comes from her heart. I find myself reaching out to touch the lines it leaves on her pale face.

I gently stroke her cheek, and she subconsciously leans into my touch.

"That's good, Kens."

She nods, her brown eyes bouncing between mine.

"I'm taking off tomorrow," I whisper, and she freezes. "Just for a few days, work stuff for the Tomahawks." She pulls away, so I let my hand drop to my lap. "I talked to Lolli. Payton will be good here while I'm gone."

She nervously starts rubbing at her palms, and I squint. I lift myself onto the couch beside her.

"Have you talked to Payton about it yet?" she asks quietly, glancing off to the side.

My eyes drop to her palms. "Not yet. She went to lie down for a while. I will as soon as she's up. Will you be here when I get back?"

Kenra looks to the ceiling with only her eyes, tears instantly filling them. "I don't know," she whispers.

My heart clenches, my head aching. "Kens—"

"Parker, please ... stop."

"Stop what?"

"Stop ... trying." Her voice cracks. "Stop looking at me like I'm everything."

"I can't, Kens." I reach out, grabbing ahold of her closed

fists. She tenses and tries to pull away, but my grip is firm. Gentle but firm. "Won't ever."

I run my hands over her closed knuckles. Slowly, her shaky fingers open, and I inhale deeply. Red and angry, her broken skin breaks another piece of me, steals another piece of her.

I bend to kiss her wounds, and a small sob escapes her, but she doesn't pull away. If anything, her hands open further, her body craving a soft touch … or maybe it's my touch she craves. Not that she'd ever admit to it.

I bring my eyes to hers, and she slightly shakes her head, begging me not to say it out loud.

This girl—this beautiful, big-hearted girl—is so lost inside herself and sees no way out.

She numbs her hurt with the break of her own skin.

"I—"

"No, Parker." She pulls her hands from mine and shifts to stand. "Not right now." With that, she disappears down the hall, and I'm left sitting in an empty room with a crushing heart and racing mind.

———

I watch Payton, laughing quietly to myself when her face scrunches in disgust as she slowly brings a frog leg to her mouth. Chase bends over, laughing, and she glares at him before taking a bite. I expect her to gag, but instead, she laughs lightly and takes another small bite.

Little moments like these are what I thought she was getting back home—at least with her friends, if not from my mom. I thought this whole time they were best buds, tight as could be, but Payton's comments over the last few days have me questioning everything I thought I knew about what she was getting at home. I would have never left without a fight had I known, Dad would have taken her in a heartbeat, but my mom put a stop to that before it even began.

When she claps for herself, proud she tried it, I smile and glance away, finding Lolli's eyes on me as Nate naps with his head in her lap.

She winks and looks to Payton. "She'll be all right."

I nod, hoping she's right. My eyes slide to Kenra, hating the way she secludes herself and watches the others smile and laugh in their summer gear, all while she sits there in her jeans and cardigan, fresh hair and makeup, whereas the other girls have messy ponytails and ChapStick, if anything.

I look back to Lolli, as if to ask, *What about her?*

She sighs, her brows knitting at the center. "Maybe we should take a walk."

"You know you could tell me to go away for a minute, so you two can talk, right?" Nate grumbles with his eyes still closed.

Lolli laughs, smiling at me. "Yeah, I know. But you're not exactly known for taking orders. You'd say no and give me that sexy-ass *don't test me, baby* frown you've perfected, and then I'd get distracted."

Nate's eyes pop open, and he grins up at her. "I'll do anything you want, baby ... for a price."

"Mmhmm, always, handsome. Consider it done. Now, go play."

Nate smirks and hops up, winking my way before snatching the football off the deck and throwing it at the back of Mason's head.

"Hey, dick!" Mason laughs and then turns back to his conversation with some random beach girls.

Lolli laughs, bringing her blue eyes back to mine. "Ain't it funny how that works? He thinks he won something when, in the end, it's me who gets what I want."

"Trust me"—I pop a brow— "he knows."

She laughs loudly, pulling her knees up to rest her chin against them. "All right, Hero, talk to me. What the fuck do we gotta do here? I'm new at all this, so you've gotta help me out."

"I'm not sure what I can do, Lolli Bear."

"I might or might not have told her to figure out what she really wants before she leaves again."

My eyes jerk to hers, and she covers her face, peeking between her fingers. I can only chuckle. "Always got my back, don't you?"

"I've got your all, Hero. Always. What hurts you hurts me."

I can feel the truth in her words. She's the first person who has truly been in my corner—at least since a certain someone walked out of it.

"When are you leavin' again?"

"Tomorrow—two, three days, max. Making a quick trip to San Francisco to meet with one of the owners before the season starts."

"You'll be gone for the Fourth?"

I nod, eyeing her.

"Take her."

My brows dart up. "Take her? To San Francisco?" I shake my head. "She'd never go."

Lolli narrows her eyes. "Ask her."

"Lolli … there are so many things wrong with that. One being, do you realize the questions Nate would ask?"

She nods, glancing his way and then to me, meaning, when he asks, she'll tell him all he wants to know.

"Look, let's be real, all right?" Lolli gets serious, sitting forward on her seat. "You've literally got two options here, and one sucks."

"I'm listening." I can't help but grin despite the shittiness of the situation at hand.

"One, everything stays how it is now." She tips her head. "That's the sucky one, obviously."

"Agreed."

"Second, you flip the fucking switch on her."

My brows jump, and she smirks.

"Go balls out. She doesn't think she needs you. Make her.

She knows she wants you. Show her what having you feels like. Be her hero, Parker."

I think it over for a moment, my eyes cutting to the lonely brunette and back. "Go for it?"

"Fourth down, five seconds on the clock. Offense is down by a touchdown. No choice but to go for a pass. What's the safety gonna do?"

I inhale deeply, feeling a flare of possibility light inside me. "Interception time."

"Damn straight."

"This is the bad choice."

"It's the only choice."

When I hesitate, Lolli sits forward, her blue eyes determined and bright. "You have to try."

My eyes flit between hers, soaking in some of the courage she's fighting to give me. "All in?"

"Defense, baby."

I sit back, my eyes once again finding the brown-eyed beauty alone at the edge of the water.

With a sigh, I look back to Lolli, and she tips her chin.

"If anyone could save her from herself, it would be you, but I can guarantee, it won't be any kind of easy. I don't know what's happening or how bad it is, but I know those things for sure. And I know you. If you don't do this, Parker, you'll regret it. I can't have that. I need you. *She* needs you."

"How can you be so sure, Lolli Bear?" I whisper, swallowing past the lump threatening to clog my throat.

"Because I see you in her eyes, just like you saw Nate in mine."

An unexpected, heavy chuckle leaves me, but for some reason, I stand, and her watery eyes shine with pride.

"Make her see, Hero."

I don't stop to think about it, afraid I'll come to my senses, and I make my way to her.

There must be something in my strides that tells my intentions because Nate's arm freezes midair as he and Mason both turn to watch me, but I keep going. It only takes a moment for her head to turn, for her brown eyes to lift and meet mine.

The breeze blows her golden-brown hair across her cheek, a few strands sticking to her lips, and they part with her gasp. She must see it, too.

I step right in front of her, and her hands drop to her sides. She holds her breath, begging me with her eyes not to do or say whatever it is she's expecting.

Well, I'm done standing here, watching her crumble.

She falls; I fall.

Might as well fall into each other.

"I'm leaving at five a.m." My words are a rushed whisper but strong. "I'll wait outside, in my truck, until five ten exactly. For you."

Her eyes flit between mine and I see the shock, understand the confusion.

"Come to me, Kens," I whisper, compelling my hands to stay at my sides, demanding my feet to walk backward, and then forcing myself to turn around and head back for the house.

I don't look back. I can't.

Defense. That's what Lolli called it.

But that's the problem, isn't it?

Because, when it comes to Kenra Monroe, I've always been defenseless.

CHAPTER 14
PARKER

SEVEN MONTHS AGO

Buttoning my shirt, I smooth it down and reach for my tie right as there's a light tap on the door.

I glance over my shoulder at my dad, who gives a tight smile and makes his way in the room.

"Mind if I help you with that?"

I hesitate for a moment before turning and handing it over.

He places it over my neck and starts to tie it. "You got a date for tonight?"

"I did, yeah, but she and her family ended up heading out of town early for vacation, so she had to cancel last minute. I don't mind though. We were only going together to get her ex to back off."

"Well, that was nice of you. I thought maybe you'd ask Lolli's friend to go with you?"

"Who?"

"The little redheaded one I see often. She can't seem to keep her eyes off of ya." He taps the tie and steps back, nodding in approval.

I chuckle and reach for my jacket. "Mia? Nah, we're just friends, and she's dating Austin."

"I don't know …" he teases.

"Trust me, nothing would ever happen there."

He stares a moment before nodding slowly. "Because of Lolli, right?"

I clear my throat and turn around.

It's true—partially. I could never be with Mia when my feelings for Lolli are still sometimes confusing. That, and I've never thought of Mia in that light. Not once, but I know I'd never even consider it now, them being cousins and all.

"I didn't mean to pry."

I turn back and offer him a grin. "It's all good. But that's a no on Mia. She's a good friend, but that's all."

"You know," he starts, glancing away, "those last few years at your mom's, I was worried about you. And then, when you left the life you knew, had to leave Payton, I was afraid you'd never ... I don't know ... be truly okay, I guess. You'd lost your spirit a while before that, and I thought I'd never see you enjoying your teenage years like I'd hoped you would."

"Dad—"

He cuts me off by lifting a hand. "You've had it tough, Parker. From a mother who tried to use you for her own personal gain, tried to force you to be what she wanted, and never stopped to show you what a mother was supposed to be ... to a dad who disappeared when he got scared that he'd failed you."

I watch my father's eyes grow watery.

"I didn't want people to treat you differently or bully you, accusing you of things you probably didn't even understand because your dad was gay. I let your mother's threats and fake worries decide what type of father I was, and I lost our relationship because of it. Lost my daughter completely because of it." He takes a minute to clear his throat and gather himself. Then, he continues, "Anyway, what I was trying to get at is, after all this bad and ugly and people walking away, I have to say, I've never been more grateful for anything as I am for Lolli showing up when she did. She's good for you, Parker. She's put that light back in your eyes. When I look at you now, I see hope."

Pressure builds against my chest, and I look away. "Dad, Lolli and I aren't … we're not …"

"I know. But just because she's not *in* love with you doesn't mean she doesn't *love* you. You know that, right?"

I nod. I do know that. And I love her just the same. I can't help but think she and I would be good together, but the fact of the matter is, at the end of the night, when I climb in bed and close my eyes, it's soft brown eyes that stare back at me, mocking me. Reminding me of all the things I want but can't have.

I look back to my dad. "I'd better get going."

"Parker, there's something you should know. Your mom showed up here one day last year just after you'd gone up to bed. I didn't let her in."

I eye him, suddenly uneasy. "Okay …"

"She got upset, like always, and said she'd make sure none of us could have what we wanted if she couldn't. I know I've learned of some things she's done over the last few years to me, and, son, I hate to say it, but I wouldn't put it past her to pull something on you either."

"What are you trying to say exactly?"

"I just … I wonder if she's had a hand in anything that maybe didn't work out for you since you've left. And I worry she might try to pull something now that you're getting close to graduating. She doesn't want to see us succeed if it's not at her hands."

My chest grows heavy at his words because it's true. She's my mother. She birthed me, but she has never been a mom. All she wanted was to have a child she could brag about. She had to have the smartest, most athletic, best-looking kid at the country club. If she didn't, if you weren't what she expected, you were worthless.

I got tired of being her Ken doll. She pumped me full of

Adderall to help me "focus" and chose all my sports and activities. Dressed me the way she saw fit. Forced me to dinners with possible "matches" and drove off all the girls I actually enjoyed talking and hanging with because feelings wasn't the "objective" and would complicate the "purpose." She was crazy.

So, when my dad finally found the courage to divorce her, to search for his own happiness, I begged him to take me with him. He agreed instantly, and we tried to get Payton. But my mom fought us to the core. She dug up any and every skeleton of mine and my father's she could. There weren't many, but in the end, Payton was to stay with my mom and me with my dad. It was hard to leave her there and even harder when my mom found a way to make her cut all ties with us. She was so innocent in all of it. She had no idea none of us were unhappy because, surprisingly, since my mom had been running my life, she'd left Payton's alone.

As soon as we moved, she pulled Payton from Alrick Junior High. She was an eighth grader at that time, so that couldn't have been easy.

With a sigh, I drop onto my bed, scrubbing my hands down my face. I look to my dad, deciding to share my decision with him. "I'm leaving after graduation."

He inhales deeply, sadness crossing his face, but he gives a small smile. "I always knew you would. You never wanted to be here. But that's what I mean when I talk about your mom. She's gonna fight us somehow. She's still executer of your college fund—"

"I don't need it."

His forehead creases in confusion, and he moves to take a seat in my desk chair across from me. "What do you mean? Do you have a scholarship?"

I shake my head, unable to hold the smile in. "Dad, Lolli, she owns half of the San Diego Tomahawks. Embers Elite, the number one sports photography company, the one that covers all the games?" My eyes widen in excitement. "That's hers, too."

Still not quite understanding, he lightly shakes his head.

"When her family died, everything was left to her. Well, after graduation, she's going back to California, and she asked me to come with her. Said she has a place for us there. Dad, she wants me to take over for her CEO when I'm done with school. They're gonna put me through college, help me stay on track, and I'll intern and shadow the entire time, all starting this summer."

"Holy shit," he whispers, crossing his arms. "Really? And it's all legitimate?"

"I don't have every detail yet, but yeah, Dad, it's real." My eyes shift between his. "This is it, my out. *Finally.* I don't have to play Mom's games anymore. Lolli's offering me a whole new life. I haven't told her yet, but I'm gonna take it."

He nods, glancing away as he clears his throat. A low chuckle leaves him as he looks back and stands with his arms out.

A weight is lifted off my shoulders in that moment, and I wrap him in a hug.

"This ... this is great news, bud. Great news."

I smile and step back, making him chuckle when I smooth my tie and jacket back down.

"I, uh, I'd better get going."

He nods, his eyes glossy. "You know I'm happy you've been here, right? I know we never saw much of each other, but knowing I shared a home with you meant a lot to me. I wish things could have been different, and I'm sorry for that, but Parker ... I'm so proud of who you are despite what we gave you."

"It wasn't all bad, Dad. And being here with you was a hundred times better than being there with her."

He smiles. "Go. Have a good time tonight."

With a nod, I walk out and make my way toward my truck.

But the second I put the key in, my shoulders slump, and I drop against it.

That was a loaded conversation, one I wasn't prepared to have just yet, if ever.

Maybe I shouldn't, but I feel for my dad. He was a good man, a great dad, for most of my life. He was always around. He taught me how to play football and was at every game and practice when I was little. Then, one day, he wasn't. It hurt, but he never necessarily did me wrong.

He had demons he battled on the inside, much like most of us, that eventually made their way to the surface.

The saddest part is, he felt he had to hide who he was for so long. Somewhere along the way, my mother made him think he was dirty. That he was somehow bad for it, that he'd "ruin" me if I saw or knew he was no longer in love with my mother but was now in love with a man. A good mother would want to show her children that being true to themselves was the most important thing, that we should all strive to be the best versions of ourselves and love strong and live happy.

I hate her and everything she did to our family.

My mother was raised in a basic home with blue-collar parents. They were getting by, at best. When she met my dad, she got a taste of what money felt like. He wanted no part of the high-society life his family led. All money and greed. All he wanted was a happy family in a quiet town, someone to love.

And he thought he'd found it with her. But after everything, her taking him to the cleaners in the divorce—not that he fought her for any of it—and the hate she'd spewed over the years, I wonder if she ever loved him at all. If she ever even loved me.

With a weak laugh, I pull my door open, unbutton and pull off my suit jacket, then toss it on the seat. I grab my gym bag with my overnight things and close and lock my door.

Fishing the bottle I bought for tonight out, I start sipping on it and make my way to the hotel where the after-party will be.

It's a solid three miles away, but I could use the fresh air. I don't need to be at the dance tonight.

It's Lolli's first one, and even though she seems not to care, I know she's excited, and I don't wanna bring her down.

I only make it a few blocks up the road, still on my street, before stopping to sit on a bus bench.

Stuffing what's left of the Jack in my bag, I scrub my hands down my face, wishing the empty place in my chest would hurry up and fill with the numbing juice I've fed it.

Then, as if the night hadn't already done me in, a voice soft as silk wraps around my throat, making it hard to breathe.

"Hi."

My pulse instantly strums in my ears, my body tingling all over as I feel her grow near, and I slowly lift my head. Every bit of air escapes me, leaving my lungs starved, the moment my eyes land on Kenra. I shift to stand.

Her hair is longer now and lays in curls down her back. There are more copper pieces shining through it than before. The long black dress she's wearing almost brushes the floor as she steps toward me, a white sweater dressed over her arms.

When she reaches me, her shaky hand lifts to my cheek where she slowly glides the tips of her fingers across my jaw. Her eyes follow her hand, those lips twitching when my body jolts from the feeling.

Her brown gaze lifts, connecting with mine. "You're taller," she breathes.

An airy chuckle leaves me, and I grab ahold of her hand, slowly bringing it to my lips to kiss her palm. Then, I drop our joined hands to hang between us. "You're here."

Her eyes flit between mine, and she nods. "I was headed for your house, but I saw you sitting here ..."

My heart starts beating out of control as she steps closer to me. "Why are you here, Kens?"

"To dance," she whispers, bringing our hands to cover her heart.

"You came here to dance?"

"I came here to dance with you." Her eyes fall to my lips.

The alcohol is starting to take over, convincing me I'm not close enough—nothing is ever enough when it comes to Kenra —so I step in even more. The tips of my fingers run across the satin-like material, keeping me from feeling what I've always imagined to be the softest of skins.

Her sharp inhale isn't missed. Neither is the way her lashes sweep with her slow blink.

"Why do you wanna dance with me?" I speak low, and she licks her lips. "Hmm?"

"Because, last time, I never got the chance."

We're standing on an empty corner in front of some stranger's house. We have no music and no dance floor. But none of that matters.

If she wants to dance, we'll dance.

My hand slides around her too-thin frame, and I gently push on her back, bringing her chest against mine. Right against me.

And, just like that, my heartbeat blends into hers. Every breath she forces past her lips, I inhale. Every tremble from her body ripples through mine. Every crease that starts to form at the edges of her eyes, the pinch that takes over her forehead, I feel the pain that created them. Our slow and subtle sway feels like the end of something that hasn't even begun.

I sense it. Her final good-bye. That's why she's here.

With a shuddered breath, I tighten my hold, burying my head in her neck as she begins to cry into mine. This is it. She's marrying Kellan.

She chose him for real. Over me.

All I ever wanted was to hold her, to love her, but I knew what would happen if I tried. I'd give her all I had, and she'd carry it with her on the way back to him.

I know she loves me; her eyes tell the truth her voice refuses to share.

We were only supposed to be friends, but somewhere along

the way, I forgot to remember she wasn't mine to keep and gave her my heart anyway.

The alcohol has officially taken control, which means it's time to go.

I can't look at her. No way I can watch the tears roll from her eyes right now.

So, without another word, without another glance, I pull my body from hers, fighting for oxygen as she whimpers in front of me. I keep my head down as she walks away, listening for her car door to open and close before I turn and head in the opposite direction.

And, once again, my heart drives away, and there isn't a damn thing I can do to stop it.

I'm in no shape to see my friends but heading home sounds like a shit idea just the same, so I continue toward the hotel, finding only a handful of my classmates here. I quietly find my room and change into more comfortable clothes, and then I sit and get trashed by myself.

A few hours of staring at the wall, thinking about nothing, must go by because the hallways are buzzing, drunken shrieks and laughter now easily heard.

I pull my heavy body from the bed and splash some water on my face before stumbling out of my room. I nod at my classmates as they say hi in passing, turning them down when I'm offered a drink. I continue down and around the hall, glancing into each open room piled high with dance-goers, and before I know it and before I can stop it, my hand comes down on the closed door of room fifty-four.

It only takes Lolli a moment to answer, and when she does, it's clear I wasn't who she was expecting.

Her grin turns flat, and a frown takes over her beautiful face.

She grips my wrist and pulls me into the room. I stumble at the edge of the bed but manage to plant my ass on the mattress.

"What's going on, Hero?" she asks, rubbing my hand.

My chin hits my chest. "I don't know, Lolli Bear."

"You didn't come to the dance."

I shake my head.

"Is it Ashley?" She asks about the girl I was supposed to bring tonight, trying to understand. "You upset you didn't get to take her to the dance or something?"

A bitter laugh leaves me before I can stop it, and I throw myself back, squeezing my eyes shut. "No, it's not Ashley. I was only taking her to help her out."

"What do you mean?" she asks, and I feel her shift beside me.

"She's in love with an asshole, and apparently, that asshole asked her to come to the dance, but she knew it was a bad idea to go with him, so she told him she had a date. I just so happened to be the first guy to walk by after the fact." I chuckle.

"Aw," she teases. "You really *are* a hero." She laughs, briefly dropping her forehead onto my chest.

"Why do you call me that? Hero?"

"You don't like it?"

A smile pulls at my lips, eyes still closed. "I like it, just wondering."

She hesitates a moment, and I know she's considering what she wants to share. She tries not to give a whole lot of herself when it comes to deep shit. But she's my best friend, so I know she'll give me something. I need something right now, and I know she can sense it.

"Because you remind me of my OG, Hero," she jokes, doing her best to take the seriousness away.

I laugh lightly, my eyes roaming her face, waiting for more.

She smiles slightly. "When I first saw you, your eyes instantly stood out, such a clear, light blue. It was more than just the color. It was the kindness behind them, the soft air around you. I knew you were a happy-go-lucky, all-around good guy. You gave me this familiar feeling of comfort I had lost."

My grin smooths out as I stare at her, and her eyes pinch slightly as she studies me, but she keeps going, "My grandpa was like you. Happy and fun, the peacekeeper between others. Kinda like you are with your parents."

I swallow, the tightness in my chest easing a bit.

"You're dedicated and eager, confident but in a respectful way. And you get me." She laughs, and I raise a blond brow in question. "You're like the epitome of the guy you bring home to mama—or maybe it's daddy since I'm a girl."

"They always say little girls grow up to marry men like their daddies." I grin, and she laughs.

"You're an idiot."

"So, what you're saying is, I'm perfect?"

"Yeah, Parker"—she chuckles, smiling down at me— "you kinda are."

I nod, a sloppy smile on my face. "I knew you loved me."

She busts up, laughing, but she sees it, how much I needed to hear her words tonight. She might not understand why, but she doesn't need a reason.

When I continue to stare, unable to pull my eyes away, she grins.

"What?"

A soft smile forms on my lips, my eyes taking her in. They lower, following the shape of her body, and slowly rise back to meet hers.

"I can't believe I didn't notice when you opened the door. You look amazing, Lolli Bear," I whisper, and worry lines take over her face. "Your eyes, they're really blue tonight."

"It's the dress," she responds quickly, trying to read me. "The contrast and shit."

I chuckle at that, my hand coming up to trace the line of her left eyebrow. "Nah, it's you." I give a small smile. "You're here right now, Lolli. All of you."

"I don't understand." She places her palm on the hand that's splayed across my stomach.

"You told me what you saw in my eyes. Well, I see things in yours, too. They always have a shadow, a little something in them, hiding a part of you." My hand lifts from under hers, coming back down to cover it. "But it's gone tonight. Your eyes … they're big and bright and beautiful." My eyes skim over her one more time. "You're beautiful. And you're happy," I say, my face pinching slightly. "Right? You're happy?"

She nods, searching my face to try to figure out what's wrong. She sees the pain and confusion but can't figure out why.

I chuckle again, scrubbing my hands down my face. "I'm kind of drunk, Lolli Bear." My head drops with a sigh. "I'm sorry. I should go."

"You don't have to. You can stay if you want."

I hop off the bed and make my way to the door. I turn back to her with a fake smile. "Come on, Lolli. Look at you." I gesture toward her body. "You, in that dress?" I playfully arch a brow. "You and I both know how tonight will end for you." I wave and open the door, revealing Nate on the other side.

Nate's head snaps up, his hand frozen midair, as if he were about to reach for the handle. His eyes narrow, and he looks from me to his key card to the number on the door and then back.

His stare shifts to Lolli and then slices back to me, narrowing in a way that tells me my being in here with her is not something he's okay with. He's pissed and with reason.

His girl is looking all kinds of beautiful and alone with another dude in a room that was meant as theirs.

"Hey, man." I nod, pulling the door open wider.

"What's up?" Nate's feet widen. Nothing I say will make this all right in his eyes. I get that.

"Just came by to hang with Lolli for a bit. I'm down the hall." I jerk my head to the left. "Room eleven."

"This is Room fifty-four." Nate's stare sharpens even more.

I scoff and shoulder past him. Okay, so down the hall and around the corner maybe, but so fucking what. He can be pissy all he wants, I'm not up for this shit right now. The alcohol is wearing off, and shit's coming back to the forefront of my mind. I need to get back to my room and knock out before I do something stupid and track Kenra down before she's gone again, assuming she isn't already.

"I'm aware, man. Like I said"—I give Nate a hard look he doesn't deserve— "I came by to hang with Lolli." I turn to look at her, my features relaxing instantly. "Night, Lolli."

I stumble a few feet down the hall, and she calls out, "Hero!"

I turn, grin in place, but the facade doesn't work on her. She sees it. The emptiness I can't fill tonight, and her brows dip.

"You okay?"

I swallow and force a nod, waving as I walk away.

I shouldn't have come here tonight. There's too much going on in my mind, and I can't think straight.

I make it back to my room and lie in the bed, alone as always.

CHAPTER 15
KENRA

I'M DROWNING. IT'S AS IF A TIGHTROPE'S AROUND MY NECK AND feet, pulling me to the deepest part of the ocean, and I wouldn't be able to break free if I tried. Not that I would try.

I wish a wave would come and sweep me under because I can't take much more of this.

I knew being near Parker would be hard, but I never imagined it would feel this way. Like the weight of the water is crashing against my chest, pushing me down while forcing me still. My lungs burn, and my eyes sting. I didn't know it would feel as if I were dying inside because I'd thought I already did.

I'm a porcelain doll, put together with special care and precision, but with the slightest push, I'll shatter.

Most days, I wait for that moment to come, beg for the final bow so I can say I tried, but in the end, it was too much.

I want to fall but only if I never have to get up again.

On the days I think I will, the nights I cut a little deeper, Parker's face appears, and my lungs open instantly. Those blue eyes of his breathe the life back into me.

And all I do is steal the life from his. But I can't stop. I'm not strong enough to walk away on my own. Not with Kellan's threats, not with the fallout Parker will have to live with.

Because not only am I weak, but I'm also selfish when it comes to time with him.

I should leave and never look back, but I can't. Being near Parker makes everything better. I don't even have to be touching him. Just knowing he's around brings a peace I can't find anywhere else.

I gave up the possibility of something good the minute I let Kellan take control of my life.

Leaving with Parker tomorrow would be a really bad idea, but my being here already is.

We'll both hurt more in the end. He knows it just as I do.

I should leave.

But, instead, at 4:59 a.m., I'm standing in the dark, waiting at the side of his truck before he's even reached it.

The smile that brightens his face when he spots me is more than I deserve, but I take it.

Just like always, I take everything he offers, giving nothing in return.

He sees the turmoil in my eyes and steps close.

"Don't worry," he whispers into the dark morning, and I breathe in his words.

"Be happy."

CHAPTER 16
PARKER

Σμιρνός

SHE CAME. SHE'S HERE, WITH ME, IN MY TRUCK.

I never would have thought she'd come, but I'm damn glad she did.

Kenra needs to remember what living feels like. So, that's my goal for the next two days. I'm gonna have fun with this beautiful girl, see her smile wide, and hear her laugh loud. I wanna watch her dance along the street and talk to a stranger. All the things the wide-eyed, lively girl she used to be would have done.

I want to remind her who she is.

I want my Kenra back.

"How much farther do we have?" she rasps through her sleepy voice as she shifts to sit up.

"Morning, sunshine." I shoot her a quick wink, and she tries to hide her grin but even in my peripheral, I caught it. "We're almost there, about a half hour out."

She nods and stares straight, fixing her little cardigan.

"So, when we get there, I figured we'd check in at the hotel and then get some food. I have a meeting at lunchtime that you're more than welcome to come to. I'd actually prefer it if you did. It should only be about an hour. Then, tonight, you pick where for dinner. Tomorrow though … I get to plan."

When I smile at her, she stares, her hand resting on the back of the seat. "Tomorrow is the Fourth of July."

I nod. "It is. And me and you? We're gonna have a good one."

It takes a few glances, but eventually, she smiles back.

"Will there be fireworks?"

"Fireworks, flip-flops, that bay breeze. All of it."

"This is crazy," she whispers slowly. "You know that?"

I shrug, not wanting to stop and think about it. "Nothing feels crazy when it's with you, Kens. We've done this a hundred times. We'll just have a better view here."

"Nate hasn't called yet."

I nod. I already thought the same thing. "That means Lolli's talked to him."

Kenra turns her head away. "What do you think she said?"

"Depends on what he asked. If he asked a direct question, Lolli gave him the answer she knows. If he asked something along the lines of why you'd leave with me, she probably answered with, *because she wanted to*." I laugh lightly, smiling wider when a small chuckle leaves Kens as well. "We're gonna have fun, Kens. I promise."

"I know we will … that's what I'm afraid of."

I swallow back the pained sigh threatening to escape and reach for her hand. "Never be afraid of what you feel when you're with me. I've got you."

"Always," she whispers.

I bite the inside of my cheek to keep from saying something that would do neither of us any good at the moment.

An hour later, we're all checked in and stepping into what will be our room for the next two nights. Kenra steps into the bathroom to freshen up, so I take a minute to gather my thoughts. Yes, I had the entire drive here to process her coming with me, but being here, knowing, at the end of the night, it'll just be her and me, is damn close to torture.

I want to go all in, like Lolli suggested, but that might push the wrong buttons at the start. I've gotta take Kenra back, make her remember who we are when we're together—just a couple of kids enjoying each other's company. Find that innocence that was us before we suddenly felt more.

"Would it be all right if we maybe walked around and grabbed something light as we go since you have lunch in a few hours?"

I glance at her over my shoulder. "Course we can. Whatever you want."

She offers a small smile before disappearing into the bathroom once again.

I shake my limbs out and pull on a pair of nice jeans and a T-shirt. The meeting is unofficial and simply a meet-and-greet type of thing. And Al told me to dress like myself, so I am.

Kenra walks out in a pair of white jeans and a loose-fitting black sweater, with her hair lying in tempting waves over her shoulder, making me wish I could run my fingers through it freely. "Ready?"

I clear my throat and glance away. "Ready."

We decide to walk a while, and she quietly takes in the buildings surrounding us. It only takes a few short blocks for her arms to uncross and her stiff movements to turn into welcoming sways.

"I've never been here before."

I grin her way. "I remember, one night when you came over, it was just after you got your research paper from Ms. Weir. You remember?"

Her mouth opens slightly, and for a moment, her feet pause, but she laughs lightly. "I remember," she whispers.

"You'd spent weeks working on it. For hours and hours, we'd researched any and all things of the Asian culture."

"And that old hag gave me a D! A damn D!" she says in surprise, and I laugh. "I was shocked."

"And what did she say?"

"She said, 'Ms. Monroe, Wikipedia is not a place to gather

your facts from.' Not once, Parker, did I read a single sentence off there!"

"Uh-huh." I grin, and she pouts a bit. "And, when you came over that night, what did you tell me you'd do?"

Her mouth pops open to answer, but slowly, she closes it as a memory flashes in her mind.

She burst through my front door that day, not bothering to knock, and tossed her paper on me from behind the couch. She narrowed her eyes and placed her hands on her little hips as she demanded I take her to China, all so she could feel better about her hard work. Of course, I laughed and agreed to take her anywhere in the world.

After an hour of junk food, we settle on Chinatown in good old San Francisco.

Her eyes grow soft as she exhales. "You're taking me to Chinatown?"

"Tomorrow."

Tears brim her eyes, so she glances away. "I'd really like that, Parker."

I smile, grabbing her hand and kissing her knuckles. "I knew you would. Now, come on. We have a city to see."

We talk and walk around Haight Street. I laugh every time her nose scrunches at the different smells the city brings. She looks my way, shock on her pretty little face, before she starts laughing with me.

We skip the food and grab a quick smoothie instead. And, by the end of the road, she is walking right beside me, her arm brushing mine with every step we take.

As we wait for the light to change, her eyes dance along the daisy-covered grass across the street, shifting to the group of teenagers when they start to laugh. She stands there for a moment, watching as they skate, grinding the curbs of the abandoned parking lot, and her lips twitch slightly.

When I step closer, her eyes fly to mine, a deep crease instantly forming in the center of her brow. I sweep her hair from her forehead, hating how much I love the way her eyes close the moment the pad of my thumb brushes across the skin of her temple.

"We need to head over to my meeting now," I whisper, trying to take my hand off her but failing to actually do it. "Will you come with me?"

She slowly steps back, and my hand drops to my side. "I don't want to be in the way."

"You could never be in the way."

She inhales while nodding. "Okay, sure."

When I smile wide, a laugh leaves her, and she lifts her hand to push on my chest. I catch it and quickly spin her once before winking and checking in for an Uber, who happens to be just down the street. They're everywhere in the city.

We hop into the little Toyota, greet the driver, and then sit back.

"So, who are you meeting today?" Kenra asks. "Are these people Lolli works with?"

"Nah, this is the other owner. Lolli's grandpa was a fifty percent owner of the Tomahawks, but the other fifty is split between two other investors—fifteen to some big investment banker who likes to remain anonymous, and the other thirty-five to a man from overseas, getting ready to pass the torch to his grandkid. That's who will be there today."

"Isn't it crazy to be involved in all this? I mean, you haven't even started school yet."

"Actually, the person I'm meeting today is in the same boat as me, just starting off, so it's been nice to have someone to chat through things with. And I've shadowed Al since I've gotten here, sat in on industry meetings. I hardly know shit, but I'm learning. I spend a lot of time going over the business plans, noting things that I don't understand or want more insight on, and then Al and I go over it, sometimes even Lolli. I've got years ahead of me, but I feel like I'm off to a great start, and I'm included in everything. I wasn't so sure about it at first, but

Lolli wanted it this way. She wants me in the know as much as possible. Her only rule is, if I get burned out, I tell her and pull back immediately. Truth is, I love everything about it so far. It gives me …" I glance at Kenra, who stares at me. "It makes me feel like I'm doing something that matters. It's good for me."

She smiles lightly, trying to hide the longing that softens her features by clearing her throat. "I'm glad."

Before I can respond, the Uber driver pulls up in front of our hotel, and we step out.

"Your meeting is here?" She looks confused.

"Yep. In the hotel restaurant. I thought it would be easier for us."

She nods lightly, tilting her head back to follow the length of the twenty-six-story building. "Since we're here, maybe I'll go up and—"

"Hello again, Mr. Baylor," comes from my left.

I turn to find Dani Dameron stepping from her service car.

With a smile, I tip my chin, and she grins, making her way over. "Ms. Dameron, great to see you again."

Kenra

My eyes rake over the beautiful brunette woman as she steps closer to us. Her smile is wide, her eyes bright and alive. She's not dressed for a meeting, donned in a pair of tight blue jeans and a low-cut royal-blue blouse that matches her eyes, her tan, toned arms on display.

She's exquisite.

"What did I tell you? Please, just Dani."

"Then, I'm just Parker," he teases.

She laughs, her hand finding his forearm.

My chest constricts at the sight, but I manage to keep my smile in place as Parker steps back, placing his hand on my back. He pulls me forward, and the woman glances my way, a slight crease at the sides of her eyes.

"Dani, this is my Kenra."

When her eyes fly to his, my cheeks grow warm.

Parker either doesn't realize what he said or doesn't care to correct himself. Either way, the woman caught it, and she can't hide her curiosity.

"Kenra"—she reaches a hand out for me to shake— "it's great to meet you."

I shake her hand, returning her sentiment because her words feel genuine.

"I have the corner table reserved if we're ready to head inside?"

The woman briefly glances at me before giving Parker a smile. "Absolutely. Lead the way."

Parker nods and leads us inside the building and into the little restaurant, ROH.

"Would you excuse us for just a minute, Dani?" Parker grabs for my hand, but Dani stops us.

"Not a problem." She stands from the seat she's just taken up. "I'll take a minute to freshen up in the ladies' room."

As soon as she's out of earshot, he turns to me. "I'm sorry you got interrupted out there. Did you ..." His features tighten. "You don't wanna have lunch?"

I go to speak but pause as I look him over.

This woman likes him—I can sense it—and here he is, not jumping at the chance to rush me off but bummed at the thought of my leaving.

Kellan would be pushing me to go up to the room, feeding me Xanax and fake concerns.

"Hey"—Parker steps close, running the tips of his fingers over my temple— "focus on now, Kens. Don't think about anything else."

I turn my head, letting my cheek brush against his wrist. "How do you always know?"

"Same way you do. I'm inside you, Kens. Can't fight it. Don't want to."

Dani starts back this way, so I step back, forcing his hand to drop to his side.

"She likes you."

At that, his brows bound high, and he goes to speak, but she's already here.

"Shall we?" she asks.

When Parker motions for her to sit, her eyes slide to mine. I don't see foul intentions, but a woman knows when another is waiting for a sign. She's holding out to see what move I'll make.

I should go back upstairs and let him have this. Perhaps he'll like her, too.

When I turn to him, ready to be unselfish, just this once, his eyes keep me from speaking.

The blue of his stare melts me, his eyes sloped at the edges, pleading for me not to go. I can read what he can't say. *Don't go when I've only just gotten you here.*

He's not worried about the woman beside him or what she might think.

He simply wants me here, beside him. So, I sit.

The woman, Dani, kind and poised, looks to me with understanding and gives her attention back to Parker.

"So, Parker Baylor, let's hear it. Al mentioned Kalani wanted you to pay close attention to a Noah Riley out of Avix U."

Parker grins with a laugh. "It's Lolli, and I only correct you now because she's pretty particular about who calls her by her real name. I don't even think Al's allowed."

At that, they both laugh, and I find myself grinning as well.

And, much to my surprise, I enjoy the luncheon.

Being able to watch Parker speak, hearing the excitement in his voice as he breaks down his last few work-related trips and the things he gained from them, is by far the best part. It's hard to witness the happiness inside him, his life moving forward without me, but even harder to look away.

He's doing something he loves, and I'm so proud.

"This was great, Parker. Thank you for meeting me today. I want to be sure you and I truly understand each other before we get into the full business side of things over the next few years. Like you, I've got a lot to learn, but I think establishing a solid level of communication will be good for us."

"Of course." He nods. "Anytime I'm available, I'm all for it."

The woman glances my way, giving a small, one-sided smile.

"Kenra"—she turns to me— "it was great to meet you. I'm sure I'll see you again."

I offer her a smile. "Great to meet you, Dani."

She nods and gives a wink before making her way out of the building.

Parker shifts to me with an easy grin, having not a single clue that the woman came here to simply get to know the man he is. She was interested, and much to my surprise, tossed the idea the moment she decided I was more than just a woman who tagged along.

"Should we take another walk and go sightsee a bit?"

I don't want to share him with the world. "Pay-per-view and PJs?"

Parker's smile opens up my lungs, and together, we head to our room.

I MIGHT AS WELL CLOSE MY EYES BECAUSE I HAVE NO IDEA WHAT'S happening in this movie right now, and I know Kenra doesn't either. Proving my thought, she reaches for the remote and turns it off.

"This is useless."

I laugh and jump to stand. "Come on."

With a weary expression, she stands but doesn't ask questions.

I grab the small throw off the edge of the bed and wrap it around her shoulders, and together, we silently make our way into the elevator.

"I was planning to wait until tomorrow, but I think we need a change in scenery." I push open the door, and she looks at me before stepping past and out onto the patio.

She stares through the tall, thick plastic that acts as a barrier to the night's city lights just behind it, but this is nothing.

"Come on. The view is even better over here."

With a soft laugh, she follows behind me, and we step up into the pool area, moving to stand against the ledge. Hundreds of city lights stare back at us, neon blues and pinks, whites and yellows, with the sound of echoed horns and drifting music all around.

"Wow. It's so loud yet so quiet. Just ... soothing," she whispers.

Even though I shouldn't, I step closer, and her deep inhale rubs against my chest. Even with the blanket wrapped tight around her to keep that ever-present bay breeze from chilling her tiny body, I feel calm. But I want to feel whole, so I dare a move reserved for a man who has a right to the woman in front of him and wrap my arms around her middle, pulling her into me.

She freezes for the slightest of seconds, but then her body relaxes into mine.

I know this is painful for her—hell, it's downright torture for me, too—but it's worse having her this close and not touching her.

It's a lose-lose situation with no clear way out.

We stand there, staring at the night sky for a long while before I hear her quiet sniffs.

With a deep inhale, I slowly spin her to face me.

Full to the brim, tears threaten to spill with her next blink, but before they can fall and before I have a chance to speak, she whispers, "I think we should go inside now."

I want to fight her, push her, but I can't yet. Not yet, so I nod. "Okay, Kens."

Once in the room, she disappears into the bathroom. A moment later, the shower kicks on, so I take that time to change quickly and pull back the sheets to her bed, making the small couch out for myself.

She stays in there for a good hour before finally stepping out in a pair of thermal-like pajamas.

She slides under her sheets, staring at me when she lays her head on her pillow. "Months," she whispers, looking to her palms.

I prop my elbow up to see her better.

"I haven't laughed or smiled even in *months*, Parker. Haven't felt like myself in over a year." Her eyes slide back to mine.

"You had me smiling within two minutes of opening the door, laughing within an hour." Her eyes fill with tears.

"It's always been easy for you and me, Kens," I speak low.

A broken chuckle leaves her. "Nothing about you and me is easy ..."

"Who we are together is easy, second nature, and it always has been. All the rest?" My eyes shift between hers. "It could be, too."

"Parker ..."

I swallow, dropping my head back on my pillow. "I know. I'm sorry."

She stares for a moment, so I stare back.

"Good night, Parker."

"Good night, Kens."

I close my eyes, hoping this isn't the last time she's the last thing I get to see before I go to sleep.

Kenra

I stare at my screen and the message that woke me in the middle of the night. Rereading the text from Kellan over and over again, I wish I could tell him to fuck off. He's so careful, always tactful in messages and voice mails. Never once breaking character just in case our phone logs and such are released. He works hard to protect the pretty little image he's painted over the last few years.

Kellan: I'll be in Texas a few more days, my love. I hope your time alone is full of good choices.

He thinks he's a clever bastard, threatening me without the actual words.

And he's not in Texas. It's the first weekend of the month,

which means his favorite flight attendant is in town and has a room key with his name on it. Better her than me, but still.

I wish he'd be the man he claims and be up-front about it, messaging me to say he's with his whore this weekend and that he'll be home when he gets home.

But he never would because that's not how he works. He's a silent predator.

He studies with his eyes and plays games with his mind. Works around everything to fuck over all, and the one on the losing end never sees it coming, not until the bitter end, not until your back is turned and the knife is to your throat.

Why he chose me for a trophy, I'll never understand. I'm plain, average at best on a good day. The women I spend my days around when in his world are made-up replicas of one another. Fake boobs, fake lips, fake nails, fake hair, and fake personalities. Nothing is real. None are genuine.

It's a place with more money than needed, where more people want *in* than anywhere else, yet it's the loneliest place I've ever been.

I can't imagine how much worse it'll get once he's actually graduated college. Right now, is what he calls the grooming years, where we're seen and set the precedence.

"Make them desperate for us and what we represent." That's one of his famous lines. For some reason, he seems to think he needs me there to make it happen.

I think it started simple, with me fitting the role he needed filled, but eventually it became more of an obsession or power trip. His need to be the winner, branding me the prize.

Ever since he learned of mine and Parker's secret friendship, he's felt threatened, grown cold and nasty, or maybe he's always been a manipulating man. Either way, he's gotten bolder over the years. Braver.

And he's gone above and beyond to make sure my feet stay planted beside his.

I've learned money controls everything. Once you have

enough of it, the power is in your hands, and you can bend anyone at will. And Kellan has me and everyone I care about in his back pocket, tied up nice in his bottomless Goyard wallet.

I slip from my sheets and slide into Parker's. Slowly his eyes open, and he stares for a moment before shifting back to make more room for me. I tuck into him, and his arm slides around to pull me closer.

Our deep sighs match, and we fall back asleep, together, as we should.

CHAPTER 18

PARKER

Σμυρνιός

WHEN I TAP THE KEY CARD AGAINST THE DOOR AND PUSH IT OPEN, I inhale deeply. Kenra is sitting at the edge of the little desk, a cheap hotel room coffee cup in her hand, long, shiny brown hair lying half down her back.

She turns from the large window to smile at me over her shoulder. "Hey."

Fuck me, she's … perfection.

Her lips are a subtle pink, her face free and clear of any makeup other than a little something on her eyes to make those gold flecks pop.

Her eyes drop to bags in my hand. "Whatcha got there?"

I set one down on the counter for later and make my way to her still holding the other, not missing the way her lips part, the closer I get. "Just some pastries from downstairs and a couple of waters."

She grins, nodding. "And in the bag you ditched behind you?"

I chuckle, licking my lips. "A prize."

"A prize?" She smiles, glancing from it to me.

"Mmhmm," I tease.

She tries to play off her excitement, but a second later, she attempts to jump past me, only for me to wrap my arm around her waist and spin her back around.

Long, soft hair flies in my face and hers, and she giggles before growing silent and completely still. Her eyes connect with mine before slowly roaming my face. She studies every single inch of me from the neck up.

Her shaky little hands lift to my chest, her fingertips pushing into me with my deep inhale.

She wants to say something, but she's having a hard time. As much as I want to wait it out, hope she'll find her own bravery and share what's on her mind, like she used to, I don't want the day to go to shit before it's started.

So, I grab her hand, squeezing lightly before stepping back and pulling her with me. "Come on, Kens. I promised you Chinatown."

She gives a soft smile as she picks up her purse. I grab the snacks I bought, and we head out the door.

It takes us just over twenty minutes to make the walk, but Kenra rejected the idea of an Uber. I think she's liking the freedom that comes with simply walking down the road. All the people and the shops, she's having a good time, smiling at everyone who passes.

Once we cross through the green awnings and into the heart of Chinatown, she's glowing. She all but drags me from shop to shop, pointing out all the paper lanterns that hang from one side of the buildings to the other.

I purposely steer her to the shop I was hoping would catch her attention, and sure enough, she spots it.

"Oh my gosh, Parker, look!" She gasps, spinning to me with a side smile. "They make you fortune cookies!"

I chuckle lightly, following behind her as she skips their way.

"Oh, look at you. Beautiful girl."

Kenra blushes a bit but smiles at the woman. "Do you really make fortune cookies?"

"Course I do, sweet. Sit, sit." She urges Kenra, who smiles as she listens. The woman turns to me. "You pay?"

Kenra's eyes widen, but I wink her way and turn back to the woman. "Yes, ma'am. I'll pay."

She walks to Kenra and places her hands on Kenra's cheeks, and they stare at one another. After a moment, the woman gives a curt nod, moving back behind her little station and gets to work.

It doesn't take long before she stands and passes over a little bag of fortune cookies. "Don't open now," she tells her. "Later, when a new path is needed."

"A new path?"

The woman nods. "Color. Live in color." She hands her a single fortune cookie. "Here. This one's for today." The woman turns to me. "She's never been here?"

"No, ma'am."

"Take her to Golden Gate Park. Ride the carousel."

Kenra looks at me, eagerness in her usually solemn eyes.

I nod and offer her my hand, which she doesn't hesitate to take, and we make our way down the road.

We Uber, and she's quiet on the short drive, rolling the miniature wrapped treat in her hand.

I can see it in the way her eyebrows keep pinching at the center and the light bounce to her leg. She wants to open it so bad, but at the same time, she's too afraid.

I wish I could erase her fears and soak up all her pain. I'd drown in hurt if it meant she felt none.

The car pulls up in front of an old McDonald's, the driver practically forcing us out so that he can move on to grab his next job.

Kenra glances around. "Are we ... is this where we're supposed to go?"

With a laugh, I place my hand on her back, guiding her forward when the crosswalk light tells us to go. "Yeah, this is the place. Just wait for it."

"Uh-huh." Her eyes widen, and she sinks a bit closer to me so a woman with a shopping cart full of random items can jam past us.

Once we cross, we start down the short path that leads to the park, and Kenra's steps start to slow. She glances at me with a small smile and then starts off ahead of me. I purposefully pull back a bit, letting her lead, letting her choose.

Little things like this, independence in the city, these are things she's missing. Things she needs. Kenra was always the life of the crowd. Bubbly and bright, she was like a beacon. Every person within thirty feet of her was pulled in. Everyone wanted to hear her talk and see her smile because she had a way of making you believe it. If she was happy, the world around her was, too.

I think that's why Kellan worked his way in and fought so hard to stay there. He knew, the moment people met her, she'd draw them in. Her presence was his gain. She was the advantage he needed in his world of image and people-pleasing.

I don't think he anticipated her to withdraw the way she has. In fact, I bet he figured the money would do the work he failed and keep that smile on her face.

If he knew a damn thing about her, he'd have known that would never be enough for her.

I almost wish the bastard were here now just to see. 'Cause the Kenra giggling at the birds in the trees above her, running her fingertips across the bright pink flowers that circle the small pond at the end of the hill ... that's my Kenra.

"Parker!" she shouts through a smile, not bothering to turn to face me, still holding her fortune cookie in one hand. "Hurry, come look!"

Unable to control my smile, I hustle to her.

"Look over there, right between the branches."

I shift to glance past her, finding two squirrels stuffing nuts into a tiny hole at the root of the tree.

One spins quick, bumping the other, and it makes a loud

noise. Kenra starts cracking up, making them both pause and run off.

Smiling, I look to her, but she's still watching after them, tears in her eyes from laughing, smile marks I haven't seen in a long time shining at me.

She's the most beautiful thing I've ever seen.

She glances my way, and her laughter dies almost instantly. I make no move, hoping I don't lose her happiness, while she works through her internal debate, deciding if she's allowed this time.

She stares a moment. Then, a deep sigh leaves her, and she smiles. "Let's go find that carousel."

"See that little tunnel?" I point behind her.

She spins, looking back with wide eyes. "That tunnel with a giant iron gate blocking the entrance?"

"Yeah, that one." I grin. "Come on, they only lock it at night, probably to keep people from sleeping under it."

She nods, and together, we follow the path through the dark tunnel and into what I consider to be the heart of San Francisco.

WHEN WE EXIT THE TUNNEL, MY STEPS BEGIN TO SLOW. MY EYES can't decide where to look first, so they roam from side to side.

There's a huge, open field full of groups of people. Some playing catch while others set up for a game of cricket. There's even Frisbees and water balloons flying all around.

My ears perk, and my gaze shifts right. I squint to see through the trees that line this side of the path to find another field, but this one is full of people dancing around while a line of others play various instruments—bongos, tambourines—and some are banging on pots and barrels.

I laugh as a man bends at the knee to swoop a woman into his arms so he can spin her around. She pops her head to the music, wrapping her hands around his neck.

"Pretty cool, huh?"

I spin to Parker with a smile. "This place is amazing." I glance around again. "These people, they're all so different from each other, but … look at them, Parker. They seem so genuine. A clean-cut man in slacks, drinking and laughing with a man in ripped shoes and a band T-shirt. I don't … I wish I saw this more."

"It might not happen every day here, but I've seen it a lot," he speaks low, and I turn to him. "People here, especially in the park, they're just happy to be out. Enjoying the time away from their day-to-day lives, enjoying the sun."

"I've grown to despise the sun."

His face contorts, and he steps closer, but I turn and continue down the path. I shouldn't have said that, and I sure as hell can't handle the pain that fills his blue eyes when he senses mine.

When I start to veer right, he calls out for me to make a left, so I do, and not a foot later, a huge playground comes into view. I roll the plastic-wrapped fortune cookie in my hand as I look along the toy structures. A tall rope pyramid of sorts sits in the front, kids of all sizes doing their best to climb to the highest point, each calling out to ones standing around to watch, proud they've made it. To these little ones, having reached the top is an accomplishment they'll not soon forget. Such a small, beautiful, innocent kind of happy.

"Back behind this part"—he points to one of the larger play structures— "there's a concrete slide. The kids carry cardboard loaded down with sand to the top of that little hill and slide down."

I smile, stretching to my tippy-toes to catch a small glimpse as we keep walking. "That's so cool. They bring the cardboard?"

"Actually"—he chuckles— "I've never seen anyone bring it. Every time I've come, it's always already been there."

"Maybe someone brings it and leaves it for the kids."

He nods lightly. "Yeah, maybe. I don't know."

I glance at Parker as he looks around, smiling at the seemingly happy little families.

I sometimes forget he didn't have that. He didn't grow up in a healthy, loving family like I did.

My parents, they are amazing. More than anyone could ask for in a mom and dad. They'd be devastated to learn the daughter they raised, who they taught how to change her own tire and bait her own hook, can't so much as choose her own lipstick, let alone set her own path.

"Hey." I jolt slightly when Parker grabs my wrists, quickly pulling away and clearing my throat.

His brows dip at the center, but he swallows whatever it was he wanted to say. "We're here."

"Where?"

He points to an enclosed, circular building, so I squint to see through the weathered glass, spotting the carousel and a smile breaks free.

"Are we gonna ride it?"

"Hell yeah, we're gonna ride it."

Loud laughter flows through the building right then. I turn to see the passengers floating out the door as their ride has just ended.

Babies and their daddies, moms and their teenagers. Brand-new young couples along with older, gray-haired ones, they all smile bright as they scatter in every direction.

"I believe you beat me the last time."

My brows meet at the center as I reluctantly look away from the carousel.

"I told you I wouldn't let you win again. It was bad for my ego."

I lightly shake my head, and a smile breaks across his face.

"What—"

"One, two, three, go!" He rushes out and then takes off.

I laugh, my jaw dropping a bit before I begin to run.

I get damn close to catching him, but in the end, he beats me there, proudly swinging his arms out wide as he gloats. I slow, but keep just enough speed to knock him back as I purposely bump into him.

With a laugh, he wraps his arms around me, swaying me a moment. His grip tightens for a split second before he lets go and steps back.

"I'm gonna grab us a ticket to ride." He hooks his thumb

over his shoulder, pointing to the small hot-dog stand just behind him, so I nod and step into the line.

It only takes Parker a minute to grab our tickets, and then he's joining me in the short line. His hands grab ahold of the cheap rope at both sides of me, and he bends to speak into my ear, "Which one you wanna ride, Kens?"

My breath gets lodged in my throat at his words, and I swear, I must turn ten shades of red.

When his forehead drops to my shoulder, his body shaking with a slight laugh, I relax some and manage to elbow him.

He grunts playfully before lightly squeezing my biceps from behind.

This is what I've missed. Our time together, the easy playfulness we used to have.

I wish I could look at him and see that guy again, the happy-go-lucky, blond-haired, blue-eyed boy next door. But it seems every time his and my gaze lock, his blue eyes lose their shine, becoming clouded with emotion I can't handle seeing. All of which is my fault.

I'm toxic for him.

But he's light for me. And I'm afraid, if I lose my light, the dark will swallow me whole. The pain will need to sting longer, the cuts will grow wider.

"Miss."

I shake my head, and Parker nudges me through the door.

I start walking toward my choice, glancing behind me to see Parker still chatting with the attendant. He nods, taps him on the shoulder, and then makes his way to me.

"Everything okay?"

"Yep. Now"—he rubs his hands together— "what'll it be, Miss Monroe?"

I tap the ugly, tattered, and boring brown horse, and he raises a brow, making me laugh.

"Really? We come all the way here, and you choose an old,

boring horse instead of the majestic white-and-gold stallion or the wild king lion or something."

I laugh lightly and reach past him, tapping the one that first caught my eye, the one I want him to ride, and he drops his head back, laughing.

"Cute, Kens. Real cute." He laughs.

Then, before I can stop him, he spins me, and his large hands are around my waist. He hoists me up, so I can wrap my legs around the horse. His hands hesitate a moment longer than necessary, but then he steps back and swings a long leg over his seat. The ride starts just then, and slowly, our animals start to lift and lower as we make our way around.

"That was the last time you were at the house," he speaks low, his eyes on the frog I chose for him, before turning to me.

I nod, my throat tightening. "I remember."

"You made me watch *The Princess and the Frog*."

I nod again, too choked up to speak.

His eyes flit between mine. "I almost kissed you that night. Right after the movie. You were starting to fall asleep, so I covered you up. The moment I did, you crawled over and laid against me. It was almost too much—to hold you like that and not be able to truly hold you like it meant something."

A tear slips from my eye, but I don't bother wiping it away.

Parker watches it roll down my cheek. "But you have to know what it meant to me, Kens." He glances up then. "Every time you've ever been in my arms, from four years ago to five minutes ago, every damn time … it means something to me. *You* mean something to me."

I'm all but silently sobbing now, but he's not done.

He steels his face, his eyes narrowing a bit. "I tried to wait you out. Hoped you'd give in to the things you wanted, but I don't wanna wait anymore."

At his words, the air suddenly becomes a weight my lungs can hardly hold. Resolve and determination stare back in the form of bright sky blue.

"I want you, Kenra. Plain and damn simple."

I search for air that won't come, begging with my eyes for him to stop talking but he refuses. Pushes.

"You want me; you always have. I know this. So, I'm sorry if it'll be hard for you, but I'm going all in. No more holding back. I can't make decisions for you, but I can't live with the regret of never trying."

"Parker—"

"No talking me out of it. I need you. Want you. I've gotta try."

I look down, watching my tears stain my jeans as the ride begins to slow to a stop. "It won't work, Parker."

"Maybe not," he admits and then sighs. "Probably not, but I still have some hope, Kens. Even if you've lost yours."

He hops off when the ride comes to a full halt, and I go to step down, but he keeps me in place with a warm hand to my thigh. When I raise my gaze to his, his knuckles lift, and he wipes away the tears on my cheeks.

"You've got one more ride, Kens. Just you." He taps my palm, and I reluctantly pull my eyes from his to look to the fortune cookie in my hand. "Close your eyes and feel. I'll be just outside the door ... waiting for you."

With that, he exits the small side door with each and every other rider.

I drop from the horse. I move to the circular teacup seat that doesn't lift and lie across the bench, hidden from outside eyes. I fight to control the beat of my heart and the screams in my head, but they only get louder and louder.

My eyes squeeze shut, my fists tightening beyond reason, only letting up when heat fills my palms. Blood forces its way through my clenched fingers, dripping onto the floor of the old wood.

Finally, I can breathe, and slowly, my eyes open.

Staring at the ceiling as I go around, I focus on the sounds around me.

Laughter. It's everywhere.

Coming from every direction, fighting its way into my soul and, just as quickly, begging for a way out.

I wipe my palms on the underside of my top, having nowhere else to hide my disgrace, and then I tear the wrapper off the fortune cookie the woman gave me.

I stare at it a moment before breaking it in two, revealing the small paper in the center.

Written there in the plainest of fonts, bolded black words mock me.

Happiness is a choice.

I almost laugh and cry at the same time.

This has to be the most cliché fortune there is, one of thousands that says the same thing.

But damn if it isn't the truest statement I've ever read.

Happiness *is* a choice.

And I choose to sacrifice my own for the sake of those I love.

"THIS PLACE LOOKS A LITTLE FANCY." KENRA GRINS, GLANCING around the restaurant as she squeezes into her seat.

I chuckle. "It's not, I promise, but the food's good."

She watches tourists as they walk past the patio-style seating. "You've been in California for only a few months—Southern California, no less—yet you walk around here and talk about this place like it's your own backyard."

I smile, nodding. "I've been about six times now, but every time I get done with the business side, I can't just head straight home. I like it here. There's just something about walking down these busy city streets. It gives me a huge sense of independence I've never felt before." I look back to Kenra. "An independence that, for a real long time, I thought I'd never have."

She nods, clearing her throat. "Are you keeping in contact with your dad?"

"I don't talk to him as much as I should, but yeah. Lolli asked them to come out to the house for a few days this summer, and he says they're thinking about it."

"Good." She nods. "And your mom?"

"Nope. Not a word. But, now that Payton's at the house, I'm gonna have to sooner or later."

"I still can't believe she agreed to let you come all the way here for school." Kenra shakes her head.

I scoff. "She had no choice. In fact, I didn't even tell her. Guess she heard through the small-ass grapevine in Alrick."

Kenra drops against her seat, her brows snapping together. "But ... what?"

I stare at her, seeing her breaths coming faster now, and tilt my head. "You know better than anyone the issues I have with my mom. Why do you seem surprised?"

"I just ..." She looks off and then back. "Why would she pay for you to go to school if you went against everything she had planned for you?"

My head pulls back, and I study her, her gaze flicking between mine. "Kenra"—I shake my head, suddenly weary, the conversation my dad and I had last winter playing through my mind— "my mom—"

I'm cut off when both my and Kenra's phones start ringing.

We look at each other and then pull our phones out.

"Mine's Lolli," I tell her.

"Mine's Payton."

Kenra tosses her napkin on the table and walks a few feet away to take her call, so I answer Lolli's from my seat.

"Lolli Bear," I answer, keeping an eye on Kenra.

"Hero! What the fuck?" she all but shouts in my ear. "Why the hell haven't you been answering?" She pauses before rushing out, "Never mind! I don't wanna know the dirty deets."

I laugh lightly, and she gasps.

"Wait, is there dirty to be told? Tell me everything!"

"Baby!" Nate yells in the background. "That'd be a, *Fuck no*!"

I laugh harder, practically hearing her roll her eyes.

"Whatever," she says loudly before whispering into the phone, "You're *so* telling me later, but, dude, we've got a problem."

My spine straightens. "Talk to me, Lolli Bear."

"You need to come home. Like, right now."

"Lolli."

"Where is she?"

Kenra turns right then, her face pinching.

"Lolli, talk." Before she can, panic starts to set deep in my gut because, somehow, I already know what she's gonna say. "He's coming."

She sighs into the phone. "I don't know for sure, but I'm bettin' when Deaton shows, he'll be right behind."

"Shit." I squeeze my eyes shut.

I need more time.

"Hero ..." Lolli whispers, and I open my eyes, focusing on the beautiful girl who stands in front of me, brows drawn in concern. "Tell me you'll be okay if ... you know, if—"

"Guessing this is why Payton just called Kenra?"

"Yeah. I think she's a little scared, not sure how to tell him about the baby."

I sigh, scrubbing a hand down my face. "I bet she is. I've gotta get back to the hotel and get our stuff and my truck, and then we'll hit the road. I should be able to make it back before he gets there."

"You will. His message said he'd be here by morning, course she didn't respond so he has no clue she's actually here, but still." She's quiet for a moment before speaking again. "Hey, Hero?"

The heavy pressure on my chest has my words leaving me in a scratchy whisper. "Yeah?"

"Sometimes, in order to win, we do things we don't always agree with. Things we think are wrong. But, Hero, a good defense can only do so much against a solid offense. If you've only got one play left in you, give it all you've got. He doesn't deserve your respect."

I nod even though she can't see me, my eyes shifting

between Kenra's. I hear what Lolli's saying. Know exactly what she means.

"I'm not so sure it'd make a difference," I whisper, and Kenra looks away. "I'll see you tonight, Lolli Bear." I hang up, and Kenra steps forward.

I clear my throat, nodding. "We've gotta head back."

She agrees, and silently, we make our way back to the road to catch another Uber to our hotel. Neither of us speaks the entire way there or as we gather our things. The sun set about twenty minutes ago, so the city lights are shining through our window. Excusing myself from the room, I make my way up to the roof and look over the ledge.

I thought I had another night with her, and now, it's being cut to a few hours, all of which will be on the road. Tomorrow, Kellan might very well show up with Deaton, and if he does, Kenra will leave with him.

I can't imagine it will go over well, and she'll be even more depressed than she is now.

Something is off. I know it, feel it in my gut.

She doesn't love him, yet she stays.

That bastard is fucking around on her, grooming her to be his perfect little trophy.

It's not lost on me that her entire body is covered twenty-four / seven, but I'm too afraid of what I'll find if I look past the cashmere. Because, if it's bruises I find, I honestly don't know what I'll do. But it won't be good.

I told her today I was gonna go all in, try my damnedest to keep her, but as it always does where I'm concerned, fates come out to say, *fuck you, Baylor*, and tomorrow, she might very well be gone.

I feel her coming before she's at my side, looking off into the night with me.

"I never wanted to hurt you," she whispers after a moment. "I fought myself that first year with Kellan, tried my hardest not to go to you at every turn but wanting to more than anything. I told myself you were my friend, so I wasn't doing anything wrong by spending time with you, but I could never convince myself enough to actually believe it. Even though you and I never did anything sexually, emotionally, I was cheating every day, all day, because you were all I thought about."

"Kens—"

"That's why I let Kellan act the way he did. When he acted like an ass and broke up with me just so he could hook up with someone else for a night—not that he'd admit to that then—or just treat me like crap, I would tell myself I deserved it because, really, I'd picked fights for an excuse to leave just so I could come hang out with you. When morning came, he'd be there, waiting, telling me all the things I wanted to hear. That mixed with my own guilt for wanting someone else always decided for me, and I'd forgive him ..." She trails off, taking a deep breath, making me hold mine. "Then, right after, seconds after I just took him back, he'd kiss me ... and I'd close my eyes every single time, wondering what you kissing me would feel like."

Heavy pressure pushes against my ribs, all while a warm feeling spreads within me.

I've always sensed it, her want, but her confirming it is a thrilling, torturous kind of feeling, a confusing type of pain I'm not sure I was ready for.

"The night I found Kellan and Liv in bed together, it hurt more than I'd expected it to. I kept thinking what I could have done to keep his interest in only me."

She goes quiet a minute, and I don't dare interrupt. This is a piece of Kenra I never understood, and I don't wanna miss a word.

"That next day, after the game ... after you asked me to come to you that night—which I had every intention of doing—Kellan came to me. I had a moment during the game. Kellan had my brother run his old play with one of the receivers, and it went well. I found myself smiling, happy for him ... and then Liv ran over to the sidelines where he was helping Coach and all but jumped on him. I started to cry instantly and was moving to leave. Well, apparently, he had walked off the field the same time I stepped off the bleachers because, all of a sudden, there he was, lifting me up and carrying me off. Before I knew it, he was mine again."

"He treated you real bad, Kens, cheated on you with your best friend."

She nods, still looking out over the city. "Yeah, he did. And that hurt, but I was young and dumb and easily manipulated by everyone. By then, I already couldn't have what I really wanted, so taking him back didn't demand much thought." My brows slope at that, but she continues before I can ask what she meant by it, "I believed all his nonsense about his early college courses and the stress it caused. Believe it or not, but I hadn't slept with him at that point, and I guess I convinced myself that it was somehow my fault.

"But, after that night, everything changed for the better. He was kind and gentle, so attentive. He'd come to my house, and we'd spend time with my family when he used to complain about how he hated it there. Everything that had been bad before was suddenly perfect.

"You asked me before if I loved him. At that time, I thought I might."

I bite the inside of my cheek, my fists tightening around the railing until my knuckles turn white. I have no idea what I'm supposed to be thinking right now, have no fucking clue what I'm supposed to feel. Relief, regret, anger. Fucking gutted from all of it.

"I never shared the good with you because ..." She hesitates. "Because I didn't want you to stop spending time with me. I was afraid, if you knew there was more good than bad, you'd ignore me when I wanted to see you. When I needed you. I know it was stupid, and I was wrong." She turns to me then, but I look away. I'm not sure what she'll read in my eyes right now. "I knew deep down you'd be there, no matter what. It's just who you were, but I couldn't risk losing you."

A low, sad laugh leaves me, and I bend at the waist, my hands holding on to the ledge as I hang my head. "But you did risk it, Kens. Every day, every time, every night. You were in his arms. In his bed."

"I know," she cries softly. "And I regret every minute of it. You want the truth? I hate my life. Hate myself," she admits.

I turn to her, my chest heaving, my body heavy.

I go to step closer, but she quickly steps back, fiercely shaking her head. Refusing my advance.

She's already shared more than I ever thought she would. It's still hazy, and there are still many holes in her story, but she won't be sharing anything else tonight; I'm sure of it.

The last thing I wanna do right now is leave this rooftop and drive home, but Payton needs me there even if she won't admit it, so I wrap my arm around Kenra's shoulders and turn her shell of a body toward the gate, and together, we walk back to the room for our things.

Once we're in the truck, Kenra covers herself with my small cab blanket and closes her eyes.

And I'm left with my thoughts as I fight the holiday traffic, trying to hit the bridge before the fireworks begin.

I planned to finish dinner tonight and then walk the pier a bit before heading back to our hotel. The rooftop was always part of the plan. I figured we'd order anything we might want from the bar or room service, and then we'd relax and watch the fireworks together.

She'd lie against me, tucking her body into mine, and it would be pure torture.

Fact of the matter is … she's promised to someone else. Has a date set to marry another man.

I never should have brought her here, never should have shared a bed with her.

But the biggest problem I'm having is with myself and the fact that I don't even feel the least bit guilty for it.

She might be his as far as labels go, but I live inside her, just like she does me.

In my bed or his, it doesn't matter.

I refuse to ever see her as anything other than mine.

Σμυρνιός

THE SMELL OF COFFEE HAS ME PEELING MY EYES OPEN. I GRIN AT Lolli, who's sitting Indian-style at the foot of my bed.

"Morning, sunshine," she whispers with a smile, slowly sipping her coffee. "What time you get in?"

I rub at my eyes, twisting to look at the alarm clock beside my bed, seeing it's just after six thirty a.m. "'Bout four hours ago."

"Oh, good, that's plenty of sleep for you. Time to talk." She wiggles against the mattress, and I laugh lightly, shifting onto my side to look at her.

"I give Nate three minutes, and then he'll be in here to drag your ass off my bed."

"I was just running. I decided this whole waking up early thing has it's perks; the entire fucking house is still out for the count." She smirks. "Why do you think I'm whispering? I'm buying time here."

I laugh lightly but when it's followed by a sigh, and she pokes her bottom lip out in a pout.

"Damn."

I nod. "Yep."

"So, we just … wait for today to happen and go from there?"

"I think that's all we can do at the moment."

"Your eyes are heavy, Hero. She laid a weight on you while you were gone. I can see it."

I smile at my friend, telling her without words that she's right, but I can't give her much more. She gets it, gets me, like always, and nods.

"Payton up yet?"

"Not yet. She had a weird pregnant day yesterday, so I guess she's extra tired; I don't know."

"What do you mean?" I prop up on my elbow. "What happened?"

"I made breakfast 'cause, *duh*, it's my thing, and as soon as she walked into the kitchen, she straight vomited on the fucking floor. And then in the sink. And then all damn day. Dude, she couldn't even eat a plain-ass bagel. I thought maybe she was dying or something, so I kinda, um ..." She trails off, squishing her lips to the side.

I can see the confusion mixed with worry in the way her eyes are pinched. "Kinda what, Lolli Bear? Kinda got scared and kinda wanted to help her, and you have no idea why?"

She narrows her eyes before laughing lightly. "Well, pretty much. It's like I don't even know her, but I feel connected to her, which is just fucking weird, considering, one, pretty sure she hates me, and two, I don't, you know, do feelings and shit."

I bark out a laugh, and she uncrosses her legs to kick me with a glare.

"Lolli, you didn't *used* to do feelings. That was pre-Nate. Now, you're like a real girl."

Her jaw drops, and she gasps, making me laugh harder.

"Kalani!" comes from down the hall, and she clamps her mouth shut, her eyes widening in humor. "Baby, get your ass off another man's bed and back in the one I'm lying naked in."

When my face scrunches in disgust, she raises an eyebrow.

"That's what you get for that *real girl* comment." She shifts to stand, smiling softly at me. "Also, a man like you, honorable and just flat-out good, can't possibly fucking lose in the end.

There's still time on the clock. Make it happen, captain." With that, she winks and walks out.

I call out, "See? Real girl!" I know damn well she's flipping me off on her way down the hall.

I slip from my bed and quietly walk through the house, finding it as quiet as Lolli said. I grab a water bottle from the fridge and drop onto the couch. I close my eyes, letting sleep pull me back in.

"Payton!"

My eyes peel open when the pounding begins, not letting up for a second.

One by one, everyone files from their rooms.

Nate stomps down the hall, nodding at me with a frown. There's blame in his eyes; most likely, he feels some sort of betrayal over my and Kenra's little trip. I'm betting it's more from her than me.

"What do we do?" he asks, waiting for me to make the decision.

We both turn when a wide-eyed Payton walks around the corner from the kitchen.

"Payton, open the door!" Deaton shouts, frantic. "Please open the door. Please." He pounds again.

"Peep"—I hold my hands out— "talk to me. What do we do?"

Nate and I turn when Lolli squeezes between us and makes her way to Payton, who seems frozen in place.

"Payton," she whispers in a gentleness I've never heard, but Nate must have because his chest puffs slightly with pride for his woman. "He sounds worried. Maybe we should let him in, if only to show him you're okay."

Payton's eyes fly from the door to Lolli's to mine. She jumps when the pounding starts again. "Open it," she tells me.

Lolli shifts to stand beside her.

I nod, and the second I pull the door open, Deaton Vermont sags against the frame, his hair crazy and sticking everywhere, collared shirt a wrinkled mess.

"Please tell me she's here. I've ..." His voice cracks, and he swallows. "I don't know where else to go. She just ... she disappeared and—"

"Deaton ..." Payton speaks low from the same place she stands.

A cracked chuckle flies from him, and the second I pull the door open enough for him to spot her, he briefly squeezes his eyes shut, before he rushes to her.

His emotions get the best of him as he wraps her in his arms. Instantly, she starts to cry.

"Baby, I didn't know what had happened. Suddenly, you were gone and—" His voice cracks, and he hugs Payton tight against him. "I thought your mom ... why did you leave me there? I would have come with you if you wanted to run away. I would have come. Anywhere. I love you."

"Deaton, please." Payton pulls away, and his arms flop to his sides.

"Talk to me. Tell me what I did. I'll fix it. I promise you."

She cries harder, shaking her head.

Lolli catches my eye, asking silently if we should leave, but Payton shoots her eyes my way, asking me to stay.

"You can't fix it," she whispers.

He steps closer, but she pulls back, and the clear shock pales his face.

"What's going on?" he whispers, and I almost feel for the guy. "I don't understand ..."

"I ..." She squeezes her eyes shut. "I'm pregnant."

Deaton freezes but only for a moment before he gives her no choice of pushing him away. He bends and scoops her in his arms, deciding this is a conversation they'll have privately. He walks forward, out the sliding glass door to the patio where we all watch him gently set her on a cushion, and then he drops in front of her.

"Come on, guys." Lolli hits my shoulder and pushes on Nate's chest. "Let's give them some privacy. That has to be an awkward-ass conversation."

"I think it's cool. She's a complete part of him now; she has his blood running through her."

"She's sixteen," I remind him.

Nate shrugs, looking from them to me. "Still pretty cool."

I look to Lolli, whose brows are creased as she looks at Nate, but she turns before he can see it and heads for her room.

Nate looks from her to me and then follows her down the hall.

I stand there, waiting for the oldest Vermont to make it through the door, but he never comes. I even go as far as looking out the window, only to find an empty rental car.

I glance at Payton, who has her face buried in Deaton's shirt, and then head for the shower.

Kellan could still show. Today could still be Kenra's last day here with me.

And I have no idea how to handle either of those possibilities.

"You need to talk, Baylor." Nate steps up beside me, looking out at the girls as they dip their toes in the water.

I sigh. "Not sure what you wanna know, man."

"Are you and my sister having an affair?"

Emotional affairs are still affairs, right? But does it count when there's no love in the committed relationship? Only hate and lies.

"I don't know what I should say to you, Nate, but I'm gonna go off the bill here and tell you I might need your help." I look to him, and his scowl deepens.

"I'm gonna need you to keep talking, Parker."

"Tell me you don't see somethings off with her."

"Course I fucking do," he scoffs. "Thought it was Kellan, but now, I'm wondering if it's you fucking with her head. The guy who lost his shit and punched me in the face because he thought I'd hurt Kalani."

"I punched you in the face because you disrespected her," I remind him.

The edges of his eyes pinch as he looks away.

The time he's referring to was just after he thought Lolli had cheated when Liv set him up to think so, and he made a shitty comment out of hurt.

"I can't even think about any of that. It kills me. I start remembering the thoughts I had about her, the doubt I felt, and it fucking sickens me, man. I don't think I'll ever forgive myself for that."

"You guys both made the wrong moves when you decided not to talk it out, both learned from it, and are stronger because of it. That's how relationships work."

"Right." He sighs and then turns back. "Back on track here. What's going on?"

"Your sister means a lot to me, Nate. Always has. She and I grew close over the years, just behind everyone else's eyes."

"Why?"

"I don't really know." I shrug. "At first, it seemed strange, and then after a while, it just felt like ours."

"Fuck, dude." He scrubs his hands down his face. "You love her, don't you?"

I look away, not answering him. I've never even said that to her. I'm sure as hell not about to say it to him.

"Tell me what's happening."

"I can't lay out all her problems, but I will tell you, she's not happy."

"If she's not happy, she would fucking leave."

I nod, watching Kenra watch the others enjoy the sand as

she stays a few feet back, her shoes and socks still on. "The Kenra I know would. The Kenra you know would." I turn to him, and his features harden. "So, why won't she?"

"You trying to tell me this rich prick is somehow keeping her trapped with him?"

"It's the only thing I can think of."

"I'll kill him."

"Precisely why she doesn't want you or your family to know."

"Shit, man. I've gotta think on this a little."

I look at him. "I understand."

"What about Deaton? Do I need to fuck him up? If he makes Payton cry—"

"No, no. From what I heard, he's good to her. Course, I'll pay close attention, just in case."

"Yeah, me, too." Nate nods.

I suppress a grin. I can tell he's feeling protective over Payton, and I appreciate it. But I can't tell him that his soft sides showin', or he'll tell me to fuck off.

He walks back toward the house, stopping to glare at Deaton and Payton, who have made a spot for just the two of them a few feet down the beach.

"He getting all He-Man on her?"

I laugh at Lolli, who smiles at Nate. "He's trying not to."

"Yeah," she sighs. "I think he wants to keep her."

When I laugh harder, she nudges me and then follows after Nate.

I make my way to Kenra, who smiles as I approach.

"The water isn't too bad, you know."

She nods, looking out over the ocean. "It looks refreshing."

It's a risk, but I bend and start unzipping her little boot.

"Parker—"

"Come on, Kens. I only have you for a little longer. Trust me."

I hear her small gasp but don't look up and continue pulling off her shoe and then sock. The second her foot hits the sand, she sighs. I get the other off, smiling when her toes instinctively curl into the sand.

I stand, and she inhales deeply. I hold my hand out, and she looks to it, watching as she slides her palm into mine.

Together, we walk to the edge of the water. She tenses a bit when we hit the wet sand and then smiles as her feet start to sink just a bit, laughing lightly when the water comes up and washes over the tops of her feet, splashing lightly at her ankles.

Her eyes grow glossy, but her smile is still here.

"I don't know how you do it, but you always manage to pull me from my reality and into a brighter one."

"It would always be brighter, if you allowed it," I tell her, and her eyes tighten at the sides, her gaze not leaving the water. "I'd make it my mission to see you smile, hear you laugh, as much as possible."

She breathes deep. "I haven't felt the sand on my feet in years. Probably since the last time we went floating, and that was more like creek-water dirt. This is so nice."

"Kens ... it won't be long before everyone realizes you never take off your sweaters, and I haven't seen you wear shorts or a dress either."

"Apparently, showing your legs is an invitation for men to look. Kellan's people don't approve."

"And the sweaters?"

She smiles sadly at the ocean. "We all have demons, Parker. Some of us just wear them on our sleeves."

My face crumbles, and I step toward her. "Kens ..."

She slides her eyes to me, not moving as I grow closer.

I pull her in, hugging her small frame to me, and she cries into my shirt, her body shaking lightly as she does. After a few minutes, I lower us into the sand, her cocooned in my lap.

Hesitantly, I lift one of her hands into my palm. She doesn't stop me like I thought she would, so I run my fingers along her knuckles, slowly coaxing fingers open.

The blood has dried against the cuts from her nails, but with the slightest pressure, it would start to run again.

I run my fingertips along her marred skin. When I reach the edge of her sleeve, her muscles tense, but she doesn't pull away, so I push the material down.

A shuddered breath leaves me as her demons stare me in the eye. I anticipated bruises to line her skin, but I wasn't prepared for the dozens of markings starting a half an inch down her wrist and continuing a few inches down from there.

Each line is precise, all the exact same length and angle. The only difference is a few are a faded pink, having not been opened as recent as the angry deep red cuts.

"Kenra ..." I trail off when my voice cracks.

"I told you I haven't smiled in months." She closes her eyes and tips her chin to the sky, tears rolling over her cheeks. "I haven't felt the sun against my skin in a year."

"Does he know?"

"He knows, even bought me a set of real silver blades once," she whispers. "As long as my arms stay covered, all is well in his world."

I stare at her, so beautiful, so lost.

All this time, I've been worried that maybe Kellan has been putting his hands on her, having no choice but to believe her when she denied it. I had no idea she had been doing this to herself.

CHAPTER 22

I take a deep breath, sitting back in my chair, when Deaton drops in the one beside me.

"Any chance he knows you're here?"

I shake my head, taking a nervous drink from my water bottle.

"This is pretty risky, Kenra."

"My brother is here. My cousins are here. I'm visiting."

"He won't buy that for a second," he whispers.

Both of us are quiet for a few minutes as we watch Parker and Payton walk around further down the beach. Payton laughs at something he said, and he smiles down at her before wrapping his arm over her shoulders.

"She's missed him. It's been hard for her these last few years. You know she wasn't allowed to talk about him at home?" Deaton looks to me. "Her mom took down every picture and got rid of everything that could possibly remind Payton that she had someone else out there who cared about her. It was bad enough she'd lost her dad, but she had to pretend her brother never existed. The one person in the world who had made her feel protected and loved, and he just left her."

"It wasn't as simple as that, Deaton."

He nods. "I know that now. I've seen what their mom is capable of. And, as bad as I want to hate him, I don't. He did what he had to for himself. I can respect that, in a way." He shifts in his seat, gaining my full attention. "My point here, Kenra, is he had to do something selfish to save himself. Why is it you can't do the same?"

"There's a lot more at risk for me."

His eyes narrow. "Is there? Do you know Payton suffers from depression? Did you know that there were many times when she talked about giving up because the expectations her mom had set were impossible to reach? She does one thing and gets to that point of perfection that was demanded of her, only for her mom to set the bar higher and higher until Payton feels like she's sinking. It took me a year to get her to trust me enough, for her to see that what I felt for her was real.

I love her more than I knew a person could love someone. She might come off as bitchy and spoiled, but that's not who she is. That's her defense. She's kind and warm and the best fucking person I have ever met. She's the one who made me realize what my family was lacking. Showed me that the money and name I was proud of wasn't worth a damn if it wasn't real and honest. How she came from that fucked up woman, I have no idea.

We might be young, and some might call us crazy, but I don't care. This life, it's ours."

Parker and Payton stop halfway to the porch and turn to look at each other.

"That's beautiful, Deaton, but so different."

"It's actually not, Kenra. You know her mom showed up at my house one day last year."

My eyes shoot to his, and he stares.

"Said she'd disown Payton, send her to her dad's and strip her of the life she 'loved' if I kept seeing her." His eyes shift between mine. "Know the first thing I did when she left? I called Payton and told her everything."

Tears slip from my eyes then.

"If I had to guess, I'd say she came to you with similar threats."

I look to my lap, tears falling from my eyes. "It was the end of my junior year. He'd been with his dad a while at that point, and he couldn't care less that he had no contact with her. She was livid. She wanted him to miss her just so she could deny him. I remember him telling me a few times the messages she sent him, just nasty things a mother should never say. Somehow, she heard that he was doing well in school and football. That he seemed happy, and she couldn't stand the thought. Kellan and I were together, but we fought constantly, broke up every couple of days. Parker was my best friend at that time, only nobody knew it. We didn't exactly try to keep it a secret, but we did like it to just be the two of us.

His mom had apparently been driving by the house randomly and spotted my car a few times, so one day when I was leaving, she approached me. I instantly knew who she was; I'd seen pictures of her. When I told her we were just friends, she got in my face and called me a liar. I was a seventeen-year-old girl, and here she was, a grown adult caging me against my car. She said, if she found out that he and I were together, she'd give away his entire college fund, so he'd have no option but to stay there in Alrick and go to community college." I look back up at Deaton. "All he ever wanted was out of there, away from everything that town reminded him of. A hateful mother, a dad who didn't try hard enough, a sister he felt he had given up on." My voice drops to a whisper. "A girl he couldn't have ..."

"So, you chose for him instead of letting him decide which was worth more—a future with you or one without you?"

"At that time, yes. I wasn't gonna hold him back from his clean start. And I'd do that again. He's happy here, excited for what comes next for the first time in a long time."

"You have no idea, do you?"

"What?"

"Kenra, Parker didn't ask his mom for a damn dime. It's part of the reason she's started to push Payton so hard lately. She's pissed, and she can't figure out how to step in and ruin it for him because, for once, she has no pull."

"I don't get it." I sit up straighter, shifting in my seat to stare at him head-on. "What do you mean?"

"Parker is here on a full support from the Tomahawks. Lolli's company is covering every single expense."

All the air leaves my lungs, and I squeeze my eyes shut.

"I can't believe you didn't know."

"I … I mean, how would I? I haven't talked to him in months."

So, this is what he was getting at in San Francisco before we were interrupted. His mother had no say in his coming here because he found a way to beat her. He took his life back, took control.

My head starts pounding instantly, my body confused on how to take this news. Shock is the first thing to hit.

The very first issue that stepped in our way, Parker's future, is no longer a barrier between us, and it's as heartbreaking as it is relieving. My being here isn't a threat to his plans … but it is to his heart.

Because, even though his mother is out of the way, there's still Kellan.

"What's my brother holding over your head, Kenra?"

"You said I should be selfish, Deaton, make my own happiness even if it means someone else will hurt because of it." I look to him, my tears now dry, my heart half-empty. "Let me ask you something; would you make the selfish choice if it took from people you loved?"

"If it gave me Payton? In a heartbeat," he answers instantly.

I offer a sad smile and shift to stand.

I don't say anything else, just head for the house.

He's so full of hope and optimism. I don't wanna be the one to show him the ugly truth.

Hope and love will always lose to money.

Anger rolls through me for reasons I can't understand, and I charge into the room Parker set for me, slamming and locking the door once I enter. I rush to my bag, pulling out my makeup pouch and unzip my little hidden compartment.

Shiny, brand-new razor blades stare back at me, mocking me and my lack of control in my life, daring me to take the only piece I can.

Kellan makes every decision, holds every card, and stands there with a wad of cash at every turn. My future is set—two children, exactly a year apart, and a third if the first two are girls. I'll homeschool them until the age of ten and take them to church every Sunday. Groom the girls to be wives and the boys to be leaders.

He has it all planned, down to the color of our home and the style of our cars.

This—I pull the razor from the pocket—is the *only* thing I can control, the only choice I get to make—how deep I cut, how much I bleed, how bad I hurt.

Quickly setting the razor beside me, I pull my sweater over my head, then pick it back up, but I accidentally look up, and I'm unable to avoid the floor-length mirror that sits in front of me.

I try to force my eyes away, but fail, and slowly, they lower to my arm, skim over the monster I've created, inspect the shine of the silver in my hand, and then slide back to my face. I crumble, tossing the sharp metal across the room.

I bend, crying into my hands, wishing for a different life where the weight of others' happiness didn't bury my own.

Kellan knew right where to get me.

I learned later how he'd figured out about my friendship with Parker. It was from Ava Baylor herself. She had gone to Kellan, and together, they'd formed a plan. Keep me *from* Parker and keep me *with* Kellan.

She took away the one thing I wanted, and he found a way to take away everyone else should I stray.

Parker can move forward in life, Nate can play football, my father can keep his business ... so long as I keep sleeping with the devil.

CHAPTER 23
KENRA

"SHOULD WE FUCK HIM UP? I KINDA WANNA FUCK HIM UP." Mason stands on his tiptoes, trying to see past the pergola that Payton is showing to Deaton. "I mean, look at the dude. He keeps touching her. I don't like it."

Ari and Cameron laugh at Mason, who glares at them, and then he shifts to stand on the other side of me with his arms crossed.

"She's already pregnant, dude," Brady reminds him.

I fight a smile when Parker turns to scowl at him, making him chuckle.

He raises his hands. "What? I'm just saying, it's not like they can get into any more trouble." He laughs, and the girls laugh with him.

"I don't know. I think I'm with Mason on this one," Chase speaks up. "He does keep moving his hands around."

"Look, I don't know much about their relationship, but obviously it was serious. She's been with us for a week now trying to figure her shit out. She needs to talk to the guy," Parker tells him then looks to me. I offer a small nod, giving him the confirmation that he was looking for.

Mason literally pouts, and then a huge smile breaks across his face. He turns and smirks at Parker, whose eyes narrow

"Yo!" Mason shouts. "Kalani, beautiful!" He suppresses a laugh when Nate freezes mid-dance with Lolli and spins to flip him off. "Come down here for a minute, would ya?"

Lolli laughs and smacks Nate's chest, who spins for her to hop onto his back.

When he reaches us, she slides down and reaches into the ice chest. "Mason, Mason, Mason … the Kalani was a huge hint, but the beautiful? Boy, you've got some shit to stir, so let—" She cuts off mid-word, and Mason slaps Parker on the back, lifting his hands in the air like he's won.

I look back to Lolli, who tilts her head, her eyes narrowing slightly. Parker sighs with a laugh and drops his chin to his chest. I follow her gaze along with the others, who have yet to catch on. She's zeroed in on Payton and Deaton sitting on the swing. The swing that was once my mother's but now belongs to her and Nate. It's the center of their love story, and from what I've heard, she reserves the spot for her and Nate only.

I look back to Lolli, finding her rolling her bottom lip between her fingers, contemplating her next move.

Her head snaps to Nate, who winks at her. She stares for a long moment, and he stares back before she inhales deeply and looks away.

She takes off toward the ocean, and he, of course, follows.

Parker smiles after her and then looks back to his sister.

"Dude, the fuck just happened? That was supposed to be a guaranteed cockblock," Mason whispers loudly.

Cam and Ari smile gently at him.

Parker sighs, proud, but says nothing before he heads back to the patio.

I follow him into the house, pausing in the entryway when he drops himself into a recliner.

I eye him. "Nate told me what you did for him and Lolli in the end. How you helped him get her back."

His blue eyes lift to mine, and he waits for me to continue.

"Why would you help him, knowing what would happen when you did?"

His head jerks back at my question. "Why wouldn't I?" he counters. "You think so little of me? Think I'd do something that, in the end, would hurt the two of them *and me* more than the original issue did? I'm not a stupid man, Kenra."

"But you wish he never came to you asking for your help in finding her after she left, don't you?"

He barks out a humorless laugh. "No, Kens. I didn't. In fact" —his eyes narrow— "I thanked him for coming. *Waited* for him to come for her because I *knew* what it would mean for her. For both of them."

When my expression remains blank, he shakes his head. "*Happiness*, Kenra. I wanted her *happy*. I wanted them where they belonged, where the best versions of themselves lived, which for those two is when they're together. I don't know why you're holding on to this so badly. Clearly, you came in here to pick a fight. Just say what you wanna say. Ask what you wanna ask."

I swallow, my leg bouncing. "Fine. Do you love her?"

"Not the way you're thinking."

"Don't lie!" Undeserved anger surges through me. "It's obvious you do."

He hops to his feet and takes a step toward me, his mouth in a hard line.

"You've got nerve, Kenra. Real fucking nerve. All I've tried to do *for years* is get you to need me back because I've fucking needed you. You were the only one I had when my world fell apart. Nothing felt right if you weren't around. Then, when you were there, it wasn't as mine. I waited, Kenra. I held out hope that you'd one day knock and finally tell me you needed me back, but you never did.

"After two years of it, I realized I could never be enough for you, so I stopped waiting, but I couldn't fucking let go. I was a zombie in my own skin who ran around like a fucking clown, not a care in the world when all I wanted was the girl I couldn't have. All I thought about was how I wasn't enough for my mother to love, not enough for my dad to be brave, not enough to save my sister from the hell I lived, and not enough for you to walk away from your asshole fiancé."

"And then Lolli came along, and you fell in love all over again, right? Another girl you couldn't have?"

A bitter laugh leaves him, and he scrubs a hand down his face. "If you cared about me even a little bit, which I know you do, then you'd be happy Lolli showed up when she did."

I fight the urge not to cry and fold my arms over my chest, pinching the insides of my arms to keep my face straight. "And why is that?"

"Because she saved me, helped fix all the things you broke in me. She made me believe I was enough, that the things that had happened in my life were beyond my control. Bad happened to me, yes, but not because of who I was or wasn't. Meeting her, growing close to her, might very well be the best thing that has ever happened to me. She gave me hope without trying. Because that's who she is. I have a piece of her, just like she does me, and I'll forever be grateful for her. And, yes, Kenra, since you wanna hear me say it so damn bad ... I do love Lolli."

My heart skids against my chest, and I fear I might fall, so I shove past him and make a run for my room.

Parker

"And, yes, Kenra, since you wanna hear me say it so damn bad ... I do love Lolli."

I take a deep breath and square my shoulders. I won't allow

her to make me feel guilty for this, but when her face crumbles and she darts past me, my shoulders fall, my chin hitting my chest in a sigh.

Right then, shoes step into my view, and my head snaps up.

Nate stares at me, his expression unreadable as he flicks his gaze down the hall and then back.

He heard me.

"Nate ..." I trail off, ready to explain what he heard, but he gives a slight jerk of his head.

"Nah, man." He swallows and clears his throat. "We're good. Been through this already."

I nod, my eyes shifting between his to try to gauge his true thoughts, but I can't read him. And he's right; we did.

He knows I love her. More than that, he knows how much I respect her *and* their relationship. I'd do anything for her. She's a part of me, and she always will be. We're family.

Kenra didn't stay around to hear any of that though.

"Look, I don't know what the fuck is going on with you and my sister—heavy shit apparently—but you guys need to figure it out and quick. She won't stay forever, and I won't have either of you making Kalani uncomfortable with the bullshit tension Kenra's trying to create." He eyes me. "I love my sister, but she's not acting right. This is your home just as much as it is Kalani's. If Kenra keeps this shit up, you'll need to be the one to tell her to go." He looks off before sighing and glancing back. "We can't help her if she doesn't wanna be helped, man. But we can't let her come in here and fuck up the good thing we've all got going, sister or not."

I look off, nodding.

He's right. Completely.

But, right or not, I know myself, and I could never deny her.

He sees it, and his shoulders sag as he turns to walk back the way he came.

I get where he's coming from. He doesn't want his sister to hurt. He has no clue what she's up against, but he *does* know what it'll do to Lolli if things here change. He won't stand for that.

I know exactly what Kenra's doing. She thinks she's sly, but I see. All this—the love and support and just flat-out good living we've got going, the relaxing on the beach and bonfires and everything—it's getting to her. She's remembering what life is supposed to feel like, desperate to be a part of it instead of sitting on the sidelines, watching.

And she has no idea what to do about it.

CHAPTER 24
PARKER

"HE SAYS HE'S EXCITED ABOUT THE BABY," PAYTON WHISPERS, pulling the large hoodie that must belong to Deaton over her knees. "Says we'll figure it all out." Her voice cracks with her last word, and she drops her head, crying into her hands.

"Hey now." I wrap my arm around her, trying to pull her closer to me, but she shrugs away.

It's just her and me out here, sitting on the last step of the patio, looking out at the waves.

"I don't *want* to have to figure anything out. I *had* it all figured out before this happened! My showcase senior year and then college. Deaton was going to go to a school that was only an hour or so away, and we'd see each other every weekend and evenings we had free, kind of like Nate and Lolli do. A baby will ruin everything."

"I don't know much about it, Peep, but that can't be true. I know the timing isn't ideal, but things like this usually happen for a reason, right?"

She lifts her head to glare at me, her nose red from crying. "What, did you suddenly start going to church when you left? Are you really feeding me fate lines right now?" She scowls. "Our mother shamed our father from being who he really was and convinced him to stop loving us because of it. Mom fed you

Adderall and pumped you with performance enhancers for years—before your body was ready for the shit she gave it, almost causing you to have a heart attack. She literally taught me how to be bulimic because image was everything.

"You think she'll let me keep this baby and not find a way to groom it from birth to be all the things we're not? She'll either give it away or take it away." She cries, and I stay silent. I've got nothing good to say and flipping my shit over my mom forcing a sixteen-year-old girl to have an eating disorder is not what she needs right now. "And there's no telling what she'll do to Deaton for 'ruining me.'"

"Look, Peep, I'm sorry, but straight-up? Fuck her."

Payton rolls her eyes and looks off.

"Do what feels right, Peep. Only you know what that is."

She cries for a few moments before finally turning and letting me hold her. "I'm not ready for this, Parker. I'm not ready."

"I know, Peep. I know."

She sniffles, and we both turn when the sliding glass door opens.

Deaton steps out, shutting the door behind him as he slips his hands in his khaki slacks. He gives her a soft smile, and she sighs beside me.

I tap her knee, grab a beer from the ice chest, and head down the steps to give them some privacy. Instead of heading for my hammock, I make my way down the beach, stopping when I reach the old dock I've noticed goes unused.

An hour or more goes by before the sun starts to set, and the waves grow stronger. Right when I'm about to head back, I hear her footsteps behind and decide to sit still.

"Can I join you?" Kenra asks, but she's already dropping down beside me. Sitting Indian-style, she bends forward to peek over the edge that my legs are dangling off of.

Neither of us says anything for a while, but it's her who breaks the silence.

"I had cards made for you and Nate, little candy leis, too." My brows pull in, but I keep my eyes on the ocean. "The cards were giant ones, and each sang a song. Nate was such a cocky brat for so long, so his song was"—she laughs quietly—"'Number One' by Nelly." I chuckle, and she bumps my shoulder with hers. "Perfect, right?"

"Yeah, Kens. It is."

"Wanna know what yours was?" she whispers.

I clench my teeth, my chest tightening. "I don't know," I answer honestly.

"Can I tell you anyway?"

My body shakes with a small laugh, and I nod, glancing the opposite way from where she sits.

"Daughtry …" She trails off, and I squeeze my eyes shut. "'It's Not Over.'"

My head snaps her way, and our eyes lock.

"The cards," she whispers, "they were for graduation. I was supposed to be there. I had it all planned. I'd surprise my mom and dad, and we'd go together and watch Nate graduate, watch you graduate. And, after, I was gonna find you. Hug you. Tell you how much I missed you," she cries. "I was coming home, Parker. For good. For you."

I hop to my feet, and she's slow to follow.

Forcing my breathing steady, I shift to face her. "You were coming home?"

She nods her head, tears spilling over her cheeks. "I was coming to *you*."

I rush to her, my hands casing in her cheeks, my eyes rapidly flicking between hers.

"Parker"—her brows squeeze together, her hands shooting up to cover mine— "don't do it."

"I have to." I know it's wrong, but it's also more right than anything else.

I slightly bend at the knees, touching my forehead to hers.

Her chest heaves against me, her heartbeat blending into mine. My nose brushes hers, and a sharp breath leaves her.

"Please ..." she pleads but sways closer.

My body's vibrating as I pull her against me, step in even more, and then my lips are on hers, and if I didn't know it already, this was the sign—nobody could ever take her place.

Her soft lips melt against me, her body sagging into mine. Our mouths open at the same time, and when my tongue sweeps inside, tasting her for the first time, a shiver rakes through both our bodies.

Her hands slide up my chest and around my neck, and mine glide across her back, pulling her against me, one slipping into her hair at the base of her neck, gently tilting her head so that I can kiss her harder, show her what she does to me.

She pulls back gasping for air, a deep flush making its way up her neck and cheeks. She leans forward, sliding her shaky lips across mine before burying her face in my neck.

I cradle her to me; overcome by a calmness I've never known.

We stand there, holding on to one another, both lost in thought for a while before finally making our way back. The house is clear when we return, everyone hidden away in their rooms, and silently, we make our way to our own.

She glances at me, a small smile on her lips, before quietly shutting her door, and I do the same.

I drop onto my bed and stare up at the ceiling.

This can't be like all the times before. I can't let her go.

I need her to stay.

Kenra

Everything inside me burns. Heat and hope and hate all teeter at the edge of my skin, making me ready to explode.

He kissed me and I didn't stop him.

And I'm engaged to be married.

And I don't feel the least bit sorry for it.

It was everything I'd thought it would be, overpowering in the best way. I could hardly even breathe, my heart rate went crazy, and I was sure I'd pass out. But his large hands slid up my back, opening up my lungs, recharging my body with a sensation I couldn't control or explain. I felt his longing meet mine, and everything clicked into place for the first time.

I brush my hair out and dig to the bottom of my makeup bag, finding the one and only rubber band I own—the one I use to tie my hair back when I wash my face.

With a deep breath, I gather all my hair and tie it up, but it's so foreign to me that I frown at it in the mirror, pull it out to try again. And then I try for a messy bun, and it looks even worse.

With a groan, I pull out the tie and brush through it once more. I snatch my keys and purse from the bed, and sneak toward the front door.

"Leavin'?"

With a small yelp, I spin around and smooth my shirt down. "I ..."

Parker's shoulders drop a few inches, but his face remains blank. It makes my chest ache.

"No." I shake my head and pull myself from the door, making my way to him.

He eyes me, standing taller, the more I near. "No?"

Again, I shake my head but slower this time with my eyes on his. "No, I'm not. I'm going to Ari's. But I'll be back."

"You'll be back."

My head lowers, and I fight a grin as I look back to him. "Yeah, Parker, I *will* be back."

He swallows, cutting his eyes away. "Okay."

"Okay." I stare at him, and he chuckles lightly, bringing his eyes back to mine.

"I'm gonna stand right here, right in front of you, Kens, so if you're going, you're gonna have to be the one to move." He smirks, and I laugh, backing up toward the door.

"I'll see you in a bit, Safety."

He winks and watches me until I pull the door closed, and goddamn that wink.

As I walk to my car, anxiety starts to build.

There's so much still not right, so many things still in the way, but recklessness is inevitable at this point.

Everything's likely to blow up in my face at the end of this, but I'm not sure I have it in me to care right now.

CHAPTER 25
PARKER

"Hey, fuckface." Lolli gives me a small push in my hammock and then moves to sit on her swing.

I grin as she squints her eyes at it a moment before read-justing the cushion she's added to the seat.

"Saw you and the vagina-yielding Monroe walking up the beach last night. She looked a little sad ... but you, my dearest best friend, looked mighty ... settled." She raises a playful brow and stares at me over her coffee mug.

"Settled you say?"

"Don't fuck with me before I've had my coffee."

I laugh lightly and look out over the ocean. "Sometimes, we've gotta break a few rules, right, Lolli Bear?" I repeat her earlier words to me.

She's quiet a moment, and I know she's got me. I did some-thing that, under normal circumstances, I'd never even consider. My mother cheated on my dad for years, trying to sleep her way to a richer fortune; the six-figure monthly income my father brought in wasn't enough for Ava Baylor.

But our situation is anything but normal.

This is me and Kenra. Nothing could trump that.

"Tell me something, Hero ..." She trails off. "Say she stayed, that she and her dick of a dude split, will you ever be able to fully trust she won't leave again? I mean, would that fear ever really go away?"

My eyes pinch at the edges as I consider her question.

Could I? Would a time ever come when I wouldn't be worried I'd wake up, and she'd be gone?

I sit up to face her. "I have no idea, Lolli Bear."

She sips her coffee, her earnest gaze free of judgment and full of understanding. "I still wait for the floor to fall from under me. Every day, every *time* Nate leaves, the entire time he's gone, I feel tension in my chest." She looks off. "Like I'm constantly expecting my phone to ring, and someone on the other end will tell me he's not coming back. I hate it. Don't know how to get rid of it." She looks back to me, and I offer her a soft smile. "Me and you? We're accustomed to bad shit. I think, even in the good, we'll expect the bad."

"I think you're right."

"So, we just … deal with it … right? Nothing we can do?" Her forehead creases as she stares at the sand, and my brows dip.

I shift to stand and go to kneel in front of her. It takes a second, but her eyes shift to mine, and I see the turmoil there.

"What's goin' on, Lolli?"

"We're supposed to be talking about you right now," she whispers.

I chuckle. "Yeah, but that question wasn't just about me and Kenra. We'll cover me later, promise. But right now?" I level her with a knowing look. "Talk to me."

"Nate has to go back to school tomorrow for a few days. A two-day camp, and then he'll be back, he says."

"Okay …" I slowly coax her, and her eyes snap to mine.

"Nate won't stop talking about Payton and the baby," she rushes out. "He's like … *really* excited about it."

Oh shit.

I swipe a hand down my face, studying her. "Lolli."

She jumps off the swing, twisting her hair into a ball on top of her head, her sweater hanging down to her knees. "I mean, was I supposed to think about this stuff before? Like, were we supposed to have a conversation or something? Because, fuck me, I—"

"Stop," I interrupt her, and she clamps her mouth shut, frowning my way. "I don't think whatever you're about to say is for me to hear before Nate. You need to talk to him."

She starts frantically shaking her head, panic I haven't seen from her in months beginning to flood her blue eyes. "I can't. What if ... no, I can't."

I grab her hand and pull her in. Slowly, she hugs me back, but I can feel her labored breath as she fights against her anxiety.

I pull my phone from my pocket and quickly text Nate.
Me: *Swing. Now.*

He's the only one who can help with her panic attacks. As far as I know, this is the first one she's had in months.

"His family, Hero, they're different. They ... held hands and sang songs as kids, had bedtime stories, and made cookies and shit for Christmas. They loved different than my parents did."

I see over her shoulder when Nate steps off the porch and frowns our way. He starts toward us.

Her body starts shaking, and I squeeze her tighter.

"I don't know how to be that. I can't tell Nate—"

"Kalani," Nate rumbles, and she freezes against me.

I step back, and he steps in, bending at the knee to swoop her up, and then they're gone.

Payton and Deaton are just coming down the steps as they pass, and their gazes swing from them to me.

"Hey," she calls, trying to read what's happening. "What's wrong with her?"

I sigh and then smile at my sister. "Nothing. She's just having a bad day, is all."

Payton frowns and looks off.

I know she doesn't like it when I give her roundabout

answers she doesn't understand, but it's all I've got for her in situations like this.

"Whatever. Ari and Cameron asked us to come over for lunch. Guess Kenra's over there already. Wanna come?"

I try not to focus on the movement but can't help but notice how she gently pushes Deaton's hands away when they land on her lower stomach from behind.

"Yeah, I'll come."

Payton nods and looks off before starting ahead of the both of us.

Neither Deaton or I take a single step until she's a good fifteen feet down the beach, and then we move to follow behind.

"She won't talk about it," he speaks quietly.

"I think she's scared."

"I *know* she's scared. *I'm* scared, but she's pregnant with my child, Parker. I need to talk about it."

"What's your plan exactly, Deaton? You're seventeen years old, dude. 'Bout to start your senior year in high school. I don't know a damn thing about you, so I don't even know if I should like you. History tells me no." I stop, and he does, too, facing me with confidence. "I hear you're not him but tell me that for yourself."

He locks his stare with mine, intensity rolling off him. "I am *not* my brother. I am not my father, and I sure as hell am nothing like my mother. I was on the path toward all that, yes. I was numb to what was right and didn't give a damn. Looked for the prettiest, smartest girl I could find, one I could groom, just like my mother had instructed. Payton was exactly the type of girl my mother wanted me to pull in. Except she wasn't. She was so much more. As fucked up in the head as I was, we fought all eighth-grade year. Then, when she was pulled and moved schools, after you moved, I convinced my mother I needed to switch, too, to keep her. Took me two weeks to fall for her and took me a year to get her to trust me enough to show her. I would give up everything I have for her without a second thought. Instantly. Always."

I eye him, and damn if I don't believe him.

"I'm all alone in this, just like she is. It's just me and her. We both know our parents will toss us when they realize we plan to live our lives for ourselves. We're okay with that. This baby though, it's spooked her, and I'm trying to be patient, but I need to hear her say we've got this. Because I *know* we can do it. It'll be hard as hell, but we can do it."

With a sigh, I clamp a hand on his shoulder. "I don't know how to help you, but I believe you."

He lets out a chuckle, but it cracks. "Well, at least you're not feeding me bullshit."

I laugh lightly, and he grins.

We make it to the others' beach house, and he turns to block me from walking up the steps.

"Look, Parker, it's obvious there's history between you and Kenra, and for what it's worth, I know my brother doesn't deserve her. I have no respect for him and what he's pulled to keep her. I hope she leaves him."

I lick my lips, glancing off with a nod. I step past him and onto the deck, and when I do, I freeze in my tracks.

This time, it's Deaton who pats my shoulder as he walks by, but I don't look to him. No, hell no. I don't dare look away from the girl who has yet to spot me.

Thick, dark brown hair with golden streaks, a perfect mess on her head. No makeup, not a single fucking trace of it.

She's wearing a long, loose sweater with a tiny red string wrapped around her neck—a bikini tie. And shorts. Tiny jean shorts that make her already long legs look even longer. Legs I haven't seen in years. They might not have seen the sun in a long time, but her olive-toned skin gives them color, and she fills those babies out like never before, all wide hips and strong thighs.

My eyes travel lower to find her bare feet, fresh blue polish on her toes.

Her feet shift, one rising to rub at the ankle of the other, and my gaze slides along the inside curve of her calf to her thigh to the center of her body that's hugged by those tight little shorts.

My eyes snap to hers, and sure as shit, she's watching me, her stare burning into me while my body burns for her.

It's worse. So much worse than it's ever been now that I know what those lips of hers taste like.

Need. Pure fucking need courses through me, and I know I'm growing hard, but I can't look away, can't move my feet.

This girl in front of me—this is my Kenra. Every damn bit of her.

Every single inch is mine.

That glazed look in her eye, the slow blink of her lashes, and the deep rise of her chest tell me she damn well knows it.

HOLY SHIT, I'M IN TROUBLE.

The bad kind, the good kind. I don't even know.

But who the hell *am* I? 'Cause I want to find out.

I see it in Parker's liquid blue eyes. He's done waiting.

He said it before, and then things got sappy. He did his Parker thing and pulled back in respect, but this Parker in front of me, he's a man starved. Ready.

He's all in; no chance in hell will he hold back.

I have a feeling I'm set to see an entirely new side of Parker I've yet to learn. A grown one.

It's exhilarating in the most frightening of ways.

"Kens," he rasps, and it vibrates through my body from where I stand.

My lip twitches with a smile, but I'm too busy watching his eyes dilate to bother with responding.

I lied.

I don't know what I'm doing. I have no fucking clue, but when I got here, I knew I wanted to feel like me. And then, all of a sudden, I told the girls Kellan and I had split up months ago but hadn't announced it publicly yet. Naturally, as shit goes with my cousin and her twin and their friends, they're nosy as hell, and before I knew it, they were all sitting there, listening. I told them a few true things he'd done to make them believe it. Then, Ari asked about Parker. I gave them a little bit but nowhere near enough.

So, yeah, they know Kellan is a bastard. They think we're separated, and they know Parker and I have a background.

I stare at Parker, and the look he gives me …

I've seen hunger in a man's gaze before. The people Kellan drags me around, they're all perverted, privileged bastards with wandering eyes and occasionally even wandering hands.

But Parker's stare makes the hairs at the base of my neck tingle.

I try to swallow, but my throat has gone dry, so I end up coughing lightly.

I see the grin he tries to hide behind his cup.

This is going to be insane. Already, no more than five minutes in each other's presence in total today, and he's done a full spin on me.

Gone is that sorrow and unsure gaze I've been met with over the last year.

This Parker, he's ready to play.

"Walk with me, Kens," he says.

Just like that.

And everyone starts laughing, making me blush harder, but Parker just keeps staring until Mason grips his shoulder and physically turns him. "Down, boy. Let's eat some fucking food first, huh?"

Parker glances over his shoulder at me and smirks before stepping up to help Mason on the grill.

"Girl …" Cameron whispers to me, pulling me back by my belt loop. "That boy wants to eat you up. You should *totally* let him."

At that, I bust up laughing. I laugh so hard; my eyes start to water.

When I wipe at the tears, I catch Parker looking at me again. But, this time, the look on his face has my stomach fluttering.

His blue eyes are soft, those lips tipped up just the slightest. His gratification delivered by my laughter.

This time, it's me who winks.

I'm rewarded with a full-on devilish smirk that stirs heat in my abdomen.

The slider opens and Deaton and Payton walk back out, a fruit and chip bowl in their hands.

"Yo, where's my Lolli baby at?" Brady jokes as he snatches a watermelon slice from Payton's bowl, giving her a quick wink and kiss to her cheek as he does.

He grins wide when Deaton glares.

"Pretty sure they're having a tiff of sort." Payton shrugs, and everyone freezes mid-motion.

At the same time, they start firing off questions, and Payton's brows jump.

Parker sighs and shakes his head. "They are *not* fighting. Quit, and let's eat. But, yes, I doubt they'll be around."

He gives nothing else, and everyone respects the two enough not to ask for more.

"So, plan for tonight." Mason claps, then gestures toward Payton. "Pretty Little here has never been on a walk on the beach at night. That's a crime. So, I wanna take her."

Payton smiles, and Deaton scowls.

"Guess you can come." Mase meets Deaton's scowl, cutting a glance at his arm around her shoulders. "If you can keep your hands to yourself."

"Mason," Parker warns.

Deaton speaks up, "My hands stay where they belong—on her. And I'll take her on that walk, but you're welcome to come if you feel like showing *us* around."

Payton buries her head in his side with a smile while the boys stare each other down.

Finally, Mason nods. "All right, kid. You've got sport. We'll play your way for a while."

Ari taps Deaton's shoulder on her way by. "Sorry, Deaton.

But you're screwed. When Mason decides he cares, he's a thousand percent. No chill factor. Sorry to say ... but he *never* lets up."

"She's my sister from another mister," Mason adds, proud.

"How old are you, dude?"

Everyone cuts their eyes to Chase as he stares at Deaton with a blank expression.

"Seventeen."

"She's sixteen."

"I'm aware. Been in love with her since she was thirteen."

Chase nods, looking to Payton, who smiles up at Deaton. He licks his lips and glances away.

"Okay, they're all overprotective fools, nothing new. Now, can we eat?" Cameron whines.

Everyone gets seated.

Parker squeezes beside me, pushing a scowling Mason over a bit.

Several conversations begin among the group, but I can't focus on any of them because every time Parker moves, his body brushes mine. Be it his leg, his arm, his hip. Something.

As Parker finishes his food, he grows more lax beside me. He sits upright, laughing at something someone said, and shakes his knee under the table. The move has his skin touching mine, and my muscles lock.

His smile swings my way, and he does a quick double take, his grin slowly dropping as he reads me.

Yeah, he sees, knows what his touch—accidental and innocent—is doing to me.

"'Bout that walk, when's it happening exactly?" Parker asks, his gaze slowly sliding to Mason, who is already staring at him with a brow raised.

"Later."

Parker grins and shifts to stand. "Sounds good." He turns around and reaches for my hand. "There's a farmers market a couple of blocks over. We should check it out."

"I want to go!" Payton hops up, followed by Cameron.

"Hell yeah, me, too."

I grin when Parker fights to keep his grin. "All right, well, whenever everybody's ready then." He nods and turns to refill his cup.

I catch Ari's eye across the table, and she winks.

But, when Payton catches my eye, hers narrow. With a shake of her head, she excuses herself and stomps down the patio steps.

"She okay?" Cameron asks.

Deaton sighs, cutting a quick glance my way. "She's just got a lot on her mind."

Don't we all?

"So," Parker starts, cutting me a side-glance before looking ahead again.

I smile to myself. "So."

"Shorts, huh?" he rasps.

I can't help but laugh. "Oh, you noticed, did you?" I tease.

He grins my way. "I like 'em."

"I'll be sure to let Ari know since they're hers and all." I nudge him with my shoulder, and before I can pull back, he wraps an arm around my shoulders and pulls me in.

"Funny. Don't think I'd like 'em much on her."

I glance at him, and he winks.

"Looks like we're stopping here." Parker smiles as Payton runs for the water, laughing when Mason swoops her up from behind and carries her further in.

I look to Deaton, who scowls for a second before shaking his head with a grin.

I pull from Parker's hold and walk closer, inhaling when my bare feet hit the first part of wet sand. A soft chuckle leaves me as I continue forward until I'm stepping into warmed ocean water, captivated as it sways back and forth, splashing a little higher each time it comes near.

I close my eyelids, and moisture builds behind them as the warmth of the summer sun washes over me.

Parker's chest hits my back at that moment, and together, we inhale, our exhales reflecting each other's, jagged and wishful.

His hands find my hips, and lightly, he nudges me forward, stepping as I step, keeping his chest aligned against me. Together, we move further into the water, stopping when it reaches me mid-thigh.

I drop my head back, resting it against him, and he turns his head to brush his lips over my temple.

"Open your eyes, Kens."

"I don't want to," I whisper. "Everything is better this way." With my eyes closed, all that exists is him and me and the feel of his body against me. With them open, I have to share the feeling with the world, and I don't want to share any part of him.

"Kens—" he starts, but Ari yells out, grabbing our attention.

"Kenra!" she shouts.

Parker discreetly shifts a step away, his hands falling from me.

"Get in here!" She laughs as Chase grabs her from behind and drops them back into the water.

Instantly, I freeze and pull my sleeves over my hands. "It's too cold." I make an excuse.

Parker looks to me with an upstretched brow and playful eyes. But the longer he stares, the more he sees, and his shoulders drop an inch.

He turns and heads back for the shoreline but looks back when I don't follow and reaches a hand out.

Slipping my palm into his, I allow him to pull me behind him until we're dropping to sit on the edge of a rock firepit.

Together, my hand still in his, we watch the others goof around.

"They're a bunch of kids." I smile.

"Yeah," Parker speaks low, "the beach'll do that to ya."

My brows pinch as I turn to look at him, finding his forehead creased as he stares at my hand. His eyes rise and hold mine for a moment before dropping again.

I dig the nails of my free hand into my palm as he slowly flips the other over.

He peeks toward the water to make sure no one's looking, I'm sure, and then back to me.

I watch him watch himself as he slowly traces the markings of my palm. He cuts me another quick glace before sliding the sleeves of my sweater as close to my elbow as he can get.

He swallows thickly, and his hands start to shake as the pads of his fingers hesitantly run across my scars. He's about to ask, and I really wish he wouldn't.

"Why, Kens?" he forces out. "Why do you do this to yourself?"

Sorrow. His body and his voice are taken over by it as he formulates a thousand thoughts in his mind. My demons are stealing a piece of him, and I hate myself a little more for it. It's the only reason I answer him.

"Are you sure you wanna know?" I whisper. "You won't like the answer ..."

"Why?"

I fight to keep the tears away as I stare at the man beside me. "You."

"Me ... what?" His face slowly contorts as his head draws back an inch.

"Every time I think of you, I feel like I'm on the verge of a heart attack," I admit. "My chest grows tight, and my airway swells. I get dizzy, helpless. I literally can't breathe when it happens. Breaking into my skin helps bring me back. It's the only control I have. It makes everything easier."

It's as true as it is unfair for him to have to hear.

Everything reverts back to Parker. When I'm angry in my life, I think of him. When I'm sad, it's because I've thought of him. When I'm happy, it's because he's on my mind. When I find myself relaxing in my new life, guilt comes because I know I should be with him.

He fights to keep his face neutral, but I know he's getting angry and rightfully so. "It's dangerous and unhealthy."

A sad smile forms on my lips, and I shake my head. "Don't be so quick to judge, Parker. Sometimes, it's more dangerous *not* to have an outlet at all."

He drops my hand and hops to his feet, pacing in front of me. "This is bullshit, Kenra." He stops in front of me. "You do that when you think of me? Seriously?" His brows shoot high, and he beats on his chest. "I'm right fucking here. I've *been* right fucking here. For *years*. *You* walked away. *You* refused to acknowledge what I've basically been begging to give you."

"I know. And I'm so sorry," I whisper, tears slipping down my cheeks. "I made choices I can't take back—"

"Why?" He crouches in front of me. "Why can't you take them back? Why can't you let me love you?"

When I don't respond, he nods, a frown on his face as he turns and starts to walk away.

"I'm sorry," I rush out, quieter than I intended, but he hears me and stops.

He doesn't turn to face me but waits for me to continue.

"I'm sorry I can't be who you deserve. I'm sorry I keep coming back," I admit. "But, mostly … I'm sorry I ever left in the first place."

His shoulders lift with a deep breath. I know he's trying to talk himself into walking off, but he can't do it and turns to me. "Are you?" he asks, staring at me dead on. "Are you really?"

"Of course I am."

"Then, fix it. Right now."

His eyes flit between mine, and my pulse quickens.

"What are you asking me exactly?"

"I'm asking you to pick me."

My heart drops as I stare at this man. The only man I've ever truly wanted.

"It's not that simple."

"Does it have to be?"

"I …" I pinch my lips together, unsure of what to say.

"I'm not looking for easy here, Kenra. Don't need it. I can work harder, longer." His arms shoot out. "Shit, I'll work forever if it means I'll have you in the end."

"Don't do this."

"Don't do what?" He moves closer. "Push you? Fight for you? Fucking beg you? Because I will, and I am. For too long, I've sat back and waited for you to admit what I know you feel, and you refuse. Every time, you go back to him. I used to think it was me, that maybe I just wasn't enough for you, but I know now that's wrong. I know for a fact I can be everything you could ever need. I fucking feel it, Kenra. With everything inside me … I feel you."

"Parker …" I trail off. I want to tell him how much I believe him. How I know, just as sure as he does, that he and I are meant to be, but the words won't come out. All I can do is cry harder.

He licks his lips, his face pinched as he glances off. "I'm afraid to ask, Kens, but I have to." He looks back to me, anguish in his eyes. "What was that last night? And today? What are you doing, Kenra? Do you even know?"

Again, I find myself unable to speak, and he nods. His shoulders drop.

"I didn't mean to upset you, but damn … I don't want this for you. I've stayed back because I thought you loved him despite everything, but now, I know that can't be it."

"I wish I could give you-"

"Nah," he interrupts shaking his head. "Don't wish anything for me. Don't *do* anything for me. Do it for you. Be happy *for you*. What I want, shit, what I need? Is to know that you're happy."

"Parker—"

"I, uh," he cuts me off, unable to meet my gaze now, "I'm

gonna head back. Make sure you stay with the group, okay?"

"Okay," I whisper.

And he walks away.

The second he does, I crumble, a crippling feeling I'm all too familiar with taking over, and I slide down into the sand.

What the hell am I doing?

I'm ruining him all over again. He was happy here, starting a new life for himself, and now, here I am, painting his new life black with mine. Giving him hope then taking it away.

I wipe my face and look to the water, scanning each smiling face I see.

I want this. All of it.

And I want it with him.

Σμυρνιός

"Did she tell you?"

I open my eyes, finding Nate scowling at the ocean in front of my hammock.

"Did who tell me what?"

Nate laughs bitterly. "Right, my girl *and* my sister seem to talk to you before me nowadays, don't they?"

When I scowl at him, he groans and runs his hands down his face. "Sorry. Lot going on in my head."

"I think we're all a bit on edge right now."

"Yeah, no shit."

I stare at his profile as he moves to sit on his and Lolli's swing. "Can I ask you something?"

"Honestly?" he spits, swinging his head toward me. "I don't fucking know, man. I'm ready to lose my shit right now, and I'm not sure I have the right to or not. I don't wanna fuck up again."

"How about you ask me what you wanna know then?"

"Are you fucking my sister? My *engaged* sister?"

"No."

"But you want to. Or you would."

"It's a helluva lot more than what you're trying to make it, Nate. But, if you wanna demean it down to that, sure. Yes, I would."

185

"So, that ring on her fucking finger means nothin' to you?"

I sit up to face him better. "We still talking about Kenra here?"

His eyes harden. "Who else would we be talking about?"

"Man"—I hop down, and he hops up. Then, we're in each other's faces— "don't fucking start. This?" My brows jump. "This is you 'fucking up,' as you called it. You standing here, saying this type of shit ... I know I'm not Austin, who you'd normally talk to about this shit, and you and I, while we're friends, we aren't that kind of close. But you can say what you need to, and I'll listen. Just because Lolli and I are close like we are, it doesn't mean you can't talk to me if you need it."

His eyes narrow even further, his jaw clenching, but then he steps back and runs his hands through his hair.

He's quiet a minute, so I wait it out, and eventually, he drops back onto the swings seat.

"Kalani's nineteen years old, man. How could she be *so* certain about the things she doesn't want in life? I mean, she could change her mind, right?" He's slow to bring his gaze to mine.

"Would it matter if she didn't? Change her mind, I mean."

He stares at me, his eyes pinched at the sides. "Not even a little bit."

"Then, what are you worried about?"

"Her selflessness," he answers instantly, and it clicks.

"Nate." I shake my head.

He looks away. "She disappeared on me once. I know that shit was different, and we're solid as fuck now, but what if she does it again because she wants me to have all the things she thinks I need or want? I don't need a damn thing but her. Not a damn thing," he mumbles.

"You tell her that?"

"'Bout every day since you brought me back to her."

"Then, I say you're all right."

He nods, clearing his throat. "Yeah." His eyes come back to

mine. "I've been gone only a few weeks of the summer so far, and I hate it. I don't think I can be at UCLA and her be here."

"It's only a few hours away. You could commute if you really wanted."

"There's no way. Not with practice and schoolwork. Games."

"She said she'd be there to see you as much as possible."

"I don't want her to get tired of making the drive and start doing it because she feels she has to."

"Get the hell outta here with that, Monroe. She *wants* to. You and football in the same place?" I tease. "That's Lolli's brand of heaven."

He laughs lightly, but I hear the fear in his voice. "I wanna quit. Go to SDU with you. Be here with her every night. I can't do this shit for a single season, let alone four full years."

"She'll kick your ass, Nate, and you know it. You quit that team for her? Not play your first year in college? She'd never forgive herself even though it'd be you making the choice."

"Yeah, I know. Fuck, I don't know."

He grows quiet, and I realize it took a lot for him to talk to me about this.

Lolli and me? We're tight. Me and Nate? We're all right but no more than basic friends.

"I pretty much asked Kenra to leave Kellan for me today."

Nate's eyes flash to mine.

"I'm in love with your sister."

"*In love* with my sister?"

"Like I told you, we've been close for years. We became accidental friends, secret friends, and eventually, it turned into more. She was with Kellan, so I stayed back, but she kept showing up, and I kept falling deeper until, eventually, I was gone on her. So far gone, I've never been able to come back. Every time I thought I was ready to let go; she'd show up again." It was like, subconsciously, she knew I was slipping away. Like we were connected somewhere deeper, and we both felt it when it started to lessen.

"She know you love her?"

"I've never said it, if that's what you mean, but she knows."

"She love you back?"

"She tries real hard not to."

His eyes close, and he drops back in the swing. "Fuck."

"Yeah."

After a few minutes, Nate asks, "Where's Kellan fit into all this? She just ... you *both* would just do him wrong?"

"You'll have to ask her about that one."

His jaw twitches, his frown deepening. "He's a piece of shit, isn't he?"

When I only stare, he curses to himself. "She's different."

"She is."

"No"—he turns to me— "she's been different the last few days, here, with us. With you."

I lick my lips and look away.

"Maybe you should tell her how you feel."

I laugh lightly. "I did."

"And?"

"And I'm poutin' over here now, aren't I?" I grin at him, and we both laugh lightly.

Nate lifts his fist, and we bump knuckles before he turns to head back.

"Hey, Baylor?"

"Yeah, man?"

"I'm glad Kalani has you. She loves you."

I nod, smiling to myself, and he heads toward the house.

I laid it out for Kenra today, told her what I wanted. I might end up worse off when this is over, but it's a risk worth taking. Because I know who she wants, and it's not Kellan.

But she has to be brave enough to make us happen.

I know her, and I *know* I pushed all the right buttons today. It may have hurt her to hear, but it was necessary.

She told me those things yesterday for a reason. Let me kiss her because she knows it wasn't gonna be our first kiss and our last.

From now on, I'll be right here, fighting. Every day until the day she—*if* she—marries him.

And maybe even after.

Kenra

"You're in love with him," Ari whispers.

More tears fall from my eyes.

I don't say anything, and she shifts to face me on her bed.

"You don't have to say it. I always sort of thought it."

"Yeah," Cameron adds as she climbs up next to us. "It's like with Ari and Chase. We all see it, have been seeing it, but nobody talks about it."

"Shut up, Cam." Ari rolls her eyes, and Cameron wiggles her eyebrows. "Besides, we talk about my relationship with Chase all the time … and the fact that it doesn't exist, so … not the same."

At that, we all laugh.

"For real though, Kenra. What's up with you two now that the boys aren't in here, listening?" Cameron asks.

I sigh. "I want him," I admit, plain and simple and for the first time out loud. "For keeps."

The girls scurry to a sitting position, and I chuckle lightly, pulling myself up as well.

"So, reel him in, girl. He wants you just the same. His dick told me." Cam grins.

My eyes widen and bounce to hers.

"Cam!" Ari squeals. "What the hell?"

189

Cameron laughs. "What? He had on his game-day face earlier. I couldn't *not* glance south to check out if he were properly equipped. And I'll bet a hundred bucks he used an extra-large cup on the field."

My mouth drops open, and Ari's head pulls back right as we glance at one another, and then we crack up laughing until our sides hurt, and we can't laugh anymore.

"I know what we need." Cam hops up. "Be right back!"

Ari rolls her eyes through her smile and turns to me. "She's totally getting alcohol."

I grin and glance off.

"I know you lied," Ari rushes out, and my eyes fly to hers. "You and Kellan. You're not split up, are you?"

I stare at her, and she gives a small smile.

"It's okay, Kenra. I know something's off at home for you, and I have some suspicions of my own. I just want you to try to trust that everything will work out somehow, someway, if you do decide to walk away. He doesn't deserve you. I know that. And you *deserve* to be happy."

"Shots, motherfuckers." Cameron skips back in the room with a bottle in her hand, and the boys are hot on her heels, each carrying shot glasses.

Brady hands one to me while Chase hands one to Ari.

I haven't drunk hard liquor like this in a long time, but I'm ready to relax, and maybe this will help. So, when the liquor is poured and all their glasses rise, so does mine.

"To the last few weeks of summer." Cameron grins, cutting her eyes to Mason. "And getting what we want out of it."

Then, together, we toss our heads back and drink to possibilities.

Σμυρνὶδ

EVERYONE'S GETTING READY TO WALK TO THE BEACH TONIGHT, AS Mason wanted. The sun set about two hours ago, and looking down the beach, I can see tons of the firepits have already been lit, friends and families dancing around, laughing and simply enjoying each other's company.

Mason jogs past me, and down the steps of the patio. "I'm gonna head over there before that dick takes Pretty Little by himself."

"That *dick* put a baby in her. He has the right to walk her if he wants." Cameron smirks as she stops beside me.

"You guys got problems," Chase mumbles as he walks past us, and Cameron slaps his ass.

"Not as many as you're gonna have if you don't get your shit together."

Chase freezes halfway down the steps and spins to glare at Ari, who throws her hands up. He sighs with a shake of his head and takes off to follow Mason.

"Really, Cam?" Ari hisses in a whisper.

"Hey, I didn't do anything." She feigns innocence, and Ari rolls her eyes, following after Chase.

Right when I glance forward, the others come into view, and instantly, my eyes are drawn to Parker. He stands off to the side a bit, his hands in his jean pockets, a gray Tomahawks hoodie on.

He stares at the ocean a moment, and then his eyes close, and his chin drops to his chest. My gaze shifts, and I find Nate staring at me with a quizzical look, Lolli leaning against his front, chatting with Payton.

Nate's brows furrow a bit, but he gives a small smile.

When I give one in return, he glances to Parker, reaching out to hit Parker's arm.

Parker slowly looks to my brother and then follows his gaze to me.

He freezes for a moment before breaking from the group and meeting me halfway while the others continue forward.

He grins, but it doesn't meet his eyes. "Wow. Shorts and leggings in the same day, huh?"

I smile at him even though my body aches at the pain in his eyes. Pain I caused but could easily take away.

And I just might have to.

I step closer, and he pulls his hands from his pockets.

"My afternoon sucked," I tell him.

He chuckles, his smile lifting a bit. "Yeah, mine, too."

"Think we can have a better evening?"

He licks his lips, his eyes flitting between mine. "I think we could, yeah."

"Are we ready?" Payton snaps, and our attention turns to the group.

When I look to Payton, she quickly looks away.

"Yeah, we're ready. Me and my date wanna get going, whole lotta beach, not a lotta time." Mason smirks as he goes to wrap his arm around Payton but is intercepted by Deaton.

Mason glares at him and then winks at Payton behind his back.

"We stoppin' for ice cream?" Nate asks.

"Ooh, yeah … ice cream," Lolli all but moans. "I want cookie dough," she says, and both Parker and Nate laugh loudly.

"Oh, we know, Lolli Bear. We know," Parker teases.

She glances back at him, playfully scrunching her nose, leaving me wondering what the fun is about.

Parker grins, and Nate laughs, wrapping his arm around her and forcing her attention forward again.

Parker glances my way and does a quick double take before leaning in to whisper, "Lolli almost kicked Nate outta bed for some chocolate chip cookie dough." When I laugh quietly, he grins. "She's a bit obsessed."

I smile up at him, grateful he chose to let me in on their little inside joke, and he winks, lifting his thumb to touch my cheek for a moment before facing forward again.

I love this. All this fun and easy play. Just a night on the beach with friends and family, goofing off and enjoying time together. This is what my childhood was made of, laughter and good-natured fun. My cousins and their friends are one of a kind, as tight-knit as they come. And it seems, while I've been gone, they've welcomed Lolli and Parker in their crew and now, Payton.

This is what I've been missing.

I don't want to miss it anymore. I want to be a part of it.

"Hey," Parker whispers softly beside me, "you okay?"

I give him a soft smile, nodding lightly.

"Ah shit." Mason claps, gaining our attention, his face lit up in boyish excitement. He spins to face Payton as we grow closer to the beach bash of sorts going on ahead of us. He starts to take a step toward her and then licks his lips and turns to Deaton. "All right, big D—that's for Deaton, so don't be getting a big head."

Payton blushes and looks down, but Deaton smirks.

"Lemme steal your girl for a minute. Promise I'll give her back. I just want all the credit for this one."

"Maybe you should back off a bit, Mason," Chase tells him, and all eyes fly his way.

Mason's eyes start to narrow, but Deaton grabs his attention.

"Nah, man. It's cool." He stands tall, lifting Payton's hand to kiss it before looking back to Mason. "If she wants to, she can, obviously. But I appreciate you not being a dick for once."

Payton smiles up at Deaton and lifts onto her toes to kiss his cheek, and I watch as his fingers skim her stomach as she moves to take Mason's hand with a laugh.

"You with me?" He tips his head, and she sweeps a hand out in a *lead the way* motion.

They get a full four steps when Deaton calls out, "Hey, Mason!"

Mason nods over his shoulder.

"You got my family in your hands."

Respect. That's what Deaton just earned in one sentence.

Mason tips his chin and slowly turns back to Payton.

I smile at Deaton but frown when I catch my brother's eyes following Payton and then shift to Lolli, who is already staring up at him. His hand lifts so he can tuck her hair behind her ear. Then, with his eyes closed, he moves to kiss her hair, and my brows pull in.

"Let's go get in line, guys. The ice cream bar closes kinda early," Cameron reminds everyone, and we keep moving.

Deaton knocks Parker with his elbow. "Where's he taking her, and should I be worried about him?"

Parker and Ari laugh.

"He's taking her over to the band that plays under the pier. Just a group of local guys who like to entertain," Parker tells him.

"It's karaoke at best, but it's a lot of fun," Lolli adds.

"Great. So, music and moonlight?" Deaton deadpans.

Brady grins, wrapping his big-ass arm around Deaton's neck. "Now, now, sperm boy, he asked nicely," Brady teases.

Ari pulls him off. "Deaton, you have *nothing* to worry about. Mason is like the drill sergeant father nobody wants, but he forces you to have. He's completely harmless and *not at all* romantically interested."

"He's basically adopted a new little sister. So, good luck trying to get laid when he's around," Cameron tells him.

Parker frowns at her, making me laugh.

She gives him a *what* look.

"Man, you guys are a bit too candid for me," Deaton teases.

"Candid?" Brady scoffs. "Boy, you're lucky lil' Lolli baby here's got that sailor mouth of hers under wraps right now, or she'd lay you out with some real shit."

Lolli grins at him, but it's only half there, and Nate tightens his arms around her.

After we get our ice creams, we head over to meet Mason and Payton, finding them both dancing around to the music.

Everyone starts goofing off just the same.

After a couple of minutes, Parker's chest hits my back, and I gasp.

"Dance with me, Kens," he breathes against my ear, and I don't even attempt to cover the shiver that it causes.

I go to spin, but he locks my hips in place.

"Nah, like this." His arm slides across my stomach, his fingers spacing out wide across my ribs so he pulls me closer, and then he buries his face in my hair. "Just like this," he whispers.

We don't move much, just light sways, but he's shifted, so there's nothing but miles of dark ocean and bright stars in front of us.

And then I realize what they're singing—Brett Young's "In Case You Didn't Know."

"Parker ..."

"I know, baby," he whispers, and my heart beats double time. He moves my hair from my shoulder and presses a slow, warm kiss to my neck. "In case you didn't know, Kens. Always."

My eyes squeeze shut, and his chest inflates with his deep breath.

"Come on, people. Let's go get drunk at home by the fire. I'm cold," Cameron whines.

Everyone agrees and starts for the house, but Parker grabs me by the hand, nodding to the small park at the edge of the sand. He walks backward, pulling me with him over to the swing set.

He drops down, staring up at me as he lifts my wrist to his lips, lightly kissing my skin. He gently turns me and pulls me onto his lap.

His deep breaths have my chest rising with his, and his arms slide against my leggings before wrapping around my middle. I lean my head against his, and together, we watch the moon dance along the water.

"The night of the dance, when I came to see you, I really thought that would be it," I tell him in a whisper.

He patiently waits for me to continue.

"I wanted to let you go, but I didn't know how. I kept waiting, hoping the next time I looked into your eyes, you wouldn't be staring at me the same way you always had. I thought maybe, because of Lolli, that time would be different. That you'd let go. I wanted you to look through me. Past me. I needed to forget you, Parker, and I couldn't as long as you kept looking at me like I mattered, like I was worth more than I felt. But, when I looked into your eyes, everything was *right* there, all the things I was feeling—hurt and anger and pain, hope and love. It was staring back at me." My voice cracks, and his arms tighten around me. "I knew the second you walked away that night ... I never could."

"You're worth everything I have, Kens," he whispers, and a small smile takes over my lips. "Everything I am is already yours; you just have to take it."

Tears brim my eyes, and I nod.

He's right. About everything. This won't be easy. Not even a little bit.

But he's worth it.

We're worth it.

"Are you busy the next few days?" I ask, my chest growing tight.

He's quiet a moment before he answers, "I have some reading to do, emails, and stuff, but I'll be around."

"I wanna go home."

All his muscles lock beneath me.

"*Home*, Parker. To Alrick. See my mom and dad. I need to talk to them before …"

"Before what?" he whispers slowly.

"I'm ready."

He's quiet and then, "For?"

"You." I swallow. "Us."

"Kens," he breathes, and my tears fall.

His hands lift from my waist, and he runs his knuckle along my jaw, gently turning my head to face him. His eyes, so blue, hold mine as he stares up at me, searching for a sign of uncertainty but he finds none.

His hand sinks into my hair, and his chin lifts as he pulls me closer, bringing my lips to his.

He kisses me with a loving care I've never felt, so tender.

When I sigh against his mouth, his chest rumbles, and his hand moves to slide against my leggings until he's gripping my thigh, and heat takes over. He senses it and shifts me as much as the small space will allow. Instantly, our kiss grows hungry.

Desperate and deprived for way too long, we attack each other's mouths. He claims me with his fevered kiss.

He grows hard beneath me, and my pussy walls clench in response. His hand slides higher until it rests at the bend where my thigh meets my pelvic bone, and I push against him.

When I shift slightly, attempting to bring his thumb closer to where I want it, he growls in my mouth, kissing me hard, and then he pulls back and jumps from the seat, carefully setting me on my feet.

His breathing is labored as he stares at the sand and then lifts his eyes to mine.

He gazes at me a moment before pushing against me. His hands case around my back, and he kisses me once more before dropping his forehead to mine. "Go home, Kens. Do whatever you need. I'll be here, waiting, when you're ready to come back to me. But ... maybe don't take too long." He laughs lightly, skimming his lips over mine.

I slide my hands up his chest, loving how his eyes close when I do, and whisper against his lips, "Come with me."

His lids pop open, and I swear, I'd fall if he wasn't holding me against him.

There's a shine to his eyes I've never seen, a cover of hopeful wishing. Complete and total vulnerability. He's given everything to me. Literally, his heart is in my hands. I feel it.

"Come with me, Parker."

He swallows, giving a small nod. "I can do that."

We stare at each other a moment before he pulls me in and hugs me tight against him. And I hold on, praying I'm stronger than I believe. Hoping I'm as strong as he thinks.

And knowing damn well it doesn't matter if I am or not because, at the end of it all ... I can't be me without him.

CHAPTER 30
PARKER

Σμυρνίδε

Kᴇɴʀᴀ sᴛᴀʀᴛs ʀᴜʙʙɪɴɢ ᴀᴛ ʜᴇʀ ᴘᴀʟᴍs ᴀs ᴡᴇ ʜɪᴛ ᴛʜᴇ ᴇxɪᴛ ɪɴᴛᴏ Alrick, so I reach over and slide my hand into hers.

She gives me a side grin before facing forward again.

I know she's nervous. Shit, I'm nervous for her. As far as we know, her parents think she's in some busy, happy, fairy-tale relationship, and she's about to let them in on whatever secrets she's been keeping, tell them she's leaving Kellan.

"I'm gonna drive to my dad's and have you take his car to your parents' house. Then, tomorrow, you can call me, and we'll see what we need to do."

"Are you sure? It's okay if you drop me."

I glance at her. "I can, if you want me to … but something tells me you need to do this on your own, and I don't wanna confuse them right away by showing up with you."

"Yeah, you're right."

A few blocks down, and we're stopping in front of the house.

She shifts in her seat, pulling herself closer to me, and I watch her from the corner of my eye, a nervous, numbing sensation shooting across my chest. She senses it, and her little hand lifts to bring my eyes to hers.

"You think I'll change my mind."

I shake my head. "I know you're scared. And I worry it might take a little more than you're ready to give for them to understand. But they deserve to know everything, Kenra." I lift her hand to kiss her wrist. "Everything."

"I …" She chokes, shaking her head. "I want to tell them everything. Maybe I can start slow since I'll be alone, and then maybe tomorrow… you could be there with me?"

I'd pull her in, kiss her hard right now, if I didn't think we'd end up upstairs, and then nothing would get done.

"I'll do whatever you need me to. Be wherever you need me to be."

Her cheeks grow warm, and she nods lightly.

I run inside, quickly grab my dad's car keys, and pull it from the garage for her.

When I step out, she steps forward, so I lean in, softly kissing the side of her mouth.

With a slight smile, she moves to sit, and I close the door behind her. Rolling her window down, her hands coming up to cover the top of the steering wheel, she stares at me. "I don't wanna be away from you yet."

I can't help but smirk at that. "Good. Then, I did something right. Go, Kens. I'm only a call away."

She nods, hope shining in her eyes. "See you soon, Safety."

With a laugh, I watch her drive off and then head inside.

It's clear my dad's gone, so I send him a quick text, just in case. He calls me almost immediately.

"Hey, Dad," I answer, tossing my bag onto the couch.

"You're home?"

I chuckle at his excitement. "I'm at your place, yeah. But only for a night I think."

"Damn. I wish I'd have known. We could have tried to be there, one of us at least."

"It's all right. Last-minute trip." My mind shifts to Payton, and I sigh. "Dad, I need to talk to you about a few things. You think maybe we can FaceTime in the next day or two?"

"Are you okay, son?"

"Yeah, I'm good. But I need to talk to you about some stuff."

"Course then, yeah. I can't tomorrow, but I'm free the next. That be all right, or you need me to make it happen sooner?"

"No, couple of days is fine." Gives me time to find out what all Payton plans to let me say.

"Okay. Be safe, son. Talk soon."

I drop onto the couch right as a text comes through.

Lolli Bear: Yo. You make it, or you pull over to do the dirty on the way?

I laugh and text her back.

Me: No doing the dirty. Just got here.

Lolli Bear: Your daddy and his daddy home?

My face scrunches, and I picture her laughing her ass off, knowing damn well she made me cringe.

Me: You're a pain in the ass, and no, gone as always. How's Peep?

Lolli Bear: Locked in her room with Deaton since last night, so I'm betting she's pretty damn good.

"Ah fuck," I mumble to myself. I get ready to toss the phone when a video call comes in.

Lolli's laughing when her face pops up. "Sorry!" she rushes out. "I'm sorry. I couldn't help it."

"I was about to ignore you."

"Oh, I know. Why do you think I called?" She smiles and laughs lightly. "So, where's Kenra?"

"Had her take my dad's car to her parents' house."

"Good idea. Her parents will be surprised to see her as it is. No need to confuse 'em off the bat with you being her ride."

I nod.

"You feel okay about all this, Hero?"

I take a deep breath. "I do, Lolli Bear. Before, it was always that we wanted each other but never said it out loud. This is different."

"Good. That's good," she whispers.

I eye her. "Nate go home today?"

201

"Yeah." She pulls her sleeve over her hand. "Pretty much had to push him out the door though. He wanted to stay, but he needs to be at camp. It's not exclusive to the quarterbacks, but he needs to be seen as much as possible. I'm telling you, Parker, he's gonna start as a freshman. I know it."

"Lolli?"

Her blues lock on to mine through the screen. "Hmm?"

"You okay?"

She's quiet a minute and then, "Yeah, I'm good. Getting ready to go for a run."

My gaze narrows, and I drop my head back on the couch. "I think we should get a dog."

She laughs out loud at that, and I grin. "You think Nauni, the devil cat, would appreciate a *dog*?"

"Nauni's become more of the neighborhood cat now that you let her out into the sand. Maybe you need a buddy there with you during the day."

"I'll be fine, Hero. And I'm good, I swear. I did have an idea of something I kinda wanted to talk to you about though."

"Let's hear it."

She shakes her head. "When you come home."

"You sure?"

"Yep. Hey, I gotta go, but, Hero?"

"Yeah?"

"Use a condom." She smiles wide when I laugh.

"Bye, Lolli. Call you tomorrow."

"Better." Then, she hangs up.

I take a deep breath, considering taking a quick nap when an idea hits. I hop up, snatch the keys from the glass bowl by the door, and head out.

It only takes a solid two minutes to get there, and I'm knocking before I know it.

The door swings open, and Mia's eyes widen, her brows disappearing under her bangs.

"What the hell?" she drags out.

Right then, her mom, Kara, steps up behind her, pulling the door open the rest of the way.

"Parker!" She steps outside with open arms. "So good to see you, honey. Please tell me my niece is with you?"

I glance at Mia and she shrinks into herself, regret taking over her features. Her mom must not be aware Lolli and Mia haven't spoken since our trip to Mexico this past spring break.

"No, ma'am." I look back to Kara. "Lolli's at home. I'm in town for a night, so I came to take Mia to lunch."

Kara's eyes thank me as she steps back, patting her daughter's shoulder, and then she disappears into the house.

"I—" Mia starts the second her mom is out of sight, but I shake my head, and she closes her mouth.

"Come on, Mia. Please?"

She licks her lips and nods, stepping inside to quickly grab her purse.

Together we climb into my dad's car and make our way to Wicker, the hometown diner we frequented all through high school. It's the place the team would go to hang out after practice and the place we'd all have breakfast at on the weekends— assuming Lolli wasn't cooking for us.

"Does Lolli know you're here?" Mia asks and then rethinks her question. "Scratch that. She *knows* you're here. Does she know you came to kidnap me?"

I laugh lightly, and she smiles out her window.

"No, Mia, she doesn't have the slightest clue that I showed up and politely asked you to lunch." I turn into the restaurant parking lot, pulling into the first spot I find. "She'd kick my ass if she did."

"She'll still kick your ass when she finds out you did."

I grin at her, and she laughs, shaking her head, as we hop out and head inside.

We grab a table, and Mia glances around, smiling at a hostess I've never seen. "Most of our friends have taken off already," Mia offers, seeing the confusion on my face as I look over the place, noticing all the fresh faces.

This was a place that brought comfort to a lot of us throughout school. Good day or bad day, many of us ended up here before going home.

"It's weird, right?" Mia asks, tearing the paper from her straw into little pieces.

I nod, leaning my forearms against the table. "Yeah, it, uh … it's kind of like that last piece that made this place my home is gone now." I look around the room, finding a bunch of small groups of teenagers, some I recognize, laughing and goofing around like we always did. "Guess it's their turn now."

"Everything here feels off now."

I look back to Mia, and she gives a fake smile.

"You need to call her, Mia. She misses you."

"Did she say that?"

"Does she have to?"

Mia smashes her lips together, her face drawn tight as she looks off.

"Look, you know her about as well as I do. She's not calling because she thinks *you* need time. She didn't write you off, Mia. You wrote her off, and that tells her she needs to give you space. Personally, I don't think you need space. You're just being stubborn."

At that, Mia starts crying, her face dropping into her palms. "Ugh, I was such a bitch, Parker, not calling her, not checking in on her … nothing."

"You know how she is, Mia. She doesn't care about all that. She'll give you shit for five whole minutes, and then it'll be back to normal."

She looks at me and then drops her eyes to the table. "My cousin had lost her parents and grandpa, the only family she had outside of me and my parents. Then, she fell in love and thought she'd lost him, too, after Liv lied, making both Nate and Lolli look guilty for things that they weren't. And I abandoned her, just like that, because I was … angry. I thought she'd led you on, taken advantage of your relationship, and slept with you because she didn't know what else to do, and it pissed me off. I know, if it had happened, you'd hurt because of it, and that wasn't right." Her cheeks grow pink, and she looks up, locking eyes with me.

I offer her a small smile. "I had no idea, Mia. You never said anything, and I never saw it before."

She shrugs and looks off again. "I've thought a lot about it, and I know I was irrational. It wasn't even about you, like I had thought it was. I mean, it'd started with you because the two of you were instantly connected, and I—" she cuts off before continuing, "God, this is embarrassing."

She looks to me. "I was jealous. Of *her*. Of *you*. I had a small thing for you and couldn't get you to see it, but you instantly saw her. And then I was trying to build a stronger relationship with Lolli, and she *instantly* saw you. Between you guys, and constantly being divided between my mom and Lolli, trying to keep peace but hurting because my mom only seemed to worry about her niece, and mad at Lolli for always treating my mom so cold. It's shitty of me, I know." She shakes her head, pinching her lips to the side. "I mean, I understood. Lolli lost her mom who was my mom's identical twin. I can't imagine how hard that was on either of them. I don't know." She shrugs, looking back to me. "Everything sort of hit at once and I didn't know how to deal. By the time I really thought about it, I felt stupid and now I don't know how to take the first step in fixing things between us."

"I get it. I really do. But forget about all that, Mia. You didn't hear it from me, but she could really use you right now."

Mia sits up straight, throwing her red hair over her shoulder. "What do you mean? What's wrong?"

I glance out the window a moment, then slowly bring my eyes back to her.

After a few seconds, she rolls her eyes and laughs. "Man, you are seriously a badass friend to have, aren't you?"

When I grin, she nods.

"Okay, Baylor. I hear you."

"Good." I pat my stomach. "Can we eat now?"

Mia laughs and flags down the waitress, who walks over with a smile.

"You guys ready?" She looks between the two of us.

"Yeah." Mia nods before smirking my way. "I think it's time for some French toast."

I nod with a smile. "Good choice, Mia. Good choice."

Σμιρνόϛ

My legs won't stop bouncing as I make my way down my childhood driveway.

I smile when it comes into view.

This home, this is what true love is about. My dad built this place from the ground up for my mom—a perfect replica of the Forrest Gump house. My dad jokes that it was to feed her Tom Hanks obsession, but it's so much more than that.

It's what the home represents.

Complete and total fearless love.

Nobody loves like my parents.

They're the strongest, bravest people I know. So loyal and caring. Damn good people.

And I'm the apple that fell so far from the tree.

The sad thing is, when I tell them the truth about everything with Kellan—his lies, my lies, the things he's holding over me and them—they won't even be upset with me. They'll be devastated I've lived unhappily for as long as I have.

All they ever wanted for Nate and me is for us to be happy. They were so scared for Nate for a while. He was partying constantly, hooking up with all these random girls, and then bam, there was Lolli, and he was gone. Consumed and forever changed.

I turn the engine off and fight off the wave of emotion threatening to steal my breath. I step out of the car, wiping my hands across my shorts, and slowly walk up the porch steps.

Right as I reach for the screen, the door is yanked open, and my mother stares back at me, her hand flying to cover her mouth as tears fill her brown eyes.

"Oh, baby ..." she croaks.

I can't handle it. I start to cry and move into her. She wraps her little arms around me, and I hug her back just as hard, softly sobbing into her chest.

She soothingly runs her hand down my hair. "Hey, shh," she coos. "It's okay. Everything will be okay. He told us everything."

My forehead scrunches in confusion for a moment when I remember Nate knows I was headed here. I didn't expect him to give them a heads-up though, and he doesn't exactly know what all I have to share.

I pull back and wipe my eyes as my mom's hands find my biceps, and she squeezes. "There's so much more to it, Mom," I cry.

She gives a sad smile. "I know, sweetheart. And I want to know everything you know so far."

We make our way into the kitchen, and she notices me glancing around, so she points out all her little projects.

"With both you and Nate gone, I have a lot of time on my hands, so I've been tryin' to redecorate." She glances around with a frown. "I'm not real good at it." She laughs, making me smile.

With a sigh, she places her hand over mine, her eyes roaming my face. "Let me look at you." She touches my hair and my face, her eyes growing glossy again. "I've missed you."

I swallow past the lump in my throat. "I miss you guys, too."

Right then, the back door opens, and voices fill the room.

My mom pats my hand. "Here they come."

Right then, my dad walks around the corner, and a huge yet somber smile takes over his face. I shoot toward him as his arms open for me, and I throw myself against his chest. Strong, protective arms wrap around me, bringing a peace only my dad can give. His chest inflates with his deep breath.

"Baby girl," he whispers into my hair.

I choke up again. He kisses my head and pulls back to look at me, his eyes holding a sadness I can't remember ever seeing in him; it's a deep-rooted pain he can't hide.

"I'm so sorry to hear," he speaks, his voice cracking slightly.

And then a hand slides down my back, and I turn.

Everything in me freezes, my heart included, when I lock on to a pair of dark eyes.

"Kellan," I think I say out loud but too stunned to know.

"Baby."

My breath lodges in my throat, and my bottom lip starts to tremble.

No ...

"It's okay," he speaks so soft and delicate as he steps closer, and the dam breaks, tears bursting from my eyes. "We'll find a way; don't worry." He wraps his slimy arms around me, and my head falls as uncontrollable sobs rip through me.

Nobody says anything for a few minutes, and when I pull back, I find my dad comforting my mom, his protective arms wrapped around her as silent tears fall from her eyes.

Kellan drops one arm from around me but forces me to stay glued to his side with a tight grip on my hip, and at this point, I'm so fucked in the head, I let him because I have no strength to stand. No idea what's happening around me.

"Let's talk in the living room."

I say nothing as Kellan directs me to the couch, my parents choosing to sit on the ottoman directly in front of us.

He clears his throat. "Baby, I'm so sorry. I knew you'd be emotional when you got here today, so I filled them in a little beforehand. I just wanted this to be as easy on you as possible."

Tears continue to fall as I stare at nothing.

"Kenra, honey, it's okay. This doesn't mean there's anything wrong with you, sweetheart," my mom says quietly.

I start to shake slightly.

The cutting? Has he told them what I do to keep control?

"That's what I've been telling her, Mrs. Monroe, but she's been so hard on herself; it breaks my heart. The doctors said it wasn't anything she did, that, sometimes, as devastating as it is, there's no reason or answer to why. We just have to keep trying. Right, baby?"

My stomach lurches, vomit threatening to come up as I realize what he's done.

My eyes fly to his, angry tears blurring my vision, and he stares back, seemingly merciful to the outside world, but pure malice is all I see.

This bastard knows why I came here.

"Don't worry," he speaks low, never taking his eyes off mine as he delivers his underlying message. "We'll get past this."

My jaw clenches, and I'm ready to throw it all out, but the slight pinch that finds the edges of his eyes warns me something worse is in the works, and mine squeeze closed.

Although I'm too ashamed to face them head-on, my eyes slide to my mom, finding her hand over her mouth, her eyes closed tight in pain, as my dad cradles her in against him, rocking her in an attempt to soothe. I lift my eyes to his, and my heart cracks open wider.

With his eyes brimmed red at the edges, and his mouth in a firm, forced line, my dad fights to stay strong.

For me.

Because he thinks his baby girl has lost something she never had.

Their grandchild.

They sit there, mourning a little part of themselves that never even existed.

I look to Kellan, begging him not to make me go along with this.

He's breaking them down, filling their happy, love-filled lives with sorrow for their only daughter. He's come in and taken away the most precious wish a mother could ever have.

"Daddy ..." I whisper, my voice cracking at the end.

Tears fill his eyes as his cheeks inflate, and he blows out a harsh breath. "It's okay, baby girl." He chokes, his nostrils flaring, as he tries to hold it all in. "It'll all be okay."

And I cry harder. This is so fucked up.

"Mr. and Mrs. Monroe, I know she only just got here, and you've both missed spending time with her, but maybe she and I should get a hotel room tonight. She's so upset. I'd like to just ... hold her for a little while. It's been really painful for us, dealing with the news."

"We understand, Kellan, sweetheart."

I lift my head to look at my mother, who dislodges herself from my dad's arms.

My body lies limp and defeated against the couch cushion, my eyes following my mom's as she drops to her knees in front of me.

"Kenra," she whispers, her hands coming up to push my hair from my face, "trust me when I say, we will get through this, together."

My chest caves in when she reaches over and squeezes Kellan's hand in support.

I can only stare, dead-eyed and motionless.

"Thank you, Mrs. Monroe." Kellan stands, and my mother follows.

She steps back, reaching a hand out, and my dad is already there to take it, to give her the strength she's losing watching me so lost.

Constant support—that's how they love.

"Pumpkin, you sure you don't wanna stay upstairs? Your room's still sitting there," my dad asks quietly.

He doesn't want me to leave. Worried about how long it'll be before he sees me again if I do.

"I ... I need to leave with Kellan," I whisper, unable to look my dad in the eyes, but I see the curt nod he gives after I say this, and he runs a hand across his jaw.

"Okay, baby girl. Whatever you need."

As quickly and quietly as possible, I hug my parents, feeling the tension and worry in my dad's firm hold, and then I all but run out the door.

Kellan says proper good-byes and then meets me out front.

His hand finds my lower back, and I fight not to jerk away from him as he pushes me toward Parker's dad's car but instead of leading me to the driver's door, he tells me to get in the passenger seat. Then, he makes his way around and slides behind the wheel. Obviously, he had a car service drop him off knowing he'd give himself away if I saw his car here.

I press my body against the door, turning to stare at him.

I don't glare. I don't speak. I just stare.

I know his game, the dramatic effect he likes to give, so I know it's coming.

And then he gives a small smile.

"Hello, *baby*." His eyes shift between mine. "We need to talk."

"So, talk."

His lips tip slightly, his eyes narrowing for half a second before he masks his anger and laughs lightly.

He pulls an envelope from his laptop bag and holds it out for me.

I don't take it. I don't take my eyes off his.

"It's a contract I had drawn up. I've already signed and had it filed away." When my brows pinch, he continues, "It's time I make a change in our relationship. I've decided to leave your parents and your brother alone. For good. No more threats, no more moves to keep them in my pocket. I've already sold the building your dad's shop is in, so I no longer have the power to

212

shut him down. I've called my guy at UCLA, and Nate's original roommate will be reassigned to his room. I made a hefty donation to get my guy transferred out, so you won't have to worry about him going after Nate on the field either. His career is safe. I no longer control it."

"Why would I believe you?"

"Because it says in here"—he taps the envelope he's dropped onto my lap— "if I do, you get half of my inheritance, no questions asked, and I have to go public about my threats on you and your family. I've also eliminated the prenuptial agreement to make you feel more stable in our home and in our life. Everything I have will also be yours."

Dread. It zaps up my spine, raising the hairs along my neck, because I know this man in front of me. I have watched him play this game for the last year. This means there's something so much worse coming.

"Why?"

"So, you can see how much you mean to me, how much I want this to work between us. Kenra, I love you. I always have. So much so that I"—he jerks his chin to the side, clucking his tongue— "can't let you go. I went about it wrong before; I know. But I can make you happy, Kenra. I know I can. But I'm not stupid." He shakes his head. "It will only ever work with *him* gone."

My breath noticeably lodges in my throat.

His dark eyes harden. "I know this car, Kenra."

"How did you know I was here?"

He ignores me and hands over a second envelope.

I don't take this one either, and he drops it on top of the other.

"Another contract?"

"Of sorts, yes. I'm quite proud of this one. Just sent the email two nights ago, and it's already a done deal." His eyes bounce between mine. "My offers were *more* than generous, so I wasn't too worried."

He leans toward me, and when I start to pull back, he speaks through clenched teeth, "Your *daddy* is watching, *baby*. Make this believable, would ya?"

I dig my nails into my palms with as much force as I can find, forcing my body toward his.

I don't even feel his lips when they land on me. I don't move my mouth to match his, and he growls against me, anger hardening his jaw.

He pulls back and shifts the car into drive. "Buckle up, Kenra. We have somewhere to be."

When I make no move, he scoffs and heads toward the road.

He hits his knuckle against the envelope. "You might wanna read over this before we get to where we're going. It'll save us a lot of time."

With shaky hands, I run my fingers along the edges. Then, I flip it open and pull the freshly printed forms out.

At first, it's unclear of what I'm looking at, so I start to skim. When I do, a few key words catch my eye, and all the air is knocked from my lungs.

My hands fly to my throat as I start to choke on nothing, and the papers fall to the floorboard.

Kellan chuckles in his seat, his hand sliding over to tap my knee once. "Yeah … I figured that would do the trick." He flicks his eyes to mine and then back to the road. "Nobody will ever have to know if you can learn how to walk a straight line for once, Kenra. It'll be our little secret, everyone else can carry on none the wiser."

My head starts to pound, my pulse beating behind my eyelids in merciless thumps. I can't see, can't hear. Can hardly breathe.

And he smirks beside me, reaching over to turn the stereo up.

With my energy gone, tears cried out, I drop my head against the seat, closing my eyes tight as I search for a deep breath I can't find.

I don't open them again until the car comes to a complete stop, and when I do, reality stares back at me in the form of a giant brass bell.

Shock doesn't even begin to cover it. I'm struck by his nerve.

He's making bolder moves than I ever thought possible.

He's locked me in.

"I've been patient, let you set the pace, but no more. You were mine first, and you will stay mine. *I* do not lose. Now, get out of the fucking car, Kenra."

I do as he said and follow him up the steps and into the tiny room where a few people stand, waiting for us.

No one looks at me. Not once. But why would they? I'm not the one with the black card.

Twenty minutes later, we're exiting, headed back for the car.

Right then, a town car pulls up, and Kellan parts from me. He tosses the keys at my feet with a glare. "Tie up your loose ends. Now. I expect you to be at my parents' by lunch tomorrow

I watch him pull away. Then, I open the car door and drop into the seat.

I'm not sure how long I sit there and stare at nothing, but when the parking lot lights shut down, I put the car in drive.

I flip around and head for the old country roads that line this town.

It's well after midnight now, so there are no cars around.

I roll all the windows down and push my foot all the way to the floor, listening to the wind as it whistles by, the engine as it fights to keep up. Papers fly all around; some might even fly out, but I don't care.

Everything is ruined.

I start to scream in anger as I grow closer to the end.

I bite into my cheek, the taste of metal coating my mouth, as I will myself to keep going, but for some reason, I slam on the brakes, and the car skids out.

Once it finally stops, I drop my head against the steering wheel, and the tears return.

I gave Parker hope. Made him believe we could be, even fooled myself into believing it.

Kellan said to tie up my loose ends, basically saying to get rid of Parker, as if it were simple.

I should just leave now.

Go back to Kellan's parents' and accept what is.

But this is Parker. My safety.

And I'm a stupid, stupid girl.

Σμυρνός

"What's the matter?" Lolli drops her chin onto her palm as she stares at me through the screen.

I sigh. "You ever wonder what it would have been like had your grandpa not gotten sick? He wouldn't have been in the hospital, and your parents wouldn't have been on their way there. You'd have spent your birthday with your family, like you were supposed to, and never have had to go through all the shit you did."

"Honestly? I never thought about that until after Nate," Lolli admits, and my head tilts in question. She chuckles lightly, glancing away. "I never let myself think about my family after they died, Hero. Not once until Nate and I got deep, only then because it was like, once I started to feel again ... I felt everything. If I were to try to shut it off, it would have meant shutting out Nate, too." She looks back to me. "It makes me feel guilty now when I think about it, but as bad of a daughter and granddaughter as it makes me, I ... wouldn't change it if I could." Her blue eyes bounce between mine. "I wouldn't bring them back if I could because then I never would have found Nate. Kinda sick, but ... it is what it is."

"You don't think, if you were meant to be with him, that it somehow would have happened?"

She eyes me, her gaze sharpening. "No, I don't. Bad shit happens, Hero. Some so bad so that, in the end, we're stronger. So that we're strong enough to be who the other person deserves. What the hell is going on? That wasn't some random thought."

I give her a sad smile. "I just … I feel like I haven't earned my right to have everything I want yet. And that tells me—"

Lolli pops up on her bed and points a sleeve-covered finger at me. "Knock that shit off *right now*. That is bullshit. Straight-up, Parker." Her brows rise. "Yeah, I said Parker. Look, you've *lived* in hell, whereas I *fell* into it. It's why you're my person. You *deserve* to be happy. And, truthfully …" She trails off, pinching her lips to the side and then rolling her eyes. "Fuck it. I'm gonna say it. Sorry in advance. But, Hero, you were well on your way to a solid happiness before she showed back up. I know you still had your internal battles, mainly missing *her*, but you were happy. Genuinely happy, not like in Alrick."

I stare into her blue eyes, so passionate and honest. "Because you showed up."

She takes a deep breath, a soft smile on her lips.

"You brought me back."

Tears form in her eyes. "You'd do it for me."

"I would."

She nods and then glances at her door and then back. "Payton's knocking. She wants to have a girls' movie night," she whispers, rolling her eyes. "Guess Deaton's knocked out cold. Supposedly, he tried to keep up with Mason on the alcohol front. Dumbass. Why do you think we're all still awake?"

I laugh, and she glares. "I'm sure it'll be loads of fun."

"Ha! Yeah, right. I don't know how to do this stuff. I'm gonna say something super off-color, and she'll ditch me."

"Is that nerves I'm sensing?" I tease.

Her jaw drops. "Fuck off! No! I just …" She covers her face, peeking out her fingers. "I can't believe I'm admitting this, but I need her to like me. She's important to you, and I kinda like her."

"That why you were going runnin'?"

She shrugs. "Among other things."

"Lolli Bear," I speak softly, and her shoulders slump, "she'll love you. And, if she asked you, that's big. That means she's trying. Just do what you do best and be you."

"Yeah?"

I grin. "Yeah."

"You okay over there? Heard from Kenra yet?"

"Not yet, and I'm fine. Have fun. And text me if Payton gets to acting all drama queen on you."

"Oh God," she groans.

I laugh. "Night, Lolli."

"Night."

I end the video call and strip out of my clothes before dropping onto my bed.

The second my back hits my mattress, I hear the lock rattling. I lift my head to hear better, and the sound of the front door opening and closing has me sitting up.

My brows pull, but then I remember Kenra is the only one it could be; she has the keys on the car key ring.

She's not supposed to be here. The plan was for her to call me in the morning.

My muscles constrict as I listen to her hushed movements.

The keys are placed back in the bowl with a quiet clink, followed by a light thud, telling me she's kicked her shoes off.

I settle my breathing when her footsteps are all that's to be heard, each step bringing her closer to me.

Ever so slowly, she curves around the hallway and continues forward until she's standing just inside my bedroom door. With her eyes on mine, she lifts the bag in her hand, and I look from it to her.

It's the sundress I bought her in San Francisco but never had the chance to give to her.

"It was sitting by the table downstairs," she whispers. "It's for me, isn't it?"

I nod.

She pulls the blue cotton dress from the bag and gently runs her fingers along the length of it, her eyes following her hand as she does. "Why'd you buy it?"

"So, you could feel the sun on your skin again."

She inhales, sliding the dress along her cheek to feel the material. "My scars ..."

"Are a part of you."

She glances toward the window. The blinds are shut, only a small light in the corner of my room bringing light. "The sun is down."

I move to stand in front of her.

She's been crying. Her face is blotchy, eyes tired.

She doesn't look to me when I lift my hand and brush her hair over her shoulder, letting my fingers brush along her sleeve until I reach the hand that holds the dress.

Her grip on the material is tight, so I don't remove it but bring it up until it meets the center of her chest, and her lips start to tremble.

"Go put it on, Kens," I whisper.

Her eyes close, her forehead pinching tight.

Finally, she meets my gaze, her free hand coming up to run across my jawline, and she nods.

With hesitant steps, she heads for the bathroom in the hall.

Blowing out a deep breath, I drop back onto my bed and wait for her to return, but when she comes out, legs and arms bare, nothing but the knee-length, thin-strapped dress I bought for her on, she stops in the middle of the hallway and starts rubbing at her palms.

My brows pull in, but when her fingers trail a few inches up her arm, my chest constricts.

She hears me stand, and while her chin still faces down, her golden eyes lift to mine. With her attention on me, I move to twist the blinds open and then pull them all the way up, doing the same to the window on the joining wall. I move to sit at the edge of my bed, reaching over to turn off the lamp on the side table, and then look back to her.

She stares a moment, and then slowly, her fingers separate, her head lifting.

And then she steps toward me, not stopping until she's directly in front of me, nothing but me and her and the moonlight.

Staring up at her, I watch as her eyes roam across my face. She's putting off a distant air, an emptiness that wasn't there this morning. I don't like it.

I need her with me when she's with me.

All of her.

I bring my hands up and run my fingertips across hers that hang at her sides, and her eyes drop to watch.

I take my time as I slide them up, gliding past her palms until I reach her wrists.

I expect her to tense, but she doesn't.

Gently closing my hands around her, I turn her arms over, so her scars are facing us both.

When my gaze lifts to hers, she meets my eyes. I keep her there, pulling her stare with mine, so she's watching when my mouth meets her demons. I run my lips across her grazed skin, softly pressing a kiss every few inches. When I get to a point where I need to stand to kiss further up, she pulls her arm away, and my eyes lift to hers.

Her head shakes lightly, her fingers moving to press against my chest. Her hand fans out, and she nudges me slightly, so I follow her order and scoot back until my knees are bent over the edge of the mattress.

She climbs up, her knees on each side of my thighs, her chest just below my chin as I stare up at her.

Her hands move to my shoulders, but she pauses there, her forehead dropping to meet mine.

My hands start at the bend of her knees and slowly make their way up the backs of her soft thighs. When I run the pads of my fingers along her skin, her chest inflates, those eyes dilating.

So, I continue, my hands gliding up further, under her dress and over her bare ass, until I find her hips, just past the line of her panties.

Her fingernails are digging into my shoulders now, her breath coming in sharper, shorter pants that match mine.

Her knees slide out further, her nearly naked body coming down to meet my groin, nothing but our underwear between us.

I'm hard as fuck, and she feels it, right against her. Her tongue pokes out to touch the tips of her teeth.

Her nails relent, and she glides her hands up my neck until her fingers are in my hair, her thumbs cased around my ear. Then, she tilts her head and brings her mouth to mine.

She licks across my lips, moaning softly as she sucks my bottom lip between hers for a moment, and my dick twitches against her, my grip at her hips tightening. Her hands come down to grab mine, and I think she's about to move me, but instead, she slides my hands down, her eyes burning into mine when I squeeze her ass, as she's asking.

I can't handle it anymore, and my lips crash against hers, one hand coming up to pull her closer, the other flexing against her skin as she starts to grind against me.

I growl lightly and sneak my hand from her ass to the crease of her thigh that meets her bikini line.

She gasps into my mouth and slightly tilts her body, leading my hand to her sweet spot.

I push the backs of my fingers against her underwear, sliding them down and across the fabric as much as the space allows for, and a tremble runs through her.

That's when it hits me.

She's in a frenzy, eyes crazed in lust, breathing completely out of control, body dripping wet and ready. She needs to come now.

I flip her over, moving her in one quick motion to the center of my bed, and she licks her lips, her legs widening for me as I settle between them.

I slide my hands up her thighs, pushing her dress up with it until I'm staring down at her little purple panties. Her hands tighten into fists around my comforter as I stare, her wild breaths heard in the air.

My eyes flick to hers, and her chin lifts, her head falling deeper into the pillow as she stares at me.

And I'm not even touching her yet. But she knows it's coming, knows what I want, and sighs out a "Yes."

My mouth starts to water, my heart rate spiking as I lower myself onto my stomach, my elbows bent to hold me up.

I trace her panty line, and she sucks in a sharp breath. I slip my finger between her panties and her skin until my knuckle is hooked around the fabric and slowly slide it down, unsticking the wet cloth from her begging pussy. My knuckle slides against her, flicking past her clit, and her hips buck slightly.

My lips twitch in response, and then I move to slide them off her completely.

I thought she'd be embarrassed, maybe try to cover herself, but she doesn't. In fact, her hands move to glide across her stomach as she eyes me.

I bend, my eyes on hers as I grow closer. I flick just the tip of my tongue against her, tasting her for the first time.

I groan instantly, and a breath hisses past her lips.

And then I'm gone on her, my tongue sliding against her, until I find her spot. The spot that makes her knees lift and her back bow, and I stay there. Sucking and pinching her clit until she's pushing me away and pulling me closer at the same time, her knees clamping tight around my head as I force her cum from her body.

She moans, deep and long and desperate, and fuck me if it isn't the sexiest thing I've ever heard.

She gasps, trying to shift her body away, the feeling too strong, but I hold her there.

I slow my pace, moving my hands to massage her thighs, slowly rolling my tongue over her clit that's still locked between my lips. I keep her there, let her ride her orgasm from start to finish until, finally, her muscles start to relax, and her legs fall to her sides.

Her breathing starts to slow, and a soft, satisfied sigh leaves her.

I shift above her, gripping my dick to soothe the ache, and she reaches for me, her hand running along my shoulder as she pulls me closer. I move up on the bed to lie beside her, and she stares at me. Her thumb comes up to swipe across my bottom lip, and I tilt my head, so it scrapes against my bottom teeth. Her eyes find mine again, and she lifts her chin, her head staying against my pillow.

I lower myself to meet her, kissing those lips while still tasting the other ones.

She hums into my mouth, her body pulling closer to mine. Her leg hikes up over my hip, and I take it as an invitation to grind against her. Then, she pulls me on top of her.

I bend my arms, my boxers soaking up her cum as I rock against her.

Her hands come down and finger the hem of the dress, so I help her out. I push it over her ribs, bending to kiss just below her bra line, and pull it over her head.

When she sneaks her hand up and under her bra cup to rub on her own nipple, I stop her with a firm hand.

Her eyes flash to mine, drunk on desire.

"When I have your body in front of me like this, I do the work. All of it. When I'm touching you"—I cup her little pussy, and she moans— "your hands are on me or anywhere else, except on yourself. I'm a greedy man, Kens."

Her eyes turn ten shades darker right in front of me. She falls flat on her back, her arms dropping beside her head, her legs widening across the bed—across *my* bed—and I'm quick to settle against her.

The second I do, she can't handle it, and her hands fly to my sides, making me chuckle against her mouth. Her warm palms slide against my ribs, up and down, until she wants more, and her fingertips slip into my boxers.

She pauses there, her eyes catching mine.

I float my lips across hers, my hand squeezing behind her to unclasp her bra. I dip my head to her neck as I free her breasts. "Touch me, baby," I whisper against her skin, grinning when she shivers beneath me. "Anywhere you want. However you want." I kiss her throat. "As long as you want."

"Mmm ..." she hums, the vibration from the sound tingling my lips.

She lifts her hips to rub herself against my dick, her hands sliding across my ass cheeks, and she squeezes. She presses me down onto her before pulling back and pushing my boxers past my waist. Those eyes close as she scratches my skin, dragging her nails down the flex of my hip bone until she meets my shaft. Her nipples harden as she grips me, and I groan, digging my fingers into her hair, as my muscles tighten. This time, it's her who chuckles. It's a husky, desire-driven sound that goes straight to my groin, and I flex in her hand.

She squeezes, and I drop my head to her shoulder, fighting and losing to keep my breathing under control. Fuck, I've wanted this for years. Wanted her. Imagined it, fucking fantasized about it.

Mmm ... all the ways I want her. All the things I wanna do to her ...

My fingertips glide down her neck on the opposite side of where my head lies. I skim across her collarbone, feathering the side of her breast, and goose bumps rise against my fingers.

She slowly pumps me when my hand cases around her tit. I

gently squeeze her and then follow the same trail on her other side but with my lips, pulling her taut nipple in my mouth when I reach it.

The second my teeth graze across her sensitive flesh, she guides me where she wants me, maneuvering so that my tip slides in before I even know it's happening.

"Fuck," I groan.

Her chest lifts to push into mine, and I slide in.

A harsh breath leaves her as her body sucks me inside. Sharp nails find the center of my back, and her legs wrap with mine.

I kiss her chest, neck, and then lips, pulling back to stare at her as I glide out and rock back in, a deep, smooth rhythm that forces our bodies to fight the hunger building. She gasps beneath me every time I'm all the way in, crying out her soft moans when I pull back. Her face is flushed and way past aroused. She's completely consumed. Enthralled in me. Gripped *by* me.

She licks her lips, lifting to flick her tongue against my neck, and our pace increases.

I still rock into her, still grind when my pelvis meets hers, but in quicker movements that have her panting.

"Mmm … so good," she whispers.

My body twitches, my right hand moving to grip her hip.

"Kens?" I whisper into her chest, and she hums in response. "Am I all you feel right now?"

"Yes," she gasps.

I tilt her head back, exposing her neck more. "Have you ever felt like this?"

She tenses for half a second.

"It's okay, baby." I kiss across her chest, hiking her knee up, sinking in further. "Tell me."

She whimpers, her thigh muscles locking around mine. "N-never."

When I growl, she grips my hair and yanks my head back,

guiding my mouth to her as she gets closer, her pussy walls squeezing around my dick. I groan and increase my pace. I slide my arm behind her back for better leverage, and her body starts to quake.

She moans long and loud, her walls throbbing, adding even more friction, and I push in as far as I can. Her grip tightens around me, and I come right with her.

She turns her head, sliding her lips across mine, as she shivers, and my sweaty forehead meets hers.

"Never," she breathes into me, golden eyes clear and on mine.

Never.

It's still dark when Kenra wakes me. I shift, pulling her little frame across me, and she gives me a small one-sided smile.

"Can't sleep?"

She shakes her head. "Can we head back now, to California?"

"You wanna go now?" My brows tug in, and I glance at the clock to see it's just after three in the morning.

She kisses my chest and nods. "Please."

I run my hands through her hair, moving to meet her halfway, and kiss her. "Whatever you want."

She gives a lazy smile, and together, we lift from the bed and slip back into our clothes.

We never bothered unpacking, so all we have to do is basic hygiene control, grab our belongings, and we're out the door.

I stuff our bags behind the seat, and she climbs in through my door. I turn the engine over and switch my phone on vibrate, reaching past her to stuff it in the glove box. When I pull back, she catches my arm and leans over to kiss me.

It's slow but strong, and I shift to get a better angle.

Kenra pulls back and surprises the hell outta me when she

moves to climb over me, her body flush against mine, her back against the steering wheel.

I glide my hands up her thighs, smirking when she moans.

"This dress is awfully convenient," I whisper as my hand slides between her legs, and she does the same, pulling me from my basketball shorts.

"I can't wait, Parker," she whispers against my lips. "It's a day's drive. I need you now."

I don't argue, just glance around to make sure there's no one up and watching. Then, I lift her hips and guide her onto me.

This time, she sets the pace, her body rolling in ways I didn't know were possible. Deep dips at the curve of her back allow me to sink deeper, and when her head falls back, mine drops against the headrest.

I close my eyes and just feel.

Warm and tight, her pussy sucks me dry until I'm jerking beneath her, and she's pulsing around me.

Her hands case around my face, and she leans forward, kissing me slowly before pulling back to stare into my eyes.

"You have to know ... Parker, I—"

I catch her lips again as I tuck myself back into my shorts and gently pull her off me, placing her in the seat beside me. I kiss her again, and she sighs into my mouth.

"You, Kenra Monroe, are amazing. Now, let's get on the road and get back to our friends and family. What do you say?"

Tears fill her eyes, and she nods, scooting as close to me as possible.

I force myself not to ask her to look at me. If she does, I'll be able to see what the tears are for.

And I'm afraid to find out.

CHAPTER 33
PAYTON

Σμυρναε

Saliva fills my mouth, sweat beads breaking out across my forehead. I run to the bathroom, barely making it before the dry-heaving starts. My stomach cramps, my muscles tightening, as my body attempts to hollow out my already empty belly.

Only it's not empty.

There's a baby in there.

My and Deaton's baby.

I flush the toilet and quickly brush my teeth before exiting as quietly as possible.

"That's the third time this morning."

I jump, my hand hitting my chest, as I spin to find Lolli leaning against the wall in her running gear.

She holds out a water bottle, and I slowly take it. "Thanks."

Her lip twitches, and she nods toward the kitchen, so I follow behind her.

She starts making coffee and then pauses to look back at me. "Is this gonna make you puke again? 'Cause, I mean, I could just … go get one …" She pouts to herself at the thought, and I find myself laughing lightly.

"It's okay. I was thinking of maybe sitting on the patio anyway. Maybe … you want to come out there with me for a while?" I ask, glancing away in case she says no.

Lolli sets her cup down and spins to face me, her long, dark hair whipping across her face. She grins. "Hell yeah, I do." She spins back around with more pep as she starts her Keurig, pulling creamer from the fridge. "You might wanna grab a sweater. The early morning waft is damn cold."

I hop from the barstool, run into the living room to grab one I saw lying on the couch, and toss it on.

When I step back in the kitchen, Lolli is just finishing making her cup and shifts to face me. Instantly, her eyes drop, her smile quickly turning into a frown.

I glance down, seeing the sweater I put on is a UCLA sweater— Nate's sweater. My eyes flick back to hers. I open my mouth to speak, but her hand flies up, and she laughs at herself.

"You're fine. For real." She chuckles again, shaking her head, and walks for the door. "I think I need to learn how to share. Well, maybe." She winks over her shoulder as she moves to sit on the little patio couch.

I laugh and take the seat across from her. "Yeah, you don't exactly strike me as the sharing type."

"I'm not. Don't want to. Especially Nate, and I am *so* okay with that decision." She laughs into her cup. "But maybe a sweater here and there won't kill me."

"You don't sound real sure about that," I tease.

She grins. "I'm not. And honestly? If that were his team sweater with his name on it … I'd have made you change." She widens her eyes, opening her mouth in a mock shocked expression, and we both laugh.

"Will he be back today?"

"I told him to stay, get some extra sleep." She glances my way with a grin. "He told me to wear my purple chonies."

We both laugh lightly, and she smiles to herself.

"You love him a lot, huh?"

Her features soften in a way I've noticed only happens when he's around. "With everything I am. But is there any other way?"

She brings her eyes back to mine, and my lip twitches.

"I don't think there is." I bring my knees up, crossing my arms over them. "People will criticize us, Deaton and me. Say we don't know what we're doing. How stupid and young we are. Already, my mother tells me I don't know what love is." I shake my head, disgusted. "She's the one who has no idea. And we might be young, but why does that have to mean it's not real?"

I look back to Lolli, and she lowers her cup, staring at me with her head tilted slightly.

"He makes me feel like I matter. Knows how to chase away the echoes of my mom's voice when they get too loud even though he has his own problems to battle. Both our lives at home are empty, but together, we're ... everything just makes sense. He's taught me so much about what love even is. He's shown me how to love and trust in someone. I didn't even believe in the word, let alone the emotion behind it, before he offered it to me." I glance back at Lolli, waiting for judgment, but it never comes.

She smiles, her eyes dropping to my belly and then coming back to mine. "You're afraid, if you have this baby, one of your guys' parents will step in and take control."

Tears slip without warning, and I nod. "I'm afraid they'll raise the baby to be what me and Deaton were. Cold. Heartless. Unloved."

Lolli sighs, a deep crease taking over her forehead. She looks over the ocean. "I'm afraid I won't be able to love a ... anyone else like I love Nate. And I know I said I *should* learn to share, but I don't *want* to share him. Not even with ..." Her eyes fly to mine.

She stares at me, and I stare at her. And, much to my surprise, she lets me see the trouble on her mind. There's so much worry in her eyes that I've never seen.

She's genuine. And she loves her people.

I glance down and then lock my eyes on hers. "I'm worried about my brother."

"So am I," she admits with no hesitation.

"This family? Every move they make is calculated. Purposeful. She's been here almost a week now."

"You're thinking he knows she's here?"

"I'm saying he's allowing it."

Anger flashes across her features. "Why?"

"Exactly."

Lolli frowns, her eyes cutting toward the house in thought before coming back to me. Her gaze drops to my stomach.

I tense. I didn't even realize I had been cradling my belly, protecting my baby without knowing it.

"You've already decided." It's not a question, just a gentle statement.

"I could never give up a piece of us. She's ours."

"Have you told Deaton?" she whispers.

"Tonight. He wants to take me on our *own* night walk on the beach."

Lolli laughs lightly.

"I'm telling him then."

Tears fill her eyes, and she rolls them at herself, her lip twitching in a small smile. "Good. That's good." She shifts to set her cup down and bends forward to rest her elbows on her knees. "Because I wanted to talk to you about something."

She's serious in an instant, staring at me with strong, capable eyes.

I drop back in my seat. "I'm listening."

It's just after dark when the front door opens.

I glance over the couch right as Parker and Kenra walk in, and it's obvious there was some sort of shift.

He's eased.

She's hiding something.

They pause in the doorway, completely unaware of our sitting here, and Kenra moves toward him.

"I'm gonna step out back to meet Ari and the others. She said they're about here."

Deaton and I glance at each other when Kenra steps into Parker, lightly kissing him.

I hop up, enraged, and loudly toss my magazine back to the table.

Both their gazes snap our way.

Parker's eyes are pinched around the edges as his gaze flicks around the room, and Kenra's quickly cut to the floor. I meet Lolli's stare as she leans back against Nate's chest. Then, I storm past Parker, out the front door.

He doesn't understand.

Συγγνώς

"PEEP, WAIT UP," I CALL OUT.

When she starts walking faster, I jog to catch up. "Payton, damn it, would you stop?"

She whips around, her long blonde braid flying over her shoulder. "What are you doing, Parker?" She scowls at me. "Seriously, what the hell? Are you *insane*?"

"No, I'm not. Things aren't how you're thinking. It's more complicated than—"

She laughs bitterly. "Don't insult me. I might be young, but I am *not* dumb. You must be though if you think for a *second* that this will all work out for you in the end. This isn't the story where the good guy wins. You need to back off Kenra."

"Payton," I drag out, shaking my head. "You don't understand—"

"No!" she shouts and steps closer to me. "*You* don't understand. *I* do. I've been the thorn they can't get rid of for the last three years, Parker. Me. And I understand *exactly* what's at stake for me. You? You have no clue what you're up against!"

"What the hell are you talking about?" I narrow my eyes, trying to read hers. "Are you—"

"We are *not* talking about me right now. This is about you!"

"What about me, Payton? Tell me what you're worried about because I can't read your damn mind."

"Do you like it here, Parker? Do you want to stay here and go to school, move forward in life?"

My brows furrow, but I nod. "Yeah, Peep, I do."

"Then, let. Her. Go."

My shoulders sag, and I glance off and then back. "I tried that before, and it didn't work. I won't fight it anymore, not for anyone. She wants this, too, Payton. It's not just me."

Tears fill her eyes, but she blinks them away. "That family? They're vicious. They won't just let her be with you if that's even what she wants. And they won't only take it out on her, Parker."

I step closer to her. "Are you saying Kenra *can't* leave?"

Payton's head pulls back, and her face scrunches. "Are you serious? How do you not know?" She chuckles in humorless disbelief.

"Know *what*, Payton?"

Her wide eyes flick between mine. "Why don't you take Mom's calls?"

"I—" My head snaps back at the sudden change in direction. "What?"

"Mom. Why don't you talk to her anymore?" she rushes out.

"I haven't talked to her in forever, Payton. Nothing new here."

"Right, yeah …" She trails off, her gaze dropping to the sand.

"Payton."

Slowly, her eyes lift to mine. "She threatened Deaton before. Did you know that?"

"What do you mean?"

"I mean, she threatened him, told him if he didn't break up with me, she would give his wrestling coach pictures of him smoking weed."

"Does he smoke weed?"

"Once! He did *once*. He was stupid and let some of our 'friends' at a party peer pressure him. Turned out, Mom had paid them to do it. His coach had a *no drugs or alcohol* policy, or you were off the team. There was *no* leniency. Without that team, he had *no* chance at getting a scholarship."

"His family's filthy rich."

"So is our mother, Parker! But you found another way, *right*? Well, for Deaton, this was his way out."

"But you're still together."

"Because he came to me!" she stresses. "Instantly. Because *I* was worth it to him. Don't you get it?"

"No!" I shake my head. "I don't!"

"Kenra!" she shouts. "She could have picked you, and she didn't!"

"Are you saying Mom threatened her?"

"Mom, Kellan, the entire Vermont fucking family! Now, Kenra's in their pockets. Do you know what that tells me? That tells me you weren't worth it to her." Payton starts crying, and right then, Deaton steps out of nowhere and makes his way over. "That tells me she doesn't love you! Don't let her ruin your life, Parker."

I go to step toward her, but Deaton swoops in, wrapping his arms around her.

He gives me a small, sad smile over her head.

Payton sniffles, grabbing on to Deaton's T-shirt. "I just don't want you to lose everything."

"Peep ..." I trail off, unsure of what to say or think.

And they start back for the house, so I follow quietly behind.

When she reaches the door, she turns, her blue eyes scanning mine, and her shoulders sag. "You'd give this all up for her, wouldn't you?"

"Yes."

She nods. "Make her tell you everything. Maybe together, if she decides she's brave enough, you guys can fight your way through it. If it's not already too late."

We step inside, closing the door behind us.

"Too late how?"

She opens her mouth to speak, but before words come out, there's a loud bang, followed by angry fists against the front door.

My brows jerk in, and Payton's eyes grow pained.

Everything inside me locks.

There's no fucking way.

I yank my door open, coming face-to-face with Kellan fucking Vermont. He shoves past me before I think to react, walking right into my house.

He spins to face me. "Where is she?"

And the shock wears off.

I step forward, ready to knock his ass out. "There's nothing here for you. Now, get the fuck out of my house."

He laughs obnoxiously, and I inch even closer. "Please, Parker, let's not pretend this ends any other way. Now"—his face contorts, and his true colors show through his glare—"where the fuck is Kenra?"

At that, Nate storms from the hall, shoving Kellan before he even sees him coming. He stands there, glaring, as Kellan regains his balance.

"Nate, my man." Kellan raises his hands, and Nate's fists tighten at his sides. "There's no bad blood here. I'm just looking to take my woman back home."

"She isn't here," I growl, fighting the urge to beat this guy to the ground.

The problem here is, Kellan would love that. He's probably hoping for it, so he can have me arrested even though he's the one who burst in here like he had the right.

Kellan lets out a half-chuckle before tilting his head in a nod. "Now, don't lie. She's here. Anytime she disappears like this, it's when you're involved. Every fucking time. But I assure you, this *will* be the last."

"You can't just barge in here like this." Deaton steps forward, shifting Payton behind him.

Kellan's gaze snaps toward his brother. "Keep your fucking mouth shut. And, while you're at it, get your shit, or it will be Mother dearest showing up next. Your ass is going home." He glances past him to look at Payton. "I'll be sure to let Ava know where you disappeared to."

My eyes narrow further. "You on a first-name basis with my mother?"

At that, Kellan stands tall with a smirk. "How do you think I kept Kenra in line while I was away at college those first few years?"

I go to rush him, but movement over his shoulder catches my eye, and I freeze. He sees it and spins.

Ari, Cam, and Kenra are making their way up the steps of the patio, their light laughter heard through the glass.

Kenra steps to the front to slide the door open, her eyes rising as she does, and her entire body goes rigid as her stare connects with the asshole who is here to get her.

Her hand flies to her ponytail and then pulls at the hem of her dress.

Nobody says a word. No moves are made until Kellan widens his stance. She takes the first step, and then he moves toward her.

I do nothing but watch him go. Nate, on the other hand, rushes behind him.

"Hero—"

"Not now, Lolli Bear."

She sighs as we watch Kenra hesitantly approach Kellan and step into his fake-as-shit welcoming hug, and my body starts to shake.

"Tell me she won't go," Lolli rushes out in a whisper, but I ignore her.

Kellan starts talking, "I'm glad you've had fun visiting your family, love, but we have some events coming up, and I would really like you to be there with me. Come home?" Their eyes are locked a moment before Kenra nods. "Perfect. Should I wait outside for you?"

Again, she nods, her lips smashed in a tight line.

He tips his chin, and I watch, completely fucking stunned and frozen where I stand as she steps into him, her lips—lips that were on *me* only minutes ago, lips that slid across *my* fucking body only last night—sliding across his.

My fists clench at my sides, and I jerk forward, but Payton's subtle touch on my elbow has me pausing to glance her way. Wide-eyed and afraid, she stares at me, begging me not to do or say anything. Truth is, I have no fucking clue what to do here.

I bite into my tongue to keep my feet still and look back to Kenra.

We all stand there, not a damn word spoken, as she steps past him, ignores all our stares, and disappears down the hall.

Kellan smooths his shirt down as he walks for the door, smirking as he passes. "I'll be out front. *Right* out front." He turns to Deaton with a glare. "Get your shit, Deaton." And then he storms out the front.

My fingers lock around the back of my head, and I start pacing.

"What the fuck, Parker?" Nate growls.

I drag my hands down my face. "Not now, man," I grumble, and then I rush down the hall, right into Kenra's room, and slam the door closed, locking it before Nate reaches and tries to pull it open.

She lifts her tearstained face to mine, and we both listen as Lolli drags a cussing Nate back down the hall.

She's changed, back into her Vermont-approved attire, fucking cardigans and slacks.

"Tell me what happened in Alrick."

She opens her mouth but quickly clamps it shut, her eyes lowering. "I can't."

"Tell me something. *Anything*. Give me something, Kenra,

because I can't just move on or wait or let you fucking go when you walk out that door. Not this time. Not after … you said you were ready. And I believed you, Kens." My shoulders sag, and she whimpers, her hand lifting to cover the sound as she cries. "If there's more going on here than just you wanting to leave, tell me. Let me help you."

"Parker," she whispers, and I fight to keep my composure when all I wanna do is drop to my knees and fuckin' beg. She lifts her eyes to mine. "Stop saving me. Let me fall."

I slowly shake my head and move to step in front of her. My thumbs come up to wipe away her tears, my fingers threading into the hair at the base of her neck.

Her hands fly up to grip my wrists, but she doesn't pull me off her. Deep creases take over her forehead as she closes her eyes.

"I won't, Kenra. I *can't*."

Her lids slowly lift, her eyes connecting with mine.

"I'll save you every chance I get. You fall; I fall."

She pulls back. "There won't be a chance after this, Parker. I won't be back. I won't be the reason you break again."

"You leave here; I break. You don't come back; I shatter. You live unhappy, unloved, and underappreciated, and I fucking *die* inside, Kenra. Please. Don't go."

She's full-on sobbing as she grabs her bag, refusing to meet my eyes as she steps past me for the door. "I'm sorry," she whispers. "But I changed my mind."

"I don't believe that," I croak, clearing my throat. "Not for a damn second, Kenra."

I step closer, until my chest is against her back, and she tenses before allowing her body to relax into mine.

"I don't believe you. There's a reason. I don't care what it is. *Nothing* is worth more to me than having you. Nothing." I wrap my arms around her, closing my eyes as I hug her from behind. Payton's words are fresh in my mind, so I lay it out there. "Tell me what's going on and let me decide. Show me I'm worth it to you."

She takes a deep breath, and I wait, holding mine.

And then my heart is pulled from my chest as she pulls herself from my arms.

And there it is.

Maybe I was never enough to begin with.

I take a second to regain myself and then follow behind her, down the hall and into the living room.

She doesn't look at anyone, doesn't lock eyes with her brother, who is desperately trying to get her to. She pauses beside Deaton, who holds Payton in his arms. "Time to go, Deaton," she whispers and steps for the door.

I glance at Lolli when I see her legs shift, and Nate's arms quickly lock around her waist.

Deaton sighs and ignores all our presence, turning to Payton, who is already crying.

"We didn't get a chance to talk," she whispers, placing her hands on his chest. "Deaton, I—"

"Shh, baby. It'll be okay." He cradles her face. "I know you're afraid, but I *know* we can do this. I promise you, Payton. We talked about getting away, starting a family later anyway. Now, we just get to do it sooner."

She cries but says nothing, and he drops his forehead to hers.

"Just you wait, baby. This is only the beginning." He rubs her belly, and her hand comes down to cover his. "I love you both. I'll take care of everything."

She nods, pulling him into a tight hug.

I lower onto the ottoman, staring at her back as she fights to keep her gaze on the floor.

The second Deaton steps back, Payton spins and runs down the hall. He looks from Kenra to the rest of us and shakes his head. He steps behind her. The second her wrist starts to turn, so she can pull the door open, Lolli yanks free of Nate's grip and hops to her feet, as expected.

"Kalani," Nate warns her to stay out of it, but knows just as well she won't.

Her tight glare flies to mine right as they step out the door, closing it behind them.

I drop my face into my hands with a deep sigh.

I knew this would happen. It always does.

I give Kenra everything I have, and she carries it with her on the way back to him.

I belong to her, but she doesn't wanna belong to me.

When Lolli's feet come into view, I drop my hands and look up at her.

"Don't ask me not to go out there because I have to."

"Just leave it, Lolli." I grab her hand and lightly squeeze. "It's okay."

"No, it's not." She crouches down in front of me. Her beautiful face is pained for me. Blue eyes clouded with emotions she's trying to hold in. My best friend's grown into a bit of a sap.

She reaches out but pulls her hand back at the last second. I know what she's gonna say. It makes sense. She wants to ease this moment a bit for Nate.

"That night in Mexico, when shit blew up in my face, you said to me, 'He doesn't get to do this to you.' I heard you. Hear me, Hero. She does not get to do this to you."

I stare at my friend, my face softening. "I invited it, Lolli Bear. It's just as much my fault."

"Why?"

"Because I love her. Always have and always will. Can't shake her. As long as she comes back, I'll be here."

"You deserve better." Her nose turns red as she fights tears.

I give her a sad smile. "I know that now. You helped me see that I should be enough. But I'm not when it comes to her, so nothing changes. I know my worth. She comes and goes, but my feelings for her stay. I can't help it."

"I hate it," she whispers, tears evident now.

"Me, too, Lolli. Me, too."

We stand there, listening to the car out front peel from the curb with a loud squeal, leaving hope in my sister's heart that everything will work out and a burning hole in mine knowing it won't.

CHAPTER 35
KENRA
Σμηρνιός

I'LL NEVER FORGET THE LOOK ON PARKER'S FACE THE MOMENT HE realized I was leaving.

There was no anger in his blue eyes, only defeat.

For years now, I've done nothing but break down his walls, tear away his hope, and I finally succeeded at destroying his defenses.

"I swear to fucking God, Kenra, you have pushed it for the last time. I didn't think you were so stupid, but something had me driving over to his house that next morning. And, sure enough, you were already gone."

"I needed to get him to go back home first. I was planning on leaving tonight."

"Don't fucking lie!" Kellan booms, cutting me a quick glare.

"I'm not," I snap. "You think I wanted you to show up there like that? I could have left quietly with no damn drama when everyone was asleep. My car is there after all."

"I already have someone picking up the car. And, speaking of asleep"—his eyes slice to mine and then back to the road—"where'd you sleep last night, Kenra?"

I meet Deaton's stare in the side mirror, and he gives a subtle shake of his head, telling me not to do it. He knows as well as I do that nothing good will come of it. But I have nothing to lose anymore.

I've lost the only thing I ever wanted, and the man beside me is the reason, so I steel my back and even out my voice as I reply calmly, "In his bed."

Kellan's hands tighten around the steering wheel until his knuckles turn white. "And where did he sleep?"

"Beside me."

Kellan snaps his eyes to me and bares his teeth. "Did you let him fuck you?"

"You guys," Deaton warns, "stop."

I don't know why, but I lift my chin and seethe back, "I *begged* him to."

"Kellan," Deaton stresses, but it's too late.

Kellan growls and yanks the wheel right, trying to catch the exit at the last second, but his speed is too high, and it's dark out, so he doesn't see the break in gravel between the road and the ramp. The car jerks.

Kellan loses control and the car flips.

I think I hear our own screams, the crush of metal as we come down hard on the driver's side and then tumble once more.

Blue eyes are all I see before everything goes black.

WHEN MY MOM TOLD ME SHE HATED ME, IT HURT. I KNEW WE didn't have the same type of relationship most other kids had with their parents. I knew I could hardly stand her as much as she seemed to only tolerate me, but to hear her flat-out admit she hated me still hurt.

Then, when my dad woke up one morning and stopped speaking to me, stopped even looking at me, that hurt worse.

Next, my sister was taken from me and then the hope of a future outside of Alrick if I didn't play by my mother's rules.

All those things sucked. But nothing compares to the crushing feeling of Kenra walking away.

She finally said it, told me she wanted me.

Gave herself to me.

Only she didn't. She basically loaned me her body. I'll never forget it but wish desperately I could.

It'd be better to never have had that piece of her than to know she'll be sharing it with him again.

Lolli sighs from her place on her swing.

I came out here about an hour ago, and she was right behind me. I lie in my hammock as she rocks in her swing, the ocean breeze the force behind our sway.

It's black out besides the shine of the moon. It's got to be after two in the morning now.

Footsteps in the sand behind us have our gazes looking that way.

Nate tips his chin, offering me a water bottle, which I take with a nod, and he turns to hand Lolli a hot cup of coffee. She smiles up at him as he tucks her hair behind her ear. He pauses there a moment before heading back for the house.

"I slept with her," I admit quietly.

She drops her head against the white wood, turning to look at me. "I know, Hero."

"I'm not. A hero. I couldn't save her. She wanted to be saved. Maybe not in the true sense of the word, but …" I think of her scars, both the ones on her skin and the ones that run much deeper. "From herself."

Lolli doesn't say anything, just stares straight ahead, clenching her warm mug between her little hands.

"Lolli Bear, tell me what you're thinkin'."

"You sure?"

"Yeah."

"I'm thinkin' I hate her. I kinda wanna kick her ass right now."

Despite the fucked up situation, I laugh lightly, and she gives a small grin.

"But …" I coax, knowing she's got more to say.

She nods, swallowing. "But I kinda think there's more going on here. Something's not right."

When her phone vibrates, she pulls it from her sweater pocket and frowns at the screen before meeting my gaze. "It's Al."

I sit up. "What time is it?"

She looks to her phone again. "Two fifteen."

"Answer it."

Her face pinches as she answers, putting the call on speaker, "Hey, Al."

"Hey, young one, did I wake you?"

"No, I'm up, but why are you, old man?" she teases, trying to calm herself, but I see her anxiety starting to kick in.

He gives a light chuckle, and she glances my way. "Listen, I need to meet with you, preferably in the next few hours."

"Is this about what I asked you to do for me, Al?" Lolli asks, cutting her eyes to mine.

My gaze narrows in question.

"Actually, I'm glad you mentioned that. No, this is something different, but I have everything you wanted ready to go. I'll bring it with me."

"Okay …"

"Listen, you and I might want to speak privately before we have a group meeting between the three of us."

Lolli is already shaking her head as he speaks even though he can't see her. "That won't be necessary, Al. He's family. In all around."

"Yes, young one," he answers quietly. "Whatever you want. I have to look into a thing or two right quick, but then I'm heading your way."

"Sounds good, Al."

Lolli hangs up and stares at me.

"What was that about?"

"I have no idea."

"What'd you ask him to do for you?"

"It's what I wanted to talk to you about. I had him draft papers for—"

"Yo! You guys need to get up here! Now!" Brady shouts from the distance.

Lolli and I look to each other, both jumping up and dashing for the house.

We run up the steps and past a crying Cam and Ari, finding Mason pacing and a wide-eyed Payton.

"What the fuck?" Lolli mutters, spinning all around until

she sees Nate in the corner, his phone to his ear, hand over his mouth.

He spots her, and they rush for each other. He pulls her against him.

"Okay." He nods, speaking into the line, "I love you, Dad. And tell Mom to ..." His eyes squeeze closed. "Just tell her I love her, and I'll see you guys there." He hangs up, and everyone wants to hear what he's about to say.

He glances from Lolli to Payton and then to me. "There's been an accident."

———

The three-hour drive to the hospital is the loudest silence I've ever heard, deafeningly so. We've gotten not a word from anyone. The only thing we were told was, "Get here," and it took a damn hour to get on the road.

Everyone was in a panic until both Brady and Chase took charge and evened us out enough to get us in the vehicles. So, it's Brady and Payton up front with me, Lolli, and Nate in the back-seat. Chase is following behind us with Ari, Cameron, and Mason.

As soon as the half-mile mark for the hospital is seen, everyone starts to shift in their seats. Lolli closes her eyes and drops her head back, her hand sliding into Nate's.

Brady pulls right up front and allows us to hop out, Chase doing the same with the others before they move to find a place to park.

"Come on, you guys, hurry!" Ari yells.

Everyone starts jogging toward the entrance, but when Lolli yanks her hand from Nate's, he whips around with a frown, and I pause to glance back.

Her eyes are wide as she stares at the large glass building, her complexion growing paler by the second.

"Baby"—Nate goes to grab her hand, and she pulls back—

"come on. We—" He cuts off, and my eyes fly to his. "Fuck," he whispers and steps into her, wrapping his arms around her.

My legs bounce to keep going, my eyes cutting to the building and then to her.

"Go," she tells me, and I start walking backward. She turns to Nate. "You, too. It's okay. I just … can't."

"I'm not leaving you out here."

"I've got her." Brady runs up with Chase, wrapping an arm around her.

Nate frowns but nods and catches up to me. Together, we run inside.

The others are waving us down at the end of the hall, so we rush to catch the elevators with them.

"They wouldn't tell us anything at the desk. Just said to go up to the fourth floor," Cameron tells us.

"Fourth floor is ICU." Mason meets Nate's stare and then shifts to comfort his sister.

I put my hand on Payton's shoulder, but she pulls away.

"Where's Lolli?" Ari asks Nate.

"Out front with the guys. She's … this is where her grandpa died. Where they brought her parents' bodies after the crash. She hasn't been back here since." He growls and kicks the side of the elevator.

"Hey, whoa, bro. Chill." Mason puts a hand on his shoulder.

"I should be out there with her," he rumbles, pissed at the world but directing it at Mason.

"Nah, man. She's a good woman. She'd kick your ass if you stayed out there. Your mama needs ya."

The doors open, and everyone fights to get out, rushing to the end of the hall where we find Mrs. Monroe already waiting with a few other women.

"Mom!" Nate shouts.

"Mom?" Ari calls out.

The women turn, and Sara rushes for Nate, who wraps her

in a hug. She starts crying uncontrollably, and my body locks tight.

Payton's hand shoots out to grab my wrist.

The others walk over to the other women—all the other moms I'm assuming.

Nate grabs his mom by the shoulders and pulls her back to look at her. "Ma?"

Tears fall from her eyes, and she shakes her head. "They said they lost control of the car, flipped it into a ditch."

"No," I breathe, and Payton's nails dig into my skin. "She's ..." I step forward, and Sara looks to me, her brows dipping just slightly.

"Mom!" Nate shouts. "Is Kenra okay?"

"Yes, sweetheart," she whispers, reaching up to cup his cheek. "She's okay." Her eyes slide to mine and back. "But we're not in the clear yet. She's unconscious. They're running tests."

I blow out a harsh breath, turning away from everyone as I squeeze my eyes shut. Pushing my palms into my eye sockets to keep myself in check.

She has to be okay ...

A tingling starts at my toes and spreads through my body, and my skin grows warm and clammy. This is a different feeling, not like her walking away.

Her leaving is one thing; her being *gone* is another.

"You!" someone shouts.

I spin around, and all our eyes snap to the privacy door that has just opened to find a polished woman pressed in a white pantsuit, rushing our way.

Her heels clink across the floor as she pushes her way between us.

"Excuse me, miss. I—" Mason is cut off when the woman's hand rises, and she shocks us all when she slaps my sister right across her face.

Everyone starts screaming and yelling. Nate moves to

restrain the woman while I pull Payton beside me, and Mason steps forward to block her.

They're still arguing, but I look to Payton to make sure she's all right. A single glance tells me she's not. Her face is void. No tears, no anger or shock. No nothing.

She stumbles then, and I catch her as her back hits the wall.

"Payton?" I call wearily.

Her eyes lift slowly, but they don't connect with any of ours. They slide right past us, landing on the solid white doors with big red letters.

She stares at the ICU entrance, and her muscles go slack.

"Payton!" I drop with her, easing her fall as her feet slide until her ass meets the hard floor. Mason's at her other side in a flash. "Payton, talk to me."

Her lids close, her hand moving to cover her stomach, and it hits me.

My head snaps to the woman, eyes narrowing in recognition.

No …

She glares down her nose at Payton, her eyes wild but free of tears. "This is *all* your fault, little girl. Every time you think of my son, remember that. I told you, you didn't deserve him. This must be the world's way of proving me right."

"Whoa, what the fuck, lady?" Mason hops up, and his mother instantly scolds him. "Uh-uh. No way, Mama. This lady just—"

"This lady just lost her son, Mason," his mother whispers quietly.

At that, Payton's body goes limp, her hand flopping to hit the cool ground as her chin hits her chest.

"Peep." I bend to look at her face, brushing her hair from her eyes, but she won't look at me.

The elevator doors burst open, and in run Brady and Chase.

"What the hell?" Chase drops beside Payton, lifting her face to look at him.

I hear Nate ask where Lolli is, but I can't look away from my broken baby sister.

My chest grows heavy, and I swallow. "Can you, uh, get her out of here, will ya?"

Chase gives a curt nod, lifting her in his arms.

His mom steps forward, placing a hand on his back in support.

"Hi, Mama."

"Hey, baby," she speaks low. "There's a small room down the hall for families; there's a couch in there."

Again, Chase nods and then glances at Ari, who offers him a sad smile, and starts down the hall.

Right then, a familiar voice grates in my ear, and the hairs at my neck stand.

"That won't be necessary."

I spin, eyes wide until they land on her. Her smirk grows as my gaze narrows. No remorse, no comfort for her daughter is found in her blue eyes. If it wasn't so disgusting to realize, I'd say I might see joy in them.

"Get the hell out of here, both of you!" Mrs. Vermont screams.

My mother rolls her eyes. "Please, Miranda, give it a rest. I only came to collect my daughter. I couldn't care less what happens to your boys."

"You bitch!" Miranda shrieks.

"Are you people insane?" Sara shrieks, hiccupping through tears. "Our children were hurt tonight! And not just the ones in that car. All of them!"

My mother's eyes fly to mine. Every muscle in my body tightens as a grin starts to form on her Botox-filled lips, but before she has a chance to throw me under the bus for my relationship with Kenra, the nurse steps out the door.

She addresses my mother, "Ma'am, if you would please make your way into the lobby to your left. This is for immediate family *only*, and it seems you have none here."

She looks down on the woman, making it a point to look from her shoes to her badge around her collar, trying to belittle her as best she can. "I will *not* be sitting in that germ-infested space. I'll step outside a moment." She locks her glare with mine. "I *will* be back, and if you want to avoid going to jail for kidnapping a minor, *sister* or not, Payton will be here when I do." With that, she spins and slowly walks back the way she came.

Nate catches my eye and then turns back to once again gain his mother's attention. "Ma, what happened? And how'd you get here so fast? Where's Dad?"

"I caught a red-eye, but there was only one seat, so Dad's coming in on the next one. Your aunt and the others picked me up at the airport. We only got here a couple of minutes before you."

"What do we know?" Brady asks, moving to kiss his mom's forehead.

"Not much," Nate mumbles.

Tears start to fall from Sara's eyes again, and Nate moves to wrap his arms around her.

"They said Kenra's unconscious, but from what they could tell, she had nothing major wrong. Nothing visibly broken, just cuts and bruises. They said she hit her head against the window, but the airbag saved her life by lessening the impact." Sara sniffs, fighting to calm her breathing. "They're running a bunch of tests on her now. They're worried about swelling in her brain, but she's expected to be okay."

"Expected?" I breathe, the wind getting knocked out of me at her words.

Sara's eyes jump to mine. "We just have to wait, honey."

"And Kellan?" I ask, a mixture of anxiousness and uncertainty causing pressure on my chest.

"He's in surgery. So far, they said he had a broken elbow and ankle, a punctured lung. They said he almost drowned in his own blood just before paramedics got there." She covers her mouth with her hand, shaking her head. "God, could you imagine? That family could have lost both their sons tonight."

"And Deaton?" I ask quietly. "How'd he ... what happened?"

"There were no airbags in the back, and when they flipped, his head ..." She gets choked up. "They said he died instantly."

"But Pretty Little ... she's ..." Mason's eyes jump to mine, his forehead creasing from the thought of her pain.

When I drop my eyes to the floor, he lifts his hands to cover his face.

"Fuck!"

"Mason, language," his mom quietly reminds him, and he storms off, punching the wall as he goes.

Sara looks to me, her curiosity lacing her tear-stained face. "Pretty little?"

"Payton."

"She and Deaton were a couple?"

"Yes, ma'am," I whisper.

She nods. "She's your sister?"

"She is."

"That poor girl ..." She trails off, and the women step forward to hug her.

That's the last thing said for the next two hours until the double doors open.

A man in a white jacket steps through, and Sara tenses and then turns to him. Everyone shields her as he comes closer, and I swear, I've never felt so heavy.

"Mrs. Monroe?"

"Yes," she whispers, gripping Nate by his arm.

"I'm Dr. Bennett. I wanted to let you know your daughter's tests have come back, and everything looks clear. She was very lucky the airbag went off when it did. We see no major damage or areas of concern. She will have a heck of a headache for a few days."

Sara starts sobbing, and Nate's nostrils flare as he tries to keep it together. And I can't handle it; moisture builds in my eyes, and I squeeze them shut to blink it away.

"She does have two cracked ribs, but those will have to heal on their own. Not much we can do but wrap them and help keep her comfortable with medication. Other than that, it just appears she has some expected bruising and fresh cuts." He glances off, tapping the side of his clipboard a moment, and my muscles tense.

Her scars.

I know that's what he's thinking about. He wants to mention it, but he has no right. I know how confidentiality works. They aren't related to the accident, so he can't say a word.

Nate sighs. "When can we see her?"

"We're getting her cleaned up and moved now. After she's hooked up and settled, we'll let you know. Few short hours." He glances around at us all. "Unfortunately, it will be immediate family only for the first twenty-four hours."

Everyone nods in understanding.

"And Kellan?" Sara asks. "How is he?"

"I'm afraid I can't share that with you, Mrs. Monroe. I realize he and your daughter were engaged; however, that doesn't give me permission to openly discuss his case with you."

She nods lightly. "I understand."

She thanks the doctor, who excuses himself and moves down the hall to Kellan's mom, and then everyone moves to shift into the private waiting room, but I slip past them, ignoring Nate's questioning frown as it follows me to the nurses' station.

The woman, the one my mother was a bitch to, glances my way. "What can I do for you?"

I clear my throat, glancing over my shoulder quickly before turning back to her.

I keep my voice low. "Kenra Monroe—"

"Are you family?" she cuts me off.

I narrow my eyes. "She's being moved into a private room right now. Her family is here, worried to death and desperate to see her. When they do, they won't be able to help the guilt they'll feel for her being in that bed even though it makes no sense."

The woman sits back in her chair, her face smoothing out as she listens.

"Because that's what good family does. They worry. She'll be in there, unconscious, and they'll wanna hold her hand and whisper how much they love her, begging her to wake up," I croak out the last two words, clearing my throat to try to get a handle on myself. "That girl has a secret they don't know about, one that might hurt her family more than this accident has."

When her brows furrow, my gaze flits between hers.

"I need you to save those people in there from any more heartache tonight."

"How?" she whispers.

"Wrap her arms from her wrists to just below her elbows. Palms if it's possible."

The woman's head pulls back slightly, and then her face goes slack as realization dawns.

Tears fill her eyes, and she slowly stands from the chair. With a small nod, she disappears through the double doors, and I turn back to find Nate leaning against the wall with his arms crossed, his eyes narrowed on me.

When I get closer, his jaw gets harder, but he kicks off and disappears into the room.

And that's good because I don't have it in me to get into anything with anyone right now.

I peek in on Payton, finding both her and Chase passed out, her in his lap, him against his fist, and I keep going.

I make my way out to the bottom floor and head out the side entrance.

I step into the cool morning air and fight for a deep breath.

It's still dark out, so I move to find a small corner beside the building, and I fucking cry.

I had her. She was mine for a night.

Then, she left me, like she always does, and the cruel world got even crueler, stepped in, and tried to take her from me for good. And I'm fucking over it.

I've *been* tested. I've loved her and lost her, and I'm still here.

Still so far gone on the girl who cries on the inside and smiles on the out.

I'm convinced I'm the only one who can bring her back to being her.

And I will. Because I'm her safety.

And I'll be her defense, protect her from anyone who gets in her—in *our*—zone even if I have to protect her from herself.

I don't care what happens today, tomorrow, next fucking month.

In the end, it's her and me.

It has to be.

CHAPTER 37
PARKER

Σμυρνας

Nate sighs for the hundredth time as he ends his call with Lolli.

"She threatened to hold out on ya again if you go out there with her?" Mason teases to try to lighten the mood. It works a little, and Ari and Cameron give half-grins while Nate chuckles quietly.

He looks off with a nod, a deep crease in his brows. "Yeah, man. Something like that." He brings his hands up to scrub them down his face. "I hate this shit. I feel like I'm picking sitting up here instead of being there for her, and I'm not. I wanna go down there, but she's stubborn as hell. Fightin' me tooth and nail."

"Yeah"—Brady leans forward, resting his elbows on his knees— "'cause she knows your mama needs you. She ain't mad, my man. She's proud you're up here, doing what's right by your family."

"She's gonna be my fucking wife. *She's* my family just as much, if not more now."

Brady nods. "Yeah. She is, but your sister's hurt, your mama's sad, and your pops ain't here yet. And Lolli?" He holds Nate's stare. "Lolli's all right."

With a huff, I move to stand, and all eyes shift to me.

259

"I'm gonna go check on Payton. See if she or Chase needs anything," I let them know and head for the private room down the hall.

When I reach the small room, I find Payton still asleep, her body now cradled in Chase's lap.

He gives me a tight nod when I open the door and step in.

"Hey, man," I speak quietly. "She ... said anything yet?"

"Not a word," he whispers.

"This is so fucked up," I mutter, lowering myself into the chair across from them, and my head drops to my chest.

"She told us they'd split up."

When my eyes lift to his, he stares.

"Kenra. She said she and Kellan had broken up, called off the wedding. Was that a lie?"

I drop back in the chair. "Yeah, man. That was a lie. Far as she told me, she was planning on leaving him. Then, all of a sudden, today happened, and she just ... left with him. Just like that."

"She's in love with you, isn't she?"

I clench my jaw and glance off with a deep breath.

"She's never said it," he realizes out loud, and my eyes snap to his. He sighs. "And neither have you."

"She knew. She knows."

"When she wakes up, you need to tell her. Don't wait any longer, man."

I eye him. "You thinking 'bout doing the same thing with Arianna?"

His gaze cuts from mine. "I don't know what you're talking about."

A chuckle leaves me. "Come on, man. Your squad's not in here."

He drops his head back and blows out a harsh breath before looking back to me. "I don't know what's going on with me and Ari. I used to be able to push thoughts aside, but lately ... all of us being at that house, having her right there all the time ..." He licks his lips and looks away. "It's not as easy to keep myself away."

"I don't think she wants you to."

"I know she doesn't. But Mason's my best friend, and I can't mess with that. Besides, you see how he is with her and Cameron and even Lolli now. Shit, he's full caveman with Payton, and he's known her for a week."

We both laugh lightly, and Payton stirs in Chase's arms.

Her blue eyes open, shifting around a moment before squeezing shut again.

I drop down in front of her, running my hand over her hair. "Peep ..." I whisper, and her empty eyes slowly fight to reach mine.

"Parker ..." Her voice breaks, and she shifts to wrap her arms around me. "Can I go home? *Home to your house* home?"

"Are you sure, Payton?" I whisper into her hair, and she starts nodding against me. "I'm not sure any of us will head back there for a while."

"I'm sure. I don't want to be here. Please."

Chase catches my eyes and nods lightly. "I'll take her home. Stay with her."

"You sure?" I ask, and Payton pulls back to look at him.

He offers her a sad smile and nods. "Yeah, man. I got her."

I thank him and stand, and he does the same, still not putting her down.

Unfortunately, when we make it a few feet down the hall, we hear the arguing, and my mother's voice shouts louder than all the others.

"Where the hell is she?"

I rush ahead of the two, quickly coming around the corner. All the yelling stops as my mother and Nate spot me, and her cold blue eyes slice to mine.

"I gave her long enough."

"She needs to be with people who care about her right now. Not someone who treats her like a puppet."

Chase steps around the corner right then, and Mason hops up from his seat, quickly moving to stand beside them, behind me.

"Put her down," my mother snaps. "She needs to learn to live with disappointment. It's *life*. And we're leaving."

"She's not going anywhere with you," Chase calmly tells her, and Brady moves to take Chase's other side.

"Put. My daughter. Down," she seethes, her face turning red.

"Get the hell out of here, Ava," I growl. "Now is not the time for this shit. For once in your life, be a good mother and let her have some time before you start your shit again. Please."

"Time for what?" she shouts. "It's not like it happened in front of her, and she's sixteen! So, her little crush is no more. Not my problem! Deaton is dead. She'll get over it!"

"Oh my God!" Nate's mom hops up, and Nate is quick to move in front of her.

And, finally hearing the words, Payton starts to wail. She is still cradled in Chase's arms, and he tucks her into him more.

My fists clench at my sides as I stare at the evil woman in front of me. "Leave, Ava. She's not going anywhere with you."

"Shall I call the police?" Her stony eyes harden. "Payton is a minor. She never should have left Alrick. And she sure as hell doesn't get to decide to stay here. *I* still control her."

"You, Ava Baylor, are a sick, twisted *bitch*."

My mom gasps, and all our heads swing to find Lolli standing just a few feet away, Al right beside her.

"Oh, look." My mom crosses her arms. "The whore who made my son fall in love with her, only to love his friend and force him to watch it."

Nate goes to step toward Lolli, but Sara places a hand on his chest, her eyes on Lolli as protective as his. But Lolli is not a weak soul; she's not like the people my mother is used to. I think Sara knows it.

Lolli's face is blank as she stares. "You need to leave."

A surprised chuckle spits from my mother. "Of course, I'll get on that. I will *leave* when Payton is following behind me, as she should."

"Payton won't be going anywhere," Lolli tells her calmly.

At that, Chase takes it upon himself to leave with her in his arms.

My mom narrows her eyes and steps right up to Lolli, who is completely unfazed. "Watch yourself, little girl, or I'll take what you treasure most. It's my strong suit."

Now, it's Sara who tries to step forward, but her son holds her back.

While Lolli's face doesn't change, there's a flare in her eyes at that. "You come within a *state* of him, and I'll flip your life upside down without thinking twice. You wanna play with no rules, lady? Fine. I'm game."

"Who the hell do you think you are? You have no idea who you're dealing with!"

"Don't care. I don't need to know you to *know you*. What you've done to your son is enough. Parker is *my* family now. Payton, too, for that matter."

"You can have the boy. Hell"—she spins to smirk at me and then Nate— "you probably already have. But Payton—"

Lolli steps forward, cutting my mother off, "Go now, or I'll share the offshore accounts my friend Al here helped me track down."

My eyes fly to my mother, and for the first time in as long as I can remember, her defenses slip a bit, her hands dropping to the strap of her bag, as if needing something to keep her standing.

"I don't know what—"

"Sure you do. But don't worry. This isn't me threatening you. We don't want nor need your money. None of us, not even Payton. We just want you to go away. If or when your daughter decides to talk to you, she'll reach out. In the meantime, Al here has emancipation papers ready for you to sign. Payton belongs with her brother, with us. People who care for her. And that's not you."

Ava's eyes fly across the group, pausing on me a moment before landing back on Lolli. She opens her mouth to speak, but Lolli cuts her off again.

"Nobody standing here gives a damn, Ava. Save it, sign the paper, and get the fuck outta here."

Ava smooths her shirt down and lightly pushes her long blonde hair over her shoulder. She eyes Lolli a moment before all but snatching the paper from her hands.

Lolli quirks a dark brow at her, and Ava spins to me and then looks to Sara and back.

"There's always a second villain." She smirks, addressing no one directly but making sure it's heard around the room. "You got rid of one, but the other won't be so easy. He *is* still alive." She tilts her head. "Right?"

"Get out of here, Ava." I glare.

"What the hell is she talking about?" Sara asks, panic in her voice, and Nate rubs her back.

Al motions for Ava to lead the way, and the two disappear. Just like that, she is trading her daughter for her money.

Everyone glances around, taking a minute to catch their breaths, while Nate rushes for Lolli.

She steps into him, turning to speak to me, "I'll explain everything."

I nod. I owe her huge for this, for everything really. She's not only saved me now, but she's also saved my baby sister.

"Family, Parker," she whispers. "You're my family."

I swallow the lump in my throat and look off.

"What did she mean about a villain?" Sara asks again. "It sounded like she meant—"

"Come on, Ma. We don't need to worry about that right now."

"Mrs. Monroe?"

All our heads jerk to the doorway we didn't hear open with all the commotion.

She grips Nate's arm. "Yes?"

"Your daughter is all set up in her room now," Dr. Bennett tells her, and a small smile finds his lips. "She's also woken up."

Sara breaks down, her head dropping into her hands, and moisture fills my eyes. I swallow to force it away, but fuck.

She's awake.

"If you hurry back, you might catch her before she's out again. She's on some heavy medications to keep her pain tolerable—that, and her body is exhausted. But please, only two at a time until the nurses finish up, should only be a few more minutes, but even then, it's still only immediate family for the first twenty-four hours."

Sara rushes forward and goes to pull Nate along with her, but right then, the elevator doors burst open, and Ian Monroe, Nate's dad, charges down the hall.

"Sara!" he shouts, his eyes wide and panicked when he sees the doctor standing there, fresh tears running down his wife's face. "My baby girl…"

"Honey, she's awake," Sara cries, her body shaking with her tears of relief.

Ian blows out a hard breath, his eyes wet and red. He yanks her into him, and their bodies mold into each other.

"Mrs. Monroe."

"Yes, sorry." She pulls back, and Ian wipes her cheeks. "We're coming." She turns to Ian. "We have to hurry if we want to catch her awake."

Ian nods and doesn't move his arm from his wife's middle as she starts walking. He looks over the room, nodding at everyone, clamping a hand on Nate's shoulder as he walks by.

When they walk through the door, everyone starts hugging and crying in joy.

Nate pulls Lolli in, squeezing her tight, and I close my eyes, my body fighting for relief among the chaos.

"Oh!" Ian shouts, and we glance to the door just before they close. "I brought a few others along; thought you could use 'em right about now." He tips his chin before disappearing, and all heads turn toward the elevator.

Austin, Nate's best friend, smirks, and Nate laughs, rushing toward him for a bro hug.

When I look to Lolli, I find she's just standing there, frozen, and then her eyes shift to mine.

My features soften, and a crease forms between her eyes.

"You went to see her, didn't you?" she asks me in a whisper. "When you were in Alrick? She never would have come if not."

"Soon as Kens dropped me at my house."

"Why?"

I shrug and offer her a gentle smile. "Family, right?"

Tears fill her blue eyes, and she nods, looking past me.

Lolli swallows and then smiles a bit. "Hey, Meems."

"Hi, Lolli," Mia whispers back.

Both girls start crying as they step forward to hug each other.

I excuse myself and head for the private room Payton was in earlier.

I lie back, stare at the ceiling, and refuse to accept an ending that doesn't give me my nightingale.

I HEAR THEM AS THEY STEP UP TO THE DOOR AND QUICKLY CLOSE MY eyes.

I can't face them yet. I have no clue what to say.

They think I lost a baby. They were hurting for me for this reason when I left them, and now, here they are, hurting even more. Having almost lost their daughter because I was too weak to walk away before Kellan grew overly calculating.

I hear my mom's soft sobs and my dad's calming comfort. I picture him holding her close, trying to take her pain.

"We missed her," my mom whispers. "She's asleep again."

"I'm sorry, Mrs. Monroe, but expect her to come in and out. At least over the next few hours."

"Did anyone explain what's happened to her? Do we know if she remembers?"

"She remembers. She was completely coherent when she awoke. Exhaustion sets in to help the body heal when a trau-matic event occurs. As far as the … condition of the other passengers, no, ma'am. We didn't quite get to that."

I fight to keep my expression neutral but can feel my brows pinch slightly, my already tight muscles constricting even more.

"It's okay, sweetheart," my mother whispers, and I wish she could pull me into a hug. "We're here. You're okay."

But am I?

I'm tied to a man I hate and can't leave. I slept with a man I love but can't have.

And I have no idea how to fix it.

So, I play the helpless coward I am and lie there, still, until the blackness takes over again.

Σμυρνιός

"I GOT A CALL FROM THE GENERAL MANAGER OF THE TOMAHAWKS, and it seems a petition has gone out," Al tells me and Lolli. "They're voting on having you removed from the board, Miss Embers."

"Al, stop calling me Miss Embers. And what the fuck does that mean? Can they do that?"

"It means you'll be pushed off as another silent investor, but decisions—the parts where I come in and what we're set to train Parker in—will no longer be in your control."

"I own fifty percent of the fucking team. I have the most shares, the most invested. This is my fucking team, Parker's future."

"I know, which is why I asked for a meeting before voting happens. But I need you to understand that, if they decide to vote and it comes down to a fight, your age and decision in bringing in Mr. Baylor will work in their favor. Nothing against you, son." He looks to me. "But, in a greedy man's eyes, you're nothing but a boy."

"I understand."

"Well, I fucking don't." Lolli frowns. "Fifty percent, Al. My grandpa worked years to get half of the team for this reason. I might be young, but I feel this sport in my blood. And Parker is the only one who can keep that passion and still make the right decisions; I know it. I won't let this happen."

"I know, and like I said, I've called a meeting for Thursday."

"It's Saturday."

"It's the best I could do, the only time everyone could be there." He sighs and offers a small smile. "We'll figure it out. Try not to worry too much."

"Right," Lolli whispers and moves to stand. She turns for the hall and disappears.

Al is slow to stand. "Hate having to tell her things like this, but it's best she has a warning, just in case."

I nod. "I get it. Thanks for coming by Al. And for taking care of all the paperwork for Payton. She'll be much happier here."

Al smiles at that. "You're welcome. And that was all Miss Embers' idea."

"I know."

"Get you some sleep if you can, son. I'll call you guys if anything comes up."

"Night, sir."

Not five minutes after Al leaves, the double doors open, and Nate walks out.

He drops in the chair beside me, letting his head back to hit the wall behind us. "She's faking it."

My head snaps in his direction, but only his eyes slide to mine.

"Kenra. She's not fucking sleeping, man. Her reactions give her away every time. My parents are too freaked out to see it, so I sure as hell didn't point it out. But she's awake, Parker. And she won't fuckin' open her eyes and give them peace of mind."

"You sure?"

"I'm positive."

When my forehead creases, his gaze narrows.

"My mom is fucked up, dude. Dad's fucked up even more 'cause she is. Kenra needs to open her eyes and show them she's still here." His eyes flit between mine, and suddenly, he hops up and starts back for the doors. He glances over his shoulder. "Come on."

I pop up, my muscles tight, and hurry behind him. "They said, immediate family only."

"Yeah, well, I'm done seeing my mom cry helpless tears."

I freeze two feet from the door, and he turns to face me.

He throws his arms out. "What? Why are you stopping?"

"Why do you want me in there?"

He frowns. "Because, man, I know she'll open her eyes for you. She won't be able to help herself."

My throat goes tight, and I glance off.

"I see it now, Parker. You and her. I get it. And I need your fucking help," he says low, and my eyes shift back to his. His shoulders sag as he stares. "I don't know what happened when you guys left or why she went with Kellan when he showed up. I have no fucking clue, and to be honest, I'm kinda pissed at her, which has made this whole thing harder for me. I know seeing her won't be easy on you, and it's probably a real fucking bad idea for it to be in front of my parents, but ... I need you, man. Please."

"I want to. More than fucking anything, I want to go in there and see for myself that she's okay, that she's alive. But you gotta know ... they won't understand, Nate. It might be worse for them."

"She'll open her eyes, Baylor, and they'll be able to breathe."

"I'm not gonna fight you on it. I want in there too damn bad. If you're sure."

His eyes flit between mine, and he nods. "Let's go inside."

When he spins to hit the button on the wall so that the nurses can open the doors, I step beside him.

We step through, and the woman looks between the two of us.

"My brother," he tells her.

Her eyes tighten around the edges, but she waves us on, and not ten feet later, we're standing in front of room 237.

A blinding pain starts at my ribs and spreads through my chest as I stand there, shaking my limbs out. I close my eyes and take a deep breath, looking to Nate.

"Come on, man," he whispers, having to force my feet the rest of the way in the room with a grip to my shoulder.

My eyes instantly land on her, and my muscles grow stiff, a cramp forming in my jaw from the pressure of my grinding teeth. She has a thick bandage around her head and a few small cuts on her cheeks, bruising at her collarbone, and a cut lip.

Nate's parents swivel around, but I don't glance their way. I slowly step to the opposite side of her.

Nate quietly cuts his dad off when he goes to speak and whispers something I can't hear over the pounding in my ears.

I carefully lower myself onto her hospital bed, sitting so I'm facing her as she lies there.

I watch her closely, not saying a word, and the crinkles at the edges of her eyes grow more defined.

She is awake.

I take a deep breath and cut my glance to Nate then Sara, her wide eyes flying between me and Kenra. And then I look at Ian, and he stares hard before giving a curt nod and looking to his daughter.

I turn back to Kenra, leaning forward a little. The closer I get, the more my pulse spikes, and her chest rises.

She feels me.

I lean in, bringing my head closer to hers until I can whisper near her ear, "Open up, baby ..."

Sara gasps lightly, so I pull back to look at Kenra's face.

Her eyes are clenched tight now, a tear slipping from the corner, but before it hits the pillow, I wipe it away, and her eyes pop open, locking with mine.

I get choked up and swallow hard. Her big brown eyes are full of heartache and remorse. Sara instantly starts sobbing, and Ian chuckles through his emotions.

I drop my head to her shoulder without giving her my weight, and she shifts slightly, so her lips brush my temple.

I shift again to see her, and her lips start to tremble. It's a sight I can't stand to see, one too strong for me to stay strong, and everyone else fades away.

It's only me, desperate to save her, and her, wishing I would.

So, I ease her the only way I know how in this moment—by shifting closer and cupping her cheeks in my hands.

Instantly, her muscles relax, and her eyes flutter closed on a shuddered exhale.

I kiss her. Simply. Softly.

Slowly.

When I touch my forehead to her bandaged one, she finally speaks.

My name falls from her lips, and I hate how helpless it sounds, but I love that she said it just as much.

Her eyes cut to the right, so I pull back, moving to sit up, as she stares at her parents, who sit there with frowns and frozen expressions, but they quickly snap out of it when Kenra croaks, "Mom, Daddy."

Her mother starts to sob and I look away, catching Nate and now Lolli standing behind them. She winks and tucks into Nate's side while he slightly tips his chin in thanks.

I move to stand, but her hand that lies still at her side quickly shifts to touch me, asking me to stay, so I do.

"Kenra, baby, you're awake," her mom cries. "Are you okay? How do you feel? What can I do, baby?"

"I'm okay," she whispers. "Sore but okay."

Nate and Lolli step forward, and she gives a weak smile. "Hey."

"Hey." Nate frowns, and Lolli gives a small side smile.

"Should we get a doctor?" her mom asks and moves to push the Call button on the hospital bed.

Kenra lifts her hand the best she can in her exhausted state.

"No, Mom, wait …" She trails off, looking between her parents. "Tell me about the others. Where's Kellan and Deaton?"

When my body grows tense against her, her eyes fly to mine, and she frowns instantly, her gaze flying back to her mom, fresh tears building. "Mom?"

"Kellan was rushed to surgery, but we're pretty sure he's out now. His mom hasn't come out of the room for us to ask, and the doctors refuse to share information since we're not technically family. I'm so sorry, baby." Sara cuts a quick glance my way.

"Deaton," Kenra rushes out. "Where's Deaton? Did they let Payton see him? He needs her in there. He hates his family."

"Honey …" Sara's voice cracks, her head tilting, as tears take over, and Ian wraps his arms around her from behind.

"No," Kenra whispers, shaking her head. "Mom, say no."

"He died on impact."

A harsh breath of disbelief leaves Kenra, and she starts sobbing, burying her face in her hands. "It's my fault."

"No, honey—"

Her eyes flash back, and Sara stops talking, slightly confused.

"It is. We were fighting, Kellan and me, and I pushed the wrong buttons. Kellan jerked the car, trying to get to the side to pull off, and lost control. It was my fault." Kenra's eyes flash back to mine, and her lips tremble. "It's my fault … and now, Payton—"

"Stop," I whisper, moving closer. "Don't even think it. Don't make excuses for him anymore, Kens."

"What the hell is he doing in here?"

All our gazes snap toward the door, finding Miranda Vermont standing there.

"*Why* is he in here? He shouldn't be anywhere near her."

I hop to my feet, and her eyes narrow.

"Whoa, now …" Ian slowly shifts to stand. "First of all, keep your voice down. Second—"

"Don't think you can tell me what to do, Mr. Monroe. It won't happen."

Sara jumps from her chair and moves to stand in front of Miranda.

Nate's forehead pinches in worry while Lolli grins.

"Don't think you can come in my daughter's room and have any damn say as to what happens in it. Especially when you refuse to give us any updates on Kellan. It would have been nice to put our daughter's mind at ease."

Miranda spits out a mocking laugh. "Please. It would ease her to hear he was dead."

Sara's brows dip, and she looks back to Kenra, who simply stares at Miranda.

"He's alive, by the way. He's still unconscious and on oxygen, but we're confident he'll wake."

"We appreciate the update, but maybe it's best if you go."

"Me?" Her lip tips up slowly. "I'm here to get settled in. Kellan is being moved in here as we speak."

I choke on my spit and start coughing, earning a glare from her.

"What do you mean?" Sara drags out. "They're letting them share rooms?"

"Of course." Her eyes harden, locking on to Kenra's.

"Don't …" she whispers desperately, and my lungs grow sore.

"It's not the honeymoon he had in mind, but … what can we do?" She pops a shoulder, and every jaw in the room drops. "You know, I could use a coffee. I'll be back in a jiff."

Honeymoon.

No.

Her parents turn to ask her something, but I know she's looking at me, and I can't bring myself to meet her stare.

I step away from the bed, dodging her touch when she reaches out.

I lick my lips, and in what feels like slow motion, I move toward the door.

"Parker, please," she whispers. So broken. So fucking shattered.

But so am I.

I'm broken down. Out of options and out of time.

Out of fucking hope.

And completely gutted.

CHAPTER 40
KENRA

I watch Parker go, my shredded heart right there with him.

This is not how he was supposed to find out. Not how any of them were supposed to find out, but Parker's face when Miranda said honeymoon …

I might have done it this time.

Ruined everything.

"Kenra, sweetheart, talk to us," my mom whispers.

I turn to look at her.

Nate walks over and sticks a straw in my face, his face blank. I take a drink of the water he's offering and smile in thanks, but he turns and walks to set it down.

I look between my mom and dad.

They're amazing people, true, honest, and good souls of the world.

They deserve the daughter they raised to be the same.

So, I suck up my pride and start with the simplest, most honest statement I have in me at the moment. "I made a mistake."

Both their expressions tighten as they will me to continue, but I can't. This is my doing, and I need time to process. Time to think.

I can't tell them all they want to hear, but I can ease their pain a little.

I reach for both their hands, and they eagerly place them in mine.

I look into both their eyes. "He lied to you."

My mom's brows furrow, and she reluctantly pulls her gaze from mine briefly to glance at my dad. My dad, however, stares right into me, digging deep until he finds it, and his head drops onto the mattress. His shoulders start to shake in silent sobs he can't fight, and my mom's eyes instantly tear up. She rubs his back, and his free hand moves to grip her knee.

She doesn't understand, but she doesn't need to in order to comfort her husband. It's pure need to ease his pain.

Nate moves to stand behind them, his eyes shifting around the three of us.

Slowly, my dad's head lifts, his gaze flitting between mine. "You didn't ... there was no baby?"

My mother gasps, her hands flying to her mouth, and tears fill my eyes.

"No, Daddy," I whisper, shame burning in me. "There was no baby."

"Why would he ... why would you ..." My mother trails off.

"He's not what you think he is, and I'm ..." I whisper, my eyes on the blanket, but before I can say more, the nurses stroll through, a bruised and battered Kellan lying lifeless in the hospital bed they're pushing.

Everything in me locks as I stare at him. Normally so attractive and charming to the outside world, he's now a helpless, unrecognizable man, swollen and discolored, cast on his arm and foot. He deserves for the world to see him this way. As ugly as his soul. As sickening as it might be, I wish he hadn't made it out.

That he'd never wake up.

Miranda strolls back in then and stops to glare at everyone before turning to the nurse. "Excuse me, but could you please ask the guests to leave? My son needs his rest. Doctor's orders and all."

The nurse frowns, looking from my family to Miranda. "This is her room, too. Her family has the right to be here."

"She's a Vermont. *We* are her family now. Get. Them. Out."

"Hey now." My dad stands tall but respectful. "I understand things are out of order right now and that you're worried about your son. But my baby girl is in here. I will go nowhere until she tells me. And maybe not even then."

Miranda cocks a brow, crossing her arms as she looks to me. "Tell them to go, Kenra."

I stare at her hard, and she doesn't budge.

This will be a small victory, one that will bite me in the ass later, but right now, I don't care.

"Actually, miss …"

The nurse grows nervous and squints at me.

"I'm really tired. Could you maybe ask the desk to keep visitors out for a few hours once my family steps out? Kellan and I could both use some sleep."

"Yes, ma'am, I can."

I look to my parents crestfallen faces and try to smile. They do the same, kiss my cheek, and then walk for the door, all three stopping to stare at Miranda.

"What?" she scoffs. "You can't seriously expect me to *leave*?"

"We damn well sure do," my mom quietly tells her, and my dad stands with his chest at her back.

She glares at them and then me and storms from the room.

The second she does, the nurse gives a small smile and then pulls the door closed on her way out.

When I try to adjust my position, I hiss in pain, my ribs sending a sharp, heated ache through me, so I give up and settle back as I was.

I ignore Kellan's presence and close my eyes to think, but I can't focus.

Everything is fucked up, and it's all my fault. All my responsibility to fix.

I owe it to my family and to Parker to make this right—at least for them. I just have to figure out how.

With a sigh, I ready myself for sleep, but right then, Kellan's machines start beeping, and my eyes pop open with the door. Two nurses rush past me to get to his side, but I don't bother looking. I don't listen to the words they speak as they talk to each other, doing whatever it is they do to get the noises to stop, to help preserve the slick bastard beside me.

One nurse walks out, and the other stops at the foot of my bed.

"We're taking good care of him," she assures me. "Try to get some sleep. Your body needs it to heal." When I don't respond, she offers a small smile. "These things take time; don't give up hope yet."

She exits, and it hits me.

I didn't embrace my new life of high society and power over the last few years, but I learned a bit from being in it.

Money goes a long way. Maliciousness pushes it further. But ruthlessness tips it off.

Maybe the accident wasn't a punishment but an out.

Kellan called for a pass.

I'm calling a blitz.

The play call was delivered on a silver platter by the asshole himself. Because the calculating bastard sharing a room with me is no longer my fiancé … he's my husband.

Parker

Lolli calls me for what must be the fifteenth time in the last few hours. Again, I don't answer. I'm not sure what she could say that would help at the moment, and frankly, I don't want to talk to anyone right now.

"You not gonna get that, brotha man?" Brady asks from his seat, and I shake my head. "You know she'll just keep callin', right?"

"Yeah, I know."

He glances my way as he hits our turn. "What happened in there, dude?"

I lost.

When I don't answer, Brady doesn't push, and eventually, we're pulling up to my house.

I glance at Cameron, who is asleep in the backseat and back at Brady, before stepping out and closing my door. I pump fists with him through the open window. "Thanks for giving me a ride back, man."

"Just a three-hour trip. No big deal." He smirks, but it holds halfway. "I need to get a shower and some sleep myself. Felt all right leaving now that Kenra's awake and talkin'."

I nod, reaching my front door right as Chase steps out. Brady let him know we were here.

"Hey, man. Thanks for bringing her back and sitting with her."

"It's no problem. I'm glad I could do it," he tells me with a nod. "Talked to Ari. She said Kenra was awake?"

"Yeah, she woke up."

"Good, good."

"How's Payton? She been up yet at all?"

He sighs and shakes his head. "Only for about fifteen minutes. I made her drink a glass of water and eat a half-sandwich, but that's it. She needs to eat, man. Gotta take care of herself and that baby."

I squeeze my eyes shut and nod. "Yeah," I croak out, looking off and then back. "Thanks, Chase."

"Yep." He clasps my shoulder as he steps out the door.

Brady hangs out his window to catch my attention. "I'mma head back this evening. Should I call you, see if you're ready to head back with us?"

I swallow. "Nah, man. I'm not going back."

Σμυρνός

It's been three days.

Three days of lying in this damn bed. Three days of dealing with Miranda and her bullshit. Three days of listening to the sounds Kellan makes in his unconscious state. Three days of my mother staring at me like she doesn't know me. Three fucking days of pretending I'm not going insane.

I need to get out of here.

But I can't get a minute to myself to plan.

There's a small knock at the door as I ease into a sitting position.

"If I could ask everyone to step out a minute, I need to check on our patient here."

Reluctantly, the others exit the room, and the nurse steps all the way in.

"Hi there." The woman smiles and moves to wash her hands. "I'm Shelli. I was here the night you came in." She dries her hands and moves to sit at the edge of my bed. "Glad to see you're awake. How are you feeling?"

"Sore. Ready to get out of here."

She nods, her gaze dropping to my bandaged arms and palms. "If you're up for it, the hospital has counselors on staff. I could ask one to step inside to speak with you."

My eyes drop to the blanket.

My scars. She's seen them.

Heat makes its way up my chest and neck, embarrassment and shame taking over.

"That boy is something special," she whispers. "That was a beautiful thing he did, shielding you and your family like that."

My eyes fly to hers, and she gives a small smile.

"What are you talking about?"

She points to my arms. "The wraps," she whispers. "I put them on myself. It's not something we would have considered, not even something that we'd have thought about in that manner, but the second your family was informed they'd be able to see you … that boy asked us to cover them for you. He said your parents didn't know, and he wanted to make it easier for all of you since so much had happened already."

"Blue eyes?" I whisper.

The woman grins. "Like no blue I've ever seen," she teases with a whimsical sigh.

We both laugh lightly.

Kellan's machine beeps then, and our gazes are pulled his way. His chest rises and falls in deep breaths, his body growing stronger by the minute. I've been told he'll wake up soon.

I'm running out of time.

Shelli stands, reaching for a bag stuffed beneath my bed and hands it to me. "In case you were wondering, this is all they gave us when you came in."

I pull open the bag to find my small purse inside.

"They probably only grabbed it for identity purposes. Your clothes were cut off by the EMTs on-site, but if you want them, I can get them for you."

Sliding my fingers across the blood streak on my stark white Coach bag—one I didn't even like, but Kellan said was classy—I open it to find my wallet and other belongings still inside.

A sliver of white catches my eye. My hands begin to shake as I reach inside, pulling the rectangular-shaped paper out.

Happiness is a choice.

"Shelli"—I look to the nurse, who stares at the fortune in my hand before bringing her eyes to mine—"I need your help."

Parker

Three days. It's been three damn days since I left the hospital. Three days since I thought I'd lost her forever. Three fucking days since I found out she was already gone.

Already forever his.

She'd warned me. That first day on the beach, she'd said it didn't matter if he found her because she'd go back to him anyway.

I should have heard her then, avoided all this unnecessary agony and optimism bullshit.

With a deep sigh, I drop my head back against the couch right as Payton shuffles from the hall, her face pale, eyes puffy and red. It's been hard to get her to take care of herself, and she isn't exactly open to listening to what anyone has to say, which is understandable, but at the same time, she has us all pretty scared.

"Dad and Clint are pulling up now," she rasps and I hop up, making my way over to her.

"You ready to see them?"

She shrugs, not meeting my eyes.

"Why don't you take a minute, have a warm shower?" I glance back at Lolli, and she nods, deep creases framing her worried eyes. "Lolli will make you something to eat real fast. Let me talk to them first."

Payton frowns at the floor a minute before nodding and heading back down the hall.

I drag my hands down my face, my chin dropping to my chest.

Lolli steps beside me. "I have no idea what to say to her," she admits then gives me a small smile before turning back to the others. "Handsome, you and Austin go play. Meems, come help me make some snacks. Parker needs the porch *without* your nosy ass ears."

"You got it, boss," Austin teases and Lolli flips him off over her head making him laugh.

With a deep breath, I meet my dad and stepdad out front just as they step out of the car.

My dad stretches his limbs as I approach, giving me a grave smile when he spots me.

He steps forward to hug me, patting my back. "Son."

"Hey, Dad."

Clint steps up next and clutches my shoulder. "How you doin, bud?"

I let out a deep sigh. "Been better, to be honest," I tell them, glancing between the two.

With his lips in a tight line, my dad pats my bicep. "Been a long week, huh?"

"The longest." I look to the left, staring at the ocean between the houses. "Never thought I'd think it, but I can't wait for summer to be over. I need school to keep me busy. Things are... real messed up right now."

"I can't imagine," he whispers quietly.

I told him everything that happened when he called the night I came home from the hospital. Turned out, my mother called him, freaking out and trying to threaten things she had no control over, but he doesn't play her games anymore, so he hung up on her, filled Clint in on the situation and then called me directly.

"Peep inside?"

I nod, looking back to him.

"She doesn't want to see me, does she?" he asks quietly, and Clint moves behind him to grip his shoulders in support.

"Truthfully, Dad, I think she could care less."

Deep wrinkles form across his forehead. "Can't blame her." He looks to me. "How is she?"

"Not good. Hardly eating, in bed most the day but hardly sleeping."

"I know it's a tired old saying, but she'll get better in time."

"Maybe, but we don't have time. She's pregnant now, needs to keep her body strong."

Both of them nod, and we all grow quiet a minute before my dad speaks again.

"I need to know something, Parker, about you and Kenra." He eyes me. "Honest-to-God truth, no holding back. How much does this girl mean to you?"

I drop my eyes to the gutter, unsure if I want to give him what he's asking for.

"You willing to give it all away for her? Lose all the things you've just discovered you wanted? A home here, a job, maybe... probably your best friend?"

When my eyes snap to his, he gives a meek smile. "Are you willing to give up everything for her?"

"Why are you asking me that?" I cut my eyes to Clint and back.

"Answer the question, son," he quietly demands.

There's only one answer. It's a question I don't even have to process, but it still saddens me to admit it.

"In a heartbeat," I tell him in a whisper.

He nods, turning back to his car to pull out a stack of papers. With a deep sigh, he hands them over to me.

I don't drop my eyes from his as I take them. "What's all this?"

"Everything you've ever wondered about. All the reasons you ever doubted who you were and what you were worth."

His eyes flit between mine. "All the reasons she stayed with him instead of choosing you."

My hand starts to shake as my heart rate spikes. I clench my teeth to keep myself in check.

"She chose you, Parker. This entire time she's been gone, been with him, it all started with her choosing you. Your happiness over hers. Then, it grew a little deeper into others' happiness over hers. And it only got worse from there. The things this poor girl has dealt with, the weight on her shoulders ... I'm surprised it hasn't buried her already."

"What the hell are you talking about?" I ask, chest so tight that I can hardly breathe.

"It's all here." He taps the papers. "She left these in the car the night you guys came to town. I read them. Maybe I shouldn't have, but when I saw your name, I couldn't help it. But, Parker, you need to understand, the question I asked you— would you give it all away for her? —it's not a joke. This is no joke. This could end a dozen different ways, but before you read this, before you make a choice on what your next move is, you have to be willing to lose it all, trying."

"I am."

"Good. That's good."

Before I can say another word, the front door opens, and my sister is standing there.

Our dad's eyes find hers, and instant tears fill his eyes.

Payton stares a minute before she rushes for him, throwing herself in his arms, letting him hold her as tight as he's always wanted to.

I walk away then, leaving them to one another. They have a lot to talk about.

With trembling hands and shaky feet, I step inside my house right as Lolli steps around the corner.

She gets one look at me and frowns. "Hero ... what's wrong?"

I open my mouth to speak, but my dad's words replay in my head.

Would I give up my best friend for her?

My mouth closes, and her eyes grow tighter around the edges, concern blanketing her face.

I turn and walk straight to my room, shut the door behind me, and spread the papers across my desk. And I read every word of every threat made on Kenra, even the one coming from my own mother. I read every contract Kellan forced her to sign and the consequences that would follow if she broke them. I read through everything until I get to the last and final two.

One, his revised statement of a promise to her, covering all the things he would no longer hold over her head—her father's business, her brother's career.

Then, the last, the one that undoubtedly got her to the church, the bill of sale. Ownership papers that deem one Kellan Vermont as a fifty percent owner of the San Diego Tomahawks.

Son of a fucking bitch.

CHAPTER 42
PARKER

Σμιρνιδς

THE SECOND KENRA EXITS THE ROOM, I TAKE THE OPENING AND SLIP inside, locking the door behind me.

He's lying there with his eyes closed, but I know he woke up yesterday. I've waited on pins and fucking needles for it to happen. It's been two days since my dad gave me those papers. Five days since I learned she'd married the man. Plain and simple, I'm done.

"Open your eyes, you piece of shit."

His lids pop right open, and he glares, glancing from Kenra's extra chair to me. "Where is *my* wife?"

I grind my teeth together and jerk to move toward him but force myself to hold back.

I came for a reason. Beating his ass would be a bonus but one that would land me in jail—not that it wouldn't be worth it.

"Kenra stepped out, and before you ask, she has no clue I'm here."

"As if I'd believe that," he rasps.

"Don't care what you believe."

"Why are you here, Baylor? I don't want you anywhere near her. If I find out you are, I'll—"

"Threaten her some more? Maybe something against her mom this time instead of her dad and brother?"

His gaze narrows. "I don't know what she's told you, but all that's a lie. She's—"

"Save it, dick." I pull the documents from my pocket, and his eyes widen slightly before he can right them.

"Those are fake. She printed them herself to—"

"You think I'm stupid? That I wouldn't run this shit by my lawyers at the company before coming in here like this? It's real. And you're a little bitch."

His jaw twitches, and he fists the blanket on his hospital bed. "What do you plan to do with those?"

"I've got copies of them scanned into an email already, addressed to every news station I could find."

"You do this, and I will—"

"What?" I shrug. "I've got nothing to lose at this point. I've already lost everything. This shit will go to the press, threats from you or not. I swear on it."

"Name your price, Baylor." He lifts his chin. "Everything has a number."

"She's my number."

His lip curls. "Not an option."

"Only fucking option you got. Time for you to decide what's worth it and what's not."

"You think that solves your problems? Did you not read that paperwork? I own half of that fucking organization that you think you'll be working for. You'll be the first to go. Then, the whore you live with. I'll end the contract with her photography company, all but pushing her out, taking everything she has left of her dead family. Then, at some point, I'll sell the shares off, one by fucking one. I'll tear that team apart from the inside out." He smirks, dropping his head against his pillow. "Can you live with that?"

"Yes."

At my instant and sure response, his brows kick high, his eyes flicking between mine.

I've caught him off guard. He expected me to pause for thought.

But my dad already asked me this. I already thought it through.

All those things will be devastating and a guaranteed way to lose my best friend and the life I have right now. But, if I have nothing, if all is gone and all that's left is her, I'll still have everything.

She is everything.

All I could ever hope for, all I could ever wish for.

"Hell fucking yes," I restate and lower into the chair beside him, so I can stare, man to man. "But what about you, Kellan, huh? You willing to give up everything? You wanna be a state senator—God fucking help us all—or you want her? 'Cause I'll tell you right now, you will *not* get both."

His nostrils flare, his jaw tight as he jerks his eyes from mine to stare at the wall. He's quiet a moment before he turns back. "I hope you know I'm not bluffing. You take her, and I'll take everything else you have and *nothing* less."

"She's worth it."

"She's hardly worth the fucking paperwork."

"Don't you worry about the paperwork." I smirk and move the top papers to the side, dropping the divorce papers on his lap. "Sign the fucking paper. Tell her it was your idea and cut her fucking loose."

"And if I don't?"

"Come on, Kellan, I'm in your role right now. You know the answer to that."

"How will you know if I did or not?"

I stand and look down at him, forcing his eyes to lift. "Don't test me, or I'll do it for the fuck of it, and still, you'll lose her. I'm giving you an option that you don't deserve, but it's cleaner. Quicker."

"Fuck you, Baylor."

"Nah, Kellan."

I grin. "Finally, this is me fucking you."

With that, I turn and walk out the door. The sureness facade I was carrying falls with my first step past his room, and I take a deep breath. I head for the elevators, freezing once I look around the corner.

Kenra is sitting off to the side in the private waiting room, silently crying to herself. *By* herself.

I wanna go to her. To hold her, tell her what I should have years ago, and show her just how much I love her, but I won't. All this must be taking its toll on her. Physically and emotionally. And she herself is still healing.

She looks to her hands, feathering her fingertips over her palms. I watch as she pushes the sleeve of her cardigan up and does the same to her wrist. Tears fall from her eyes as they close.

Right then, a firm hand grips my shoulder, and I whip around, coming face-to-face with Ian Monroe.

He glances past me, spotting his daughter crying, and I see him fight himself from going to her, as I did. Then, he pulls me backward and steers me in the opposite direction.

"Walk with me, son." It's not a request but a heavy suggestion.

Neither of us speaks as we walk through the hospital and out into the patient garden area outside.

Even when we get there, he's quiet a moment as he collects his thoughts.

"I met my wife freshman year of high school. I remember everything about that day—what she was wearing, the things she said, the way she smiled. Something told me, that very first day, that she was ... special. One of a kind, built just for me." He glances my way and then looks back to the small rock waterfall in front of us. "People thought we were crazy. Her daddy hated me for a long time, but we didn't care. She was mine, and I was hers; nothing else mattered. We'd fight the world if we had to as long as, in the end, we had each other. And we did. Time and time again, we were tested, in many ways that not even Nate and Kenra know about, but we won. Because we knew, without each other, we were only half of ourselves." He leans forward, placing his elbows on his knees, and looks off to the side.

"We tried real hard to teach our kids to be the same. To love with everything they had and fight for all the things they wanted—love especially because, if you have someone to love, someone who loves you just as much, together, you can handle anything that comes your way."

His downcast gaze locks with mine. "I've never felt like more of a failure as a father than I do right now. That's my baby girl in there. Crying by herself in the corner. Tell me, why would she do that when the man she's supposed to love, who's supposed to love and worship her, is not ten feet from where she's at? Why would she cry, alone, when she could have his arms around her, protecting her? Why would she not be in there, letting him take her pain as his own?"

"What type of answer are you looking for, Mr. Monroe?" I ask him directly.

"I *need* an honest one, Parker. Straight from your heart and nowhere else. I don't expect you to tell me things she should on her own, and really, you don't have to tell me anything at all, but I'd appreciate it if you did. I'm dying here, watching this go on. My wife is hurting, and for the first time in our lives, I can't fix it. I've been in that room every day. I've seen no comfort, no raw need, to take away the hurt that's in my baby's eyes from that man and no wish that he would in hers. Give me something to help me feel like my baby is gonna be okay 'cause, right now, I feel like we're losing her."

"I love her," I blurt out. It's instant and strong and the only clear thing in all this mess.

His features tighten as his eyes grow glossy. He knew it. He believes it.

I can't give him her truths, that she'll have to be strong enough to do on her own, but I can give him mine. So, I do.

"I've loved her for years. Can't stop and don't want to. She's the most selfless, big-hearted, beautiful woman I have ever known. She's more than I deserve but all I want. She was there for me when no one else cared to be, heard me when no one else would. She gave me hope. Made me believe there was more when all I felt was emptiness.

"For years, we've been goin' round and round with each other. The thing about that is, there's no way out. We're sealed together, running in circles with no end zone. She comes to me, I love her while I have her, comfort her as long as she lets me, and when she feels her strength is back, she leaves. I've tried not to let her back in 'cause, every time she goes, she takes more of me with her, but my heart's defenseless when it comes to her. I can't shake her. Can't deny her. She's inside me, and she ain't going anywhere. Ever."

Ian tilts his head and blows out a harsh breath, dropping his eyes to his feet as he nods. He chuckles through his emotions and sits back on the bench to look up at the sky. "Will you fight for her?"

"I might have just lost everything trying."

His head snaps to mine, and I meet his stare, understand his pain like my own.

"You don't need to ask me, sir." My eyes bounce between his. "The answer is yes. I'm sure about her and I. She has all of me."

———————

Kenra

After trying to reach Payton for the hundredth time, I sigh and look to the clock. It's been four hours since I stepped out, and that was nowhere near long enough, but if I don't get back soon, he'll send someone to find me—or have me paged, like yesterday when I slipped out. I was discharged four days ago with the help of my nurse, but of course, Kellan suggested I stay here, save face and all.

As I enter his room, he stares, anger in his eyes clear as day.

I glance at his mother, who refuses to meet my gaze.

"What is it?"

"I've changed my mind," he states simply, and worry seizes my breath. "I don't need a woman like you at my side. You're weak. I need someone strong if they're to survive in my world. Someone who appreciates all the things I can give them."

I lower myself in the chair at the foot of his bed and wait for him to continue.

He tosses a packet of papers toward me. "Divorce. Terms are we separate *quietly* and on mutual terms. I've signed already. Sign them, go pack your shit, leave the car I paid for, and get the fuck out."

My stomach starts to turn as I reach for the forms with trembling hands.

No way will it be this easy.

I scan them over, and they are what he claims them to be, an out clear and clear.

My eyes shoot to his. "Why?"

"Why do you care? It's what you've always wanted, is it not?"

"But *why*?"

"Because it will be much more fun to release you than force you to watch as I tear apart the Tomahawks, knowing you could have prevented it all from happening." He grins. "It's quite brilliant actually. A better plan than any of the others put together. With one move, I'll ruin your fuck boy's future, end yours and your brother's relationship by destroying everything his little millionaire has, which in turn will cause heartbreak to your parents. Everyone you know will suffer, but little Miss Kenra will be free of the big, bad wolf."

"My father's company and my brother's career?"

"I can't touch those things." He shrugs. "It's in the contract, but I won't need to. As I said, this works out much better for me."

I nod, unclipping the pen attached, and silently sign each area before standing.

He glares when I don't hand them back as he reaches for them.

His mother scoffs and storms from the room.

I look to Kellan, undeserved and undoubtedly unwanted sympathy coursing through me. Because, truly, it's sad, the person he's become.

"I'll never understand how you could be so cold and heartless. I mean, with me is one thing, but … Kellan, your brother *died*. He's *gone*, and you haven't even spoken his name since you woke up." My voice cracks, and his eyes thin. "Are you … are you even sorry for what happened? Do you not sit there and wonder why the innocent one in our mess is the one who lost his life, and we lived? Because I do. Every day, every few minutes, I do."

"No," he snarls, his eyes as empty as his heart. "I don't. He never should have been there in the first place." He sits taller in his hospital bed. "In fact, if it's anyone's fault, it's yours. You are the one who took the girl there, the entire reason he followed."

He's not wrong. I did bring Payton to her brother, and ultimately, yes, that's the reason Deaton followed. That's something I'll have to learn to accept as time goes on, and maybe, one day, I'll forgive myself for pushing Kellan in the car that night, but today, I still carry that weight. Today, I still feel responsible for the loss of Deaton's life, for taking him away from his girlfriend and their unborn child.

The difference though, if there is one, is that I feel remorseful. I understand the mistakes I've made and would go back and change so many things if I could. Not that that makes it better, but it's all I have to go on. Kellan, on the other hand ... I'm not so sure he would.

I should just walk out without another word, take these papers straight to the courthouse and see if they're authentic, but instead, I stand there and stare a few moments longer.

He thinks this will be clean and easy, and he'll lose nothing of value to him because he has the upper hand.

He never has been able to recognize his own mistakes.

"Tell me, what do you regret the most in all this?" I ask.

"Easy. Threatening instead of doing, Kenra. Would have made keeping you in line a whole lot easier."

I nod, his instant reply coming as no surprise. "Sounds about right. But I bet that'll change quick."

His eyes narrow in suspicion. "And why is that?"

"Because you went through a hell of a lot of trouble and spent a crazy amount of money to own part of a professional football team with the sole purpose of using it against me in one way or another."

"And I still will." Dark eyes shift between mine. "Consider the purpose well served."

"Right," I whisper, slapping the papers against my hand as I walk backward for the door. "It's a solid plan ... but you made one little mistake, dear husband."

His eyes narrow to slits, and he opens his mouth to speak, but I'm already out the door.

Done listening to his shit. Done in this place.

I make my way out to the downstairs lobby and step out of the sliding glass doors of the hospital with a deep breath.

I slide my cardigan down my arms and toss it on the small bench as I pass.

The sun warms my skin as I walk to my car, and tears fill my eyes.

I take a deep, cleansing breath, too afraid to hope but desperately needing this to be real.

TWO WEEKS. IT'S BEEN TWO FUCKING WEEKS SINCE I WAS AT THAT hospital, forcing Kellan's hand. Two weeks since the announcement hit the papers that the two had split.

Two weeks, and still, not a word from her.

Her dad called me the minute he heard, thanked me, and told me she might need time. Nate did the same. Even Mason and Brady and the others keep saying shit like, "Give her space," and, "Let her come to you."

Well, I'm not okay with that. I've waited years for this.

I'm fucking ready now. I want to hold her *now*. Love her now.

There's a tap on my door, and I turn to see Lolli leaning against the frame.

"Hey," she whispers, her lips tipping slightly.

I glance back out the window I've been sitting in front of for the last two hours. "Hey."

She pushes off the wall and walks over to drop beside me.

"Hero ... Al called."

My muscles lock, and it takes all my willpower to look her way.

She takes a minute before sliding her eyes to mine, and tears brim the edges. Her lips start to tremble, and a sob breaks out, her hand lifting to cover her mouth.

My chest grows tight at the sight, and I pull her to me, wrapping my arms around her.

Over the last two weeks, not only have I heard nothing from Kenra, but there has also been no move against the team.

I told myself he just needed time to plan his first move, and now, it seems he has.

I told Lolli everything and included Nate, so she wouldn't feel she was lying to him. I had no choice; it wouldn't be fair for her to be blindsided if shit hit the fan. It was hard to admit, even harder to see the hurt in her eyes, but she said she understood where I was coming from; she'd have done the same for Nate.

As for Nate, he was quiet the entire time I spoke, held his anger in until he couldn't handle it anymore, and stormed off, slamming the door on his way out.

I know it's a tough one for him; it's his sister who was wronged, his girl's world that's in jeopardy, and he can't do a damn thing about any of it.

One positive that came out of all this is, I do feel the line that was between him and me where Lolli was concerned is gone. Any uncertainty he might have had as far as my intentions with my best friend has been cleared.

"What'd he say, Lolli Bear?"

She sniffs and pulls back, wiping at her eyes. "He said he needs us at the stadium at one," she speaks quietly. "I called Nate, but he didn't answer."

"Lolli, I—"

"No," she cuts me off, shaking her head. "Don't apologize. We don't know what's happening yet. Let's just ... get there, yeah?" Her head stays forward but her eyes slide to mine and I nod, a heavy pressure on my chest.

"Okay." I stand up, pulling her up by hand right alongside me.

Payton and Mia are waiting by the door for us when we make our way out.

Payton gives me a small smile before stepping up to Lolli. "Ready?"

Lolli nods, and together, we all hop in Lolli's car.

The hour drive is spent talking about Mia's surprise arrival, and all too soon, we're parking in the reserved owner's space.

Lolli doesn't take a moment to breathe but jumps out and rushes up the stairs, so we hop out and run after her, but when we hit the quarters where operations sits, we all jolt to a stop.

I look to Lolli.

"Oh shit ..." Mia whispers.

There's a team of men inside, the Tomahawks lawyers and other representatives, all sitting around a table with stacks of papers in front of them, Al at the head of the row.

Lolli starts shaking her head and then turns to me, dropping her forehead to my chest. With a sigh, I pull her in and whisper how sorry I am. Ultimately, this is all my fault.

Right then, Nate bounds up the steps and swoops in. As soon as his hand touches her back, she spins into him, and he lifts her, carrying her straight into the building.

He stops at the door and turns to the three of us, still standing there, frozen. "Let's get this over with."

The three of us exchange glances and then rush behind them, stepping inside as the men start to stand and shake hands.

They offer us small nods and basic pleasantries before exiting, leaving only Al and the rest of us in the room. He motions for us to take the seats they vacated, and while all of us move to sit, Lolli remains standing. She crosses her arms over her chest and glares our way before turning back to Al.

"Thank you for coming on such short—"

"Can we skip this shit, Al?" Lolli cuts him off.

His lips twitch. "We can, young one; we can." His eyes scan

the room, connecting with each one of us before landing back on her. "We have a new partner, as you expected."

My teeth clench together, so tight that a pain shoots through my jaw, but I ignore it and wait for Al to continue.

"What's he gonna do?" she says lower than I think she intended. She clears her throat. "What's his first move?"

My pulse spikes, and my leg starts bouncing, my gaze flying between the both of them.

"Why don't you ask him?" Al tells her, his face blank as he directly stares at her.

"He's here?" Nate growls, jumping from his chair.

"He is." Al nods and lifts a packet of papers from the space in front of him. He walks toward Lolli and gently places it in front of her before walking back.

His gaze lifts to lock with mine.

He stares at me, tipping his chin just slightly, and I reluctantly pull my eyes from his and look to Lolli.

"I …" She pulls the paper closer to her face and stares. "I don't get it. What the hell is this?"

Nate and I exchange glances, both wanting to step in, both knowing she has to do this part on her own.

"That's the final paperwork. The beginning of your new partnership."

Tears roll down her face, and finally, her head pops up to look at him. "How?" she whispers.

And Al smiles, a full-on smile, stretching from one side of his face to the other.

"What's happening?" Payton whispers loudly.

Lolli starts to laugh. She spins to me then and slowly hands me the forms.

Right there, mid-page, in bold-ass print, it shows the bill of ownership.

Fifty percent belongs to Kalani Lee Embers.

Fifty percent belongs to Parker James Baylor.

My eyes snap to Lolli's and then Al's, and panic sets in.

"No …" I hop from my seat and start pacing.

"Parker, listen—" Al starts to speak.

I spin around and glare, cutting him off. "No … *fuck no*! Don't want it. Give the shit back. Now." My breathing grows labored. "I can't … she has to …" I grow dizzy and drop back into a chair, scrubbing my hands down my face.

"He didn't do this, Parker," Al tells me. "She did."

"Will someone tell me what the fuck is going on here?" Nate complains. "Baby?"

Lolli moves a hand behind her to place it on his chest, but she doesn't take her eyes from Al. "Tell us."

"Well, Kellan Vermont found a way to get two notorious men—who wouldn't sell a single share, let alone their entire hand, no matter how many times your grandfather tried to buy them out—to sell to him. This gave him fifty percent, equal to Lolli's. His plans were vile. Back-end, nasty things to make what we've built here fall."

"We know all that. Tell us how Parker now owns the other half," Lolli quietly demands.

"Holy shit," Nate whispers while the girls gasp.

"He's a sick son of a bitch. He thought he had it all figured out, and he almost did had she not found the strength he didn't know she had."

My frown falls flat, and I stare at him.

"What the asshole didn't plan on was his wife, who he forced to marry him, turning around and giving it all away, and all before he had time to stop it. See, when he married her, he did so with no prenuptial agreement, making everything he had equally hers. Well, he forgot to carve her out of his one and final play, the only up he had left on her. She called me from the hospital, tracked me down herself with the little bit of information you shared with her on your trip to San Francisco. It was a few days before he served her divorce papers when she asked me to look over some things for her.

"I didn't know what I was looking for until she gave me that last file and told me to transfer ownership. I couldn't say anything until I was absolutely certain he couldn't somehow overturn her move. I just got the final word today. It's done. The team belongs to the two of you, end of story."

I swallow past the block in my throat, my eyes shifting between his. My voice comes out scratchier than I would like. "Kenra did this?"

He nods, standing tall and proud.

Licking my lips, I look off, bringing my hand up to cover my mouth as I squeeze my eyes shut.

Kenra did this.

She fought him back, pushed his hand with her own tiny one.

And she won.

"Oh my God!" Mia shrieks behind me, running over to hug Lolli. "This is so awesome! Everything will be okay now, Lolli!"

An instant weight hits my chest, a pressure so strong I have to fight for air. My brows dip in the center, my head pounding. Slowly, I turn to look at Lolli, who, of course, is already looking at me. Undeserved understanding and forgiveness stare back at me. My best friend.

"I, uh, I need a minute with Lolli," I speak to the room but look to Nate. "Alone."

His scowl drops to the floor, and he nods as he stands. Together, they all step outside to give us some privacy.

Once the door closes, I look to her, shaking my head. "Lolli Bear …"

"Don't, Hero." She gives a small smile.

"This is my fault. Should have never happened. Shouldn't be like this."

She shakes her head, reaching up to touch my face. "You did what you were meant to do; you saved her. You gave her back the hope she'd lost, gave her a reason to be strong." She smiles softly, and my shoulders sag more. "If we had been pushed out, it wouldn't have been for nothing. As far as we know, Kenra could have ended up doing a lot worse to herself than she already has if she had to stay. If we lost the ability to be a part of the team, it would have been from trying to save someone we care about. *Never* be sorry for that."

"But your family ... this is your connection to them, and I almost cost you it all. I put it all at risk."

Lolli shakes her head, lowering her hands to grab ahold of mine. "Football is my connection. Photos are my connection. I'd still be owner; they couldn't force me to sell, no matter how hard they tried. I'd still have been at every game I could. Embers Elite photography would still have been mine. And you'd still have been with me."

I stare at her. "That's what you would want?"

"You're my family, Parker," she whispers, tears filling her blue eyes as she squeezes my hands, letting me know she's got me. "And, now ... you're her hero."

I laugh lightly, nodding my head, and then pull her in, hugging her tight.

Nate walks in and claps my shoulder, and she steps back, laughing through her tears. She wraps her arms around his neck, and he chuckles against her.

"Everything's gonna be okay, baby. Better than," he whispers into her hair, winking at me.

Al comes back in with the others and walks up to me with an unreadable expression. "Mr. Baylor, I know this is a lot to take in, but from what I know, I know Lolli believes in you; therefore, I do, too." He holds out a key card.

"What's this?" I ask, slowly moving to grab it.

"Key to the owners' box." He jerks his chin toward the door. "Go on. Let it sink in, kid. Nothing like walking in there and belonging."

I look to Lolli, and she nods, giving me the okay I need. I grip the key tight, slowly making my way around the corner, up the elevator, and into the private hall.

I shake out my limbs and wipe my palms on my jeans, and

then I let myself in.

Σμυρνιός

I WIPE MY SWEATY PALMS AGAINST MY DRESS, PINCHING THE SOFT fabric in my hand before letting go … and then the door opens.

It takes all of two seconds for Parker's blues to find mine.

He stops, frozen in place, as his stare sears into my soul, burning deeper than ever before. Or maybe I just feel it more, feel it all over with everything inside me.

"Hi," I breathe, and he jolts.

Slowly, he turns and gently closes the door, dropping his forehead against it for a moment before standing tall and turning back to face me.

He looks from my freshly cut hair, now just above my shoulders, to my dress—the one he bought for me—and my exposed arms. With a deep inhale, he slowly makes his way over, those eyes hypnotizing me more with each step.

And then he's standing right in front of me. Soul bared in his ocean eyes, he begs me to speak, shows me his hope and want and intentions.

He's like no man I've ever known. A true safety, as he played on his team.

The last guy left waiting. When his boys, his brothers on the field, can't protect, can't make the stop, Parker steps in and does it for them. The iron fist of dependability. When something or

307

someone breaks through to tear you down, he's there to stop it. To stop *him*.

And he did.

My dad told me everything, what he did for me. The things he risked for me.

I didn't deserve it. Never deserved him, but I want to.

I wanna be what he sees, the tough, beautiful girl he makes me feel I already am.

I wanna be his, have him as mine.

"Kens—" he starts, but I lift my fingers to his lips, slowly tracing the shape of his mouth to silence him.

My eyes roam over him—from his strong, scruff-covered jaw to his perfect lips and finally back up to his striking stare. "I'm so sorry, Parker, for everything. For all the hurt and pain and confusion I caused over the years. For allowing you to ever think I'd choose anyone over you and walking away when all you ever did was love me. I'll never forgive myself for all the wrong choices I've made."

"Please—"

"Shh," I gently hush him again, needing to say it even if he already knows. "I won't, and that's a weight I'll happily carry. I'm okay with it because I know for a fact that I will never allow anyone or anything to get in our way ever again." Tears fill my eyes, but still, I continue, "I've failed you, Parker, in so many ways, so many times, but no more. Never again. I promise you."

His hand slowly comes up, wiping the tear I didn't know I'd shed.

"Kens …" he whispers, his fingertips dragging from my cheek to my neck and across my shoulder.

I shiver as they continue down my arm until he grasps my hand in his.

He lifts my palm to his lips and feathers a kiss across my wrist.

When his eyes flash back to mine, he yanks me against him, his chest pressing into mine with every labored breath he takes.

"They said you needed time," he rasps, his eyes dipping to my red-stained lips and back.

"Yeah," I breathe, moving into him even more.

"Yeah." He dips his head into my neck, softly kissing me. "Way I see it … you had four years. 'Bout ready yet?" he teases, nipping at my skin.

I laugh, my head tipping back more because of it.

He grins against my neck and moves his hand to cup the back of my head, pulling back to look into my eyes.

I sigh and move my hands to his handsome face, skimming my fingers across the scruff of his jaw. "Yeah"—I nod, pulling his forehead to mine— "I'm done." I slide my lips against his, closing my eyes. "I don't wanna wait anymore."

"Wait for what, baby?" he breathes. "Tell me. Say it for me."

My eyes pop open to lock on his. "I wanna be yours … I've *been* yours."

His other arm moves to wrap around my lower back, so he can hold me as close as possible, and he buries his face into my neck. He hugs me to him, breathing me in.

"Parker …"

He pulls back, his hands moving to grip my waist. "Me and you. Fuck the world here. You try to go, and I'll drag your ass back. Don't care where or why. No excuses or reasons will cut it. Not a fucking thing, no fucking more." He pops a blond brow, making me grin. "I've got no more plays. I'm all out of defense here. Gotta keep you now."

I slide my hands up his chest, loving the rumble of his growl beneath my hand. My hands glide up until they're wrapped around his neck, and I jump up. As expected, he catches me with a firm, tight grip to my ass, one that grows tighter by the second.

"Didn't you know, Mr. Baylor?" I lick his lips, and he groans, trying to catch my lips, but I pull back. "When it comes to each other, our hearts are defenseless. No way out. No others in."

"No way out," he repeats in a cemented tone.

Then, he turns, carrying me up the small set of stairs that leads to the second-level loft area where a plush ottoman lies directly in front of the huge glass window that overlooks the stadium.

He slides me down his body, catching my dress as he does. The material bunched in his hands, he brings only his eyes to mine, asking for permission he doesn't need.

I lift my hands, and he lifts my dress, gently pulling it over my head, dropping it to the floor.

I watch him, the crease of his forehead becoming more defined as he takes in my still bruised ribs. His fingers reach out to feather over my skin, and his head tilts as the pain in his eyes grows.

"Parker ..." I whisper, and he looks back to me.

I slide my hands under his shirt, and he allows me to lift it over his head. I slide my fingertips along his pec muscles, and his muscles grow taut, more defined. I bring my lips to his.

"I'm fine," I promise, unclasping his jeans and letting them fall to the floor.

He steps out of them, kicking them to the side.

I try to push him back, and he smirks, stepping to me.

"I don't think so, Nightingale." His voice is a rough timbre that spreads through me.

His hands follow the shape of my waist until they reach my bra. His thumbs sneak inside, scratching across my hardened nipples as he glides past until he can unclasp my bra and pull it down my arms.

He lifts my arms into the air, trailing his fingertips down from my wrist, and my body shivers. He grins when he sees it, but he doesn't look to me. His eyes follow his hands as he continues to my underwear.

He bends in front of me, blowing warm breath over my

panties, making my leg muscles clench and my hands fly to his hair.

"You wore my dress, Kens," he speaks against the cotton, heat teasing every swollen, needy inch of my pussy. "You know what that does to me, baby?"

I moan lightly, my grip tightening as his teeth move to nip me. "Take 'em off already," I beg.

He chuckles, moving his hands to squeeze my ass, and finally, he hooks my underwear in his hands and yanks them down. He gives me no time or warning, and then his hot mouth is on me. One lick, and then he's got my clit in his mouth. He rolls his tongue against me, lifting one of my legs over his shoulder to get better access. Then, a finger slides inside, followed by another, and my head falls back.

The pressure inside builds along with the heat and power of his tongue. My body starts to shake against him, and I grind against his face. My moan fills the room in the next moment. The power of the orgasm has my body tightening, my ribs hurting, but I don't care. I take all he gives, and he gives his all.

He massages my ass as I ride out every last wave before gently setting my leg down and reaching out to steady my shaky body.

He wipes his mouth on his arm.

Dazed, I move to him, and he grabs my hand, leading me to the ottoman. Ever so gently, he turns me and lays me back against the soft suede before climbing up my body.

Bringing his hand up to move my hair from my face, he whispers, "Are you okay?"

A laugh bubbles out of me.

I nod, smiling softly at the blond-haired, blue-eyed man above me. So strong, so brave and loyal. "Don't worry," I whisper.

His features tighten as emotion flares in his gaze. "Be happy," he responds in just above a whisper.

And then he pushes inside me, slow and savoring every

inch I take of him. He watches me, takes in the change of my eyes and the part of my lips as he fills me.

He moves leisurely, in and out in deep grinds, his eyes never leaving mine as he rolls against me.

I lift my legs to wrap them around him and pull him down to feel the beat of his heart against mine. The warmth of his moans as they fan across my sweat-sheathed skin.

His eyes flit across my face, coming back to lock on mine, and I see it there, as I always have. His heart in my hands.

"I love you," I whisper.

He freezes above me. His jaw locks tight, and the corners of his eyes pinch with the slope of his brows.

"I love you, Parker Baylor," I repeat. "I always have. And I'm so sorry it took—"

He cuts me off when his mouth slams against me, his dick pushing as far inside as it can reach.

My back bows in response, and I kiss him back just as fierce, just as hard and claiming.

And then we're both coming together, as we should.

He makes sure not to collapse against me but holds his weight with his elbows perched on both sides of me. His forehead rests on my chest, and I run my fingers through his sweat-slicked hair.

His tongue pokes out to skim across my nipple, and I twitch beneath him, his grin spreading across my skin.

When his head lifts, his eyes anchor mine, such a deep, endless blue. So clear and alive.

So Parker, my safety.

"I love you, Kenra Monroe," he whispers. "Always."

"Always," I whisper back with a smile of my own.

This is it.

The beginning.

EPILOGUE

Six Months Later
Kenra

Nate laughs loudly, tossing a piece of popcorn at Lolli, who spins to glare at him and then shifts back around to watch the game. He grins wide, catching my eye as he looks away.

With a deep breath, he gives me a small smile, moving to sit beside me as Lolli and the others step onto the open deck of the owners' suite.

The day after everything was settled with the Tomahawks, I went home and spent a few weeks with my parents, and much to my surprise, Nate came, too.

The very first day, I sat down with the three of them and told them everything there was to tell, starting with the day I met Parker. It was hard, letting my family see inside my nightmare, but I had to do it. They deserved to know, and more than that, we all deserved to heal; only open honesty could make that happen. Even though it pained them to hear of all the things I'd hidden, they were nothing but supportive, like I had known they would be.

In the two weeks that followed, I made it a point to

remember who I was. I helped my mom in her garden and my dad in his shop. I played catch in the yard with my brother while our parents sat back on their porch and watched. It was everything I'd missed and exactly what I needed.

Then, when it came time for Nate to head back to California, I went with him.

I had no plans for when I got there but knew I wasn't willing to be away from Parker any longer, so when my cousins and their friends asked if I wanted to stay in their beach house since they'd be heading for college in the fall, I said yes.

Now, here we are, six months later, sitting in the owners' suite at a San Diego Tomahawks game with all our friends and family. Even my parents came to support the team in their championship game, as this is the furthest they've gotten in a season since Lolli's grandpa died a few years ago.

I look from my parents to my man, all of them smiling and cheering as the team gets ready to tie the game just before half-time hits, and a peace I've only wished for settles over me.

I can't remember ever feeling as whole as I do right now. For the first time in what seems like forever, I have no secrets from the world and no weight on my shoulders. Sure, I still have scars that line the inside of my arms that I'll forever carry, but they no longer hold power over me. I look at them now and see strength instead of regret.

Nate stands and offers me a hand. When he pulls me up, he gives a soft smile. "Thank you, Kenra. For everything you did for me and everyone else. You're the strongest person I know, big sister," he whispers.

I grip his hand tighter, tears pooling in my eyes. "Thank you, little brother."

Right then, the others file back in the room, ready to hit the buffet bar that's been set up for us.

And all I can do is smile at everyone around me, proud that I can finally say I'm happy in my life and mean it with every fiber of my being.

Parker

I never realized how much my and Payton's childhood differed from the people around us until recently.

While things weren't always bad in our home, we only existed and functioned as a household. We didn't live like a family. We didn't love.

Yet here we are, loving harder than we ever knew we were capable of.

I look to Kenra right as her eyes lift to mine, and she winks as she pops a Skittle in her mouth and then turns back to Lolli and Mia as they fill their plates with junk. It's halftime, literally the only time Lolli will take her eyes off the game.

With a smile, I make my way up the small set of stairs and into the newly renovated loft area.

I lean against the door, watching my sister as she rocks her newborn son in her arms.

My dad and Clint came and stayed with us at our house the last month of her pregnancy, so they could be there to help us when she went into labor—something we were all grateful for since none of us knew what to expect or how to handle it when it came. But they were so good with her, gentle and fatherlike, as they should be.

I feel for her, for what she must be going through, but she's been so strong through all of this. She's seventeen now, a single mother fighting her way through the heartbreak of losing her boyfriend, her little boy's father.

She looks up, giving me a small smile. "Hey."

"Hey," I whisper, kicking off the wall and walking toward her.

I run my hand along the crib we had put in for her, smiling at the stuffed football Lolli added. When I see the scribble on the side, I lift it up and show it to her.

She laughs lightly. "Nate signed it, and then, when Mason saw Nate had signed it, he signed *over* Nate's signature."

We both laugh lightly at that.

"I don't know how that family deals with the both of them."

Payton gives a side grin. "We're a part of that family now," she says.

I bend at my knees, bringing myself eye-level with her. "Do you feel that here with us?" I ask hesitantly. "Do you feel like part of the family?"

Tears build in her eyes, and she nods, wiping them away before they can fall on the baby. "Yeah, I do. I like it here, Parker. I love when Mrs. Monroe comes to visit and Mason and Ari's mom. They're … they're so amazing to us."

"So, you'll stay here? Even after you finish independent study?"

She nods, and then a bright smile takes over her face.

"What?"

"You know how I lost that showcase for being pregnant?"

I nod, searching her face.

"Lolli got me an interview with the board at Embers Elite. I went last week."

"And?"

"And they want to use my photos in their next young artist issue!" She squeals quietly, bouncing the baby, and his arms fly up. "Parker, I made her promise not to tell them she knew me so they wouldn't give me special treatment. I even entered under a different name, so they had no way of knowing! I did this on my own!" Her eyes tear up, and she smiles.

"That's amazing, Peep. I'm so proud of you. I'm in awe of you really. You're just …"

"The shit," comes from the doorway.

We both look to find Lolli leaning against the frame.

She makes her way inside the room and reaches her arms out.

Payton grins at her and stands, handing her little guy over. She walks out, leaving Lolli and me alone.

Lolli looks to the baby, runs her fingertips over his eyebrows, and then moves to wrap her fingers around his. "He's pretty badass, isn't he?" she speaks low.

I keep my eyes on her. "Yeah, he is."

She looks up. "I told Nate I think I might maybe want one … someday."

I try to hold in my grin, pulling my lips in. "Think so?"

"Yeah"—she nods and drops her eyes to him— "I do."

"That's good, Lolli Bear. Real good."

"These last few months have been hard," she whispers.

"With Nate away at school?"

She nods, bending to kiss the baby's head. "I don't like not seeing him every day."

"I've noticed; you've been running a lot again."

"Yeah …" She looks to me, sadness in her eyes. "I'm … gonna rent something small next to his school," she admits quietly.

"You-you're leaving?" A small ache forms in my chest.

She nods. "I need to be by him. I *want* to be by him. I was hoping maybe you'd ask Kenra to move in? I think she'd love to. I know she has Ari and the others' house while they're at school, but you're with each other every time you can be, and this way, someone will be there with Payton and the baby all the time. If you think Kenra's up for it."

The pressure settles at the thought. She's right. I've thought about it a dozen times, and I would love Kenra to be there every morning when I wake up, but that doesn't mean I want Lolli to go.

"So, you're moving then?"

"Only during the school year. We'll be back on the weekends when we can, summers and shit." Her eyes search mine. "But … I bought the place next door."

317

I laugh at that, and the baby jumps, crying for a split second before Lolli soothes him back to sleep. We both look to each other, laughing silently.

"For real, we'll be back as often as possible. Especially with this little man there. So, don't touch my swing." She playfully narrows her eyes, and I smile softly at her. "This place is still our home, yours and mine; we just have our own front doors now."

"It's okay," I assure her. "I see you feeling guilty, and you don't need to. This feels right."

She exhales with a smile. "It does." Her blue eyes bounce between mine. "I love you, Hero."

"I love you, too, Lolli Bear."

"Can I have my woman now? Halftime's 'bout over."

We look to find both Monroes grinning in the doorway.

"That baby looks good on you," Kenra teases.

Lolli shrugs.

"Come here, gorgeous." Nate holds a hand out. "And bring that baby with you."

Lolli giggles and bends to kiss his little head. "You, Deaton Baylor, will be the most loved little dude ever."

My heart both hurts and swells in pride when Lolli says his name.

Deaton Baylor, after his father and her. At first, Payton was afraid to use Deaton's name for his son he never got the chance to meet. She worried, every time she heard it or said it herself, she'd feel an emptiness inside her, and she feared she would grow resentful, but in the end, she couldn't bring herself to call him anything different. And I'm so glad because it's ended up doing the exact opposite.

When she or anyone else calls him by name, my sister gets a little light in her eye, a reminder that, even though Deaton is gone, she has a true piece of him here to love forever. Her own little miracle with his daddy's dark hair and mama's blue eyes.

Nate and Lolli walk out, and Kenra walks in.

She glances around the room, looking to the spot where the ottoman used to be. "It turned out so cute in here." She looks to the heather-gray wall with the big turquoise-blue Tomahawks logo in the center. "This boy will be so spoiled."

"He already is."

"Good." She smirks and walks toward me right as the team takes the field again.

I spin her, so I'm standing behind her, my chin resting on her shoulder, as we look out over the packed stadium. "Heard your parents say they're staying a few more days."

"They are. My mom said my dad hasn't taken this many vacation days since we were born." We both laugh at that. "That baby is good for all of us. He's helping Payton stay strong, and he's helped Lolli get over her fears of the future. I feel like, for the first time, my family feels at peace, and it has so much to do with that little boy."

I grin against her, so damn proud of her and amazed by her strength. "I love you; you know."

"Mmm …" She snuggles against me. "I know."

"Move in with me."

"I … what?" She tries to spin in my arms, but I don't let her.

"I need to hold you in *our* bed, in *our* home, every morning and night. I want you there, with me, always. Let's erase all the bad with good, Kens."

"What about—"

"Say yes, baby. Don't make me wait any longer."

"Yes," she whispers with zero hesitation.

One hand comes up to tilt her face toward mine while the other skims down her stomach until I'm cupping her over her jeans. She gasps into my mouth as I kiss her with a gentle hunger.

"Me and you, every night, Nightingale."

She grins against my lips, her eyes still closed. "Every night, Safety."

She's everything I ever wanted and nothing I thought I'd ever have.

But here she is. In my arms.

My nightingale.

NOTE FROM THE AUTHOR

Son of a beesh! You guys! I can't believe Defenseless Hearts is in your hands!
Parker and Kenra's journey took me on a ride I never expected. When I started writing this book, I thought I knew what was set to happen, but damn was I wrong! Gah! Parker loves hard, doesn't he?
THANK YOU SO MUCH FOR READING!!!
I hope you felt and loved their story as much as I do.
Did you discover Parker and Kenra's story first? Take it back to high school in Lolli and Nate's story, FUMBLED HEARTS, now to find out how the sassy new girl and cocky quarterback came to be!

WHAT NOW?
Will there be more books in the Tender Hearts series?
Read Arianna's book NOW! Turn the page for an inside look!

MORE FROM THE AUTHOR

Series:

Wicked bad boys and the girls who bring them to their knees...

Boys of Brayshaw High
Trouble at Brayshaw High
Reign of Brayshaw
Be My Brayshaw
Break Me

Standalone Books:
- The Deal Dilemma -
Brothers ex-best friend, virgin heroine, grumpy sunshine
- Say You Swear -
Sports Romance, Amnesia, Second Chance
– Dirty Curve –
Hot College jock falls for the shy little tutor.
– Fake It Til You Break It –
Hottest guy on campus becomes your fake boyfriend
– Fumbled Hearts –
New girl in town catches the eye of the school playboy

– Defenseless Hearts –
Second chance with the one who got away
– Badly Behaved –
Rich girl falls for the poor punk

Find these titles and more here: https://geni.us/BMMBA

PLAYLIST

Luke Combs – Hurricane
Linkin Park – Leave Out All The Rest
Papa Roch – Scars
Thomas Rhett – Marry Me
Alex & Sierra – Little Do You Know
Nickelback – Trying Not To Love You
Elliot Yamin – Wait For You
Luke Bryan – Crash My Party
Brett Young – In Case You Didn't Know
Taylor Swift – Back to December
Daughtry – It's Not Over
Carrie Underwood – Heartbeat
Shawn Mendes – Treat You Better
Rite Ora – Body On Me
Ella Mae Bowen – Holding Out For A Hero
Rascal Flatts – What Hurts The Most
Jana Kramer – Circles

* STAY CONNECTED*

Follow her on Facebook: Meagan Brandy Author
Join her Facebook readers group: Meagan Brandy's Reader
Group
Follow her on Instagram: @meaganbrandyauthor
Follow her on Goodreads: Meagan Brandy
Email: Meaganbrandybooks@gmail.com
Follow her on Amazon: Meagan Brandy
Follow her on BookBub: Meagan Brandy

Printed in Great Britain
by Amazon